RUNNING AWAY TO HOME
Swept Away, Book 1
Rosemary Willhide

If home is where the heart is, Nia Kelly is screwed.

The twenty-four year old fitness instructor nearly faints when Hollywood heartthrob Derek Pierce comes to her spin class at an exclusive Las Vegas sports club.

There is an instant spark, an undeniable heat between. But falling in love is not in her plan and Nia is a girl who sticks to the plan.

She moved to Las Vegas to escape her past; a past with secrets that still haunt her. A romantic entanglement with a celebrity like Derek will put both of them in danger. She doesn't know if she'll ever be safe, ever be free.

Then he looks at her with those gorgeous blue eyes, and is impossible to resist. Her world flips upside down.

Reader Advisory: Please be advised, the devastatingly handsome hero awakens our feisty heroine, she's super horny, all the time!

RUNNING AWAY TO HOME
Swept Away, Book 1

Rosemary Willhide

LUMINOSITY PUBLISHING LLP

RUNNING AWAY TO HOME
Swept Away, Book 1

Copyright © December 2014 Rosemary Willhide
Paperback ISBN: 978-1-910397-31-2

Cover Art by Poppy Designs

Dedication

This book is dedicated to the loving memory of our adopted dogs, Smuckers and Cleo. They were my first puppy loves and my inspiration for the canine characters, Sammy and Coco. This one's for you, Smuckers, my doggie soul mate and Cleo, my angel.

Chapter One

"Happy anniversary, Nia!"

"Thanks, it's like my very own Nevada Day." I'd been living in Las Vegas for exactly one year.

Julia was anxious to celebrate. "Are you done for the day?"

"Yeah, I just taught a killer spin class. I kicked everyone's ass, including my own." An hour of hard cardio on the bike was a perfect finish to my day. "I'm at the big gym on the other side of town. I'll probably be stuck in traffic. Why don't I text you when I get to the guesthouse? I'll jump in the shower and then I'll be up."

"Sounds great, I'll call the gang and let them know the plan. We know you love it when a great plan comes together."

We chuckled, because I considered myself the social coordinator of the group. We were celebrating my anniversary with a TV binge watching party and cocktails. We watched everything from classics like *The Brady Bunch* to the latest hit series on cable. Julia owned every *Blu-ray* and DVD ever made. It was quite impressive to a TV junkie like me.

I was ready to toast my new beginning, but being a bit of a control freak I asked, "So, what are we watching tonight?"

"I knew you were going to say that. I asked everyone and they said you should pick. Then, they put in their two cents. It looks like season three of *First Bite* is the big winner."

We giggled and yelled out, "The Naked Season!"

First Bite was a current popular series on cable. It had hot, naked, male vampires. I was in!

I climbed in my Honda. It was such a beautiful March day in Vegas. I didn't care about the traffic. I couldn't wait to get home. Well, it was Julia's home, but I was more comfortable in her guesthouse than any other place I lived. I was lucky to have her in my life.

We'd been best friends since we met at college in Pittsburgh. Julia was gorgeous on the outside, and even more beautiful on the inside. When I needed her last year, she was there. She rescued me from my horrific situation in Pittsburgh and helped me start fresh. What would I have done without her? For a second, I drifted to my darkest moment.

I quickly shook it off and focused on happier thoughts. Secretly, I was happy Julia's husband was away on business, because it meant she was free until tomorrow night. Of course, I adored Phillip. He was great, but I only spent time with Julia when Phillip traveled.

Our arrangement was simple. I lived in their guesthouse and hung out with Julia while Phillip was out of town. When they traveled together, I stayed in the downstairs master suite at the main house and hung out with their adorable rescue dogs, Coco and Sammy.

Their home, or should I say McMansion, was nestled in the Mountain Heights Country Club. It was resort-style living at its finest—beautiful estates right on the greens with the Red Rock mountains for a backdrop. Living there held many advantages, like major social events at the clubhouse. They had a sports club in a separate building across the street. Tennis and golf were the big draws, but there was also a small group exercise room for fitness classes. I wasn't a country club kind of girl, but for now, it all worked.

Phillip Dickson was forty, fifteen years older than Julia and I. He was a successful entrepreneur. Julia met him when she moved to LA right after college.

The rest of my gang consisted of Steve, Scott, and Brooke. Steve Larsen and Scott McMillan, a fabulous gay couple, lived next door. Both of them possessed a wicked sense of humor. We bonded instantly.

Brooke Andrews was the fitness coordinator at the Mountain Heights Country Club. Julia introduced us when I moved to town. She hired me to teach spin, Pilates and Body Sculpt.

Sometimes we were mistaken for sisters. We both had long dark hair and small, lean frames. Brooke was an excellent coordinator. I appreciated her organizing skills and attention to detail. People called us anal and crazy. We preferred to think of it as enthusiasm for a well-executed plan.

When we were together, it was like family, something I hadn't experienced in a long time.

My ringing cell phone startled me as I crept along in traffic. The freeway resembled a parking lot. I drove fifteen minutes and barely moved. Whoever called left a message. I heard my cell beeping away. I crawled off the freeway and listened to the message.

It was Brooke. "Hey, Nia, it's me. Happy anniversary! I talked to Julia and she told me the plan, but I wanted to run this by you. Someone called the fitness desk and requested a private spin class for tonight. I didn't get a name, but call Sonya and let her know if you can get here by seven. I wanted to offer it to you first, because you're the best. Don't worry about us. We wouldn't dream of starting the festivities without you. See you soon. Bye."

Well, crap! I mean, I was thrilled Brooke thought of me, because the private classes paid so well, but I'd never been a fan of last-minute changes. I was the least spontaneous person on the planet. Still, it was doable. I called Sonya Reed, aka "Madame Scowls-A-Lot," and told her I was on the way. I texted Julia the new plan and hurried to the club.

God, I hated dealing with Sonya. Her scowl seeped through the phone. For some reason Sonya disliked me from day one. Brooke said she was jealous, which made no sense.

I was the ordinary girl next door. Only I sported a giant potty mouth. I appeared innocent, but I could give a sailor a run for their money. I offered up a few gems on my drive since Sonya wouldn't tell me who requested the private class. She just said there would be two people, and they weren't my regular students. That made me anxious.

Sometimes the super-rich and fabulous vacationed for months, and their super-rich and fabulous friends stayed at their houses and enjoyed the amenities of the club. We even had a few celebrities in class. I cringed every time I thought of my private Pilates class with a famous Kate. I told her how great she was in *Titanic*! It was the wrong Kate. My mouth always landed me in trouble.

Too bad the class wasn't with one of my regular students. They were fun. I loved them.

Yes, teaching suited me. It was great to be back in top physical shape. I was stronger than ever. Little by little, I put the past behind me.

I arrived at the club with ten minutes to spare and exchanged my usual unpleasantries with Sonya and her scowling face. Sometimes she smiled at the members, but usually, it looked like she smelled a fart. Of course, she had no new information on the mystery students. She acted evasive on purpose.

I opened the equipment closet. Barely reaching the top shelf, I grabbed the rubber mats that went under the bikes to protect the hardwood floor. Then I wheeled out three spin bikes.

It was seven-ten when Larry Wall popped his head around the door.

"Hey, Nia, I requested you for a private spin tonight. Brooke said you were already booked. What gives?"

"Sorry, Mr. Wall, I was supposed to have a seven o'clock, but I don't think they're coming. I'm giving them five more minutes before I take off."

"You should join me at the clubhouse for a drink. Big Larry's buying."

I almost threw up a little in my mouth. "Thank you, but it's against the rules."

He tromped off as Sonya shot me a disapproving glare from the fitness desk. Why couldn't he pay attention to her instead of me? He should hit on someone his own age.

Larry Wall was in his late forties and a major tool. For starters, he was married, although I'd never seen Mrs. Wall at the club. I called him Larry the Letch.

What the hell, seven-fifteen and no one showed. I should be celebrating my anniversary with cocktails and *First Bite*.

I gave up and wheeled a bike back into the closet. You would think a fancy country club would have a spacious equipment closet, but not this one. The first bike was in and I shoved the damn thing over to make room.

A deep voice echoed in the room. "Sorry I'm late."

I spun around and nearly fainted. Holy, hot vampire, it was *him*!

Time stood still as I openly salivated over the most gorgeous man I'd ever seen. It was Derek Pierce, aka sexy Vampire Drake Braden on *First Bite*. This was not any run of the mill sexy vampire. He was *the* vampire. Vampire Drake totally floated my boat and powered my doughnut. He was even better looking in person.

Derek was thirty-two, six-foot-four and perfectly chiseled from head to toe. He had dark-blond wavy hair and ice-blue eyes. It should be illegal to be this hot.

My head swirled with so many impure thoughts. I should spend months in confession.

"Are you Nia?"

I may have mumbled something like, "Uh huh," but who knew?

He offered his hand. "Hi, I'm Derek, Derek Pierce."

I placed my hand in his. He gazed at me with those eyes and I practically swooned. I was also aware of how tiny my hand was in his. Yes, such lovely, large hands…well, you know what they said.

Oh shit, I had to pull it together.

Eventually an actual sentence plopped out of my mouth. "It's nice to meet you, Mr. Pierce."

"Please, call me Derek."

"Actually, the club is pretty formal, so I kind of can't."

"Very well then Miss…Miss…"

"Oh…sorry…Kelly."

Derek's gaze captured mine. "It's very nice to meet you, Miss Nia Kelly."

There was something about the way he said my name; it sounded so sexy.

Mama Mia! My body flushed with sweat and we hadn't started the workout.

Thank heavens the teacher in me returned. "They told me the class would be for two people. I'd be happy to wheel out another bike."

"I'm afraid you're stuck with just me. My girlfriend Eden, I mean, Miss Fox, couldn't make it."

He took my breath away and apparently my memory. I nearly forgot he dated Eden Fox.

I played it cool…ish. "You mean Eden Fox, the movie star? I love her. She is such a great actress." It would've been great if I'd only said that, but when I was nervous, I babbled like a freaking idiot. Derek smiled politely.

I caught myself, mid ramble. "I'm sorry, sometimes I talk too much."

"No need to apologize. Actually, I'm an actor too. I'm on a show called *First Bite*."

"Really? I've never seen it. I don't watch much television."

For the love of God, what did I just say? I touched my nose to see if it grew like Pinocchio. Clearly, my pants were on fire, because I was a big, fat liar.

He bristled. "Look, I was hoping for a solid hour of intense cardio, but I know I was late. We can reschedule if you want."

Should I reschedule? Maybe next time I wouldn't be such a moron and have on makeup and perhaps a ball gown.

I collected myself and pressed on. "Of course, we can do an hour. What kind of music do you like?"

"I like everything, surprise me."

We hopped on our bikes and spun like mad. I pulled out all stops hoping he'd sweat so profusely, he'd strip his shirt off. I was dying to see the Holy Grail of abs. Of course, he was in awesome shape. The harder he peddled, the sexier he became.

The hour flew by. Afterward we cooled down and stretched.

Derek toweled off his glistening sweat. "That was great. You really did surprise me. It was like the hardest spin class I've ever done. I'm not sure I expected that."

"Yeah, I get that a lot." *Geez*, why was I such a cocky smart ass? Although, in a way it was true, I was tougher than I looked.

He opened the door to our tiny equipment closet.

I interrupted him. "Don't worry about the bikes. It's a bit of a tight squeeze. Everything has to go in a certain way or it doesn't fit."

"I'm more than happy to help you."

"No, I got it. Have a great night."

I grabbed a mat and went to the closet. Like always, I hoisted it to the top shelf. Only this time all the mats tumbled on my head.

"Son of a bitch!"

I offered up a silent prayer. Please, Lord, when I turn around, I pray the vampire with the ass that just won't quit will be gone. I spun around and no such luck.

Instead, a grin crossed his face that nearly detonated my panties. "Are you sure you don't need any help?"

"No, I'm fine, sorry about that." Mortified, I picked up the mats and willed him to leave. He didn't. In an instant, he was right behind me. Derek gently placed his hands on my shoulders. Every cell in my body tingled and fizzed.

He was so close. His warm breath was on my neck. "Miss Kelly, I insist."

One hand grabbed a mat, and his other hand lingered. His long, exquisite fingers grazed the exposed skin on my back. A surge of electricity fired through me. I exhaled and struggled to find my voice.

I whispered. "I'm sorry I said, 'son of a bitch.'"

He whispered back. "I believe you just said it again, Miss Kelly."

Then he was engrossed in the task. He put those mats away like nobody's business. I gawked and admired the view. I should've said something like, thank you.

Like a dumbbell, I said, "Wow, you're like really tall."

He turned to me with a sly smile. "Yeah, I get that a lot."

We stood there, locked in each other's gaze. There was unexpected warmth in those icy-blue eyes. They held me in a dreamy trance.

Breaking the silence, Derek said, "You know, I'm in town for the week. I'd like to do another private class with you if that's okay."

I snapped out of my blue-eyed induced coma. "Sure, contact the fitness desk and they'll set it up."

Oh, the thrill of victory!

He picked up his bag and sauntered out the door. "Thanks. My girlfriend would love it."

And...the agony of defeat!

* * * *

"Tell us everything!"

"We want all the details!"

"Oh my hell, he is so hot!"

News of my private class with Derek/Vampire Drake Braden reached the masses. The interrogation was brutal.

"I already told you. He's gorgeous, he has a movie star girlfriend, and I made an ass out of myself. I can never watch another episode of *First Bite* again."

They protested and I begged. "Can't we watch something else like *The Andy Griffith Show*?"

It was a hopeless cause. Mayberry was out, and Derek was in. I didn't stand a chance.

Steve and Scott were ruthless every time Derek came on screen. "Nia, there's your boyfriend. He wants to bite you." I took it in my stride and played along.

By eleven o'clock, we called it a night, and said our goodbyes. I stayed and helped Julia clean the kitchen.

My emotions bubbled up. "Thank you, for the party and for everything. I don't know what I would've done without you."

Julia hugged me. "I only wish I'd gotten to you sooner." She changed the subject. "Now, you better get some sleep. You have a hot, sexy vampire to dream about."

"Yeah, right, I hope I never see him again."

On my way out the door Julia shouted, "Well if you do, you might not want to say son of a bitch…twice!"

As I walked down to the guesthouse, I couldn't erase Derek from my mind. Would I see him again? Did I even want to? I replayed our encounter in my head. The way he looked at me. How my body responded to his touch; what was that? That never happened to me before.

Maybe it was because my romantic entanglements read like a *Who's Who* of strays and losers. No wonder I chose to avoid men when I moved here. It was easy considering I had zero interest—until tonight. There was something between Derek and me.

Why did Julia have to leave town tomorrow?

When she traveled, I was lonely. In those moments, I missed my mom the most. She died in a car accident when I was twelve. A distracted driver on a cell phone ran a red light and hit her broadside. Mom was my whole world. She possessed this special, almost magical quality. Skinned knees healed faster, and the tiniest achievements were cause for celebrations. She would have doled out the best advice about men. She was charming and had Dad wrapped around her finger.

I sometimes fantasized about how life would have been if she lived. Everything would be different, the relationship with my dad, the choices I made. Instead, I was a walking disappointment.

Dad and I were lost after the accident. He checked out for a while and then remarried. I was stuck with an evil stepmother and two wicked stepsisters. They made the characters in *Cinderella* look like a trio of homecoming queens.

A noise at my patio door jolted me from my momentary funk. It was Sammy, Julia's black lab. Although Coco, Julia's other rescue dog, didn't venture to the guesthouse, from time to time Sammy snuck out the doggie door and slept with me. He was the only male in my bed for a long time now, and that was fine by me.

I opened the door. Sammy trotted in and made himself at home. I was anxious. I clicked on the television and chose a *Friends* rerun I'd seen a hundred times.

When I couldn't sleep, there was something comforting about reruns. It was my version of a sleeping pill, and it worked almost every time. Sure enough, before the credits rolled, we were asleep.

Chapter Two

I woke up in restless fog. My fitness classes did the trick. The endorphins kicked in and kicked out my anxiety and cloudy brain.

My last class on Tuesday was at the country club. It was a spin class. I looked forward to seeing my favorite students. I adored Sue and Jeff Peterson. They were in their early fifties and in amazing shape. They'd been married for over twenty years and appeared madly in love.

I also enjoyed Nancy Simmons and Sharon Gill. I called them the chorus girls. They sang along to all the songs. They joked about bringing microphones for karaoke spin. Steve and Scott said they'd be coming; better bust out a show tune or two.

Ah, crap! Did Steve and Scott already blab about my class with Derek? Why couldn't I stop thinking about him?

I ran to the fitness room to ensure the boys shut their pie holes.

I was too late. Steve and Scott told the Petersons and the chorus girls. The avalanche of questions hit the second they spotted me.

Mrs. Peterson nearly hyperventilated. "Oh, Nia, what was Derek like? Is he as good looking in person?"

Everyone but Mr. Peterson sounded like a bunch of cackling hens. There was a sudden silence. All eyes whipped to the door. I turned to find Sonya the Scowl and the most beautiful bouquet of flowers I'd ever seen. "Here, Nia, these came for you." She practically threw them at me.

Scott said, "Who are they from? Open the card." The attention was too much, but I was as curious as they were. The card read:

Son of a bitch!
That was a great spin class!
Thank you,
Derek Pierce

I couldn't believe it. I shoved the card in my gym bag so no one would see.

How was I going to get out of this one? I had to fess up. "The flowers are from Mr. Pierce."

They cheered and high-fived. My face blushed in shades of red. I was relieved Sonya exited before I said the flowers were from Derek. That scrunched up face loved to gossip.

Steve chimed in. "I think someone is quite smitten with our Nia Kelly, or should I say Nia Pierce."

Oh man, this was out of hand. I seized control of the situation. "Okay, guys, I'm sure Mr. Pierce's assistant sent the flowers. It's not a big deal, and we don't need to mention them again. What happens in spin, stays in spin."

* * * *

After class, I rushed home to drive Julia to the airport. Phillip was in New York finishing a seminar, and she was joining him for a little fun in the city.

"Julia, am I crazy for thinking he felt something too?"

"No, I think he is totally into you and why not, you're amazing in every way."

She was always my biggest cheerleader.

"I doubt it. He's dating Eden Fox. She's one of the most beautiful women in Hollywood."

"She doesn't hold a candle to you. Plus, beautiful people in Hollywood break up all the time."

That was true, but Derek and Eden were dating for two years, now. Before that, he dated Gisela Monet, who played Victoria on *First Bite*. Derek broke up with her. At least that was what they said on *TMZ* and they knew everything.

I sighed. "I'm sure in a week or so I will forget all about it. I'll be fine."

When I dropped off Julia, she told me she would text me when she landed and I'd see her Saturday morning.

Could Julia be right? Could Derek be into me? By the time I pulled in her driveway, I convinced myself just this once Julia was wrong, and Derek hadn't given me a second thought.

Since I was on dog duty the next few nights, I scurried it to the guesthouse to grab a few essentials, like my pajamas. I always wore a T-shirt and boxers. It wasn't very sexy, but Coco and Sammy never complained.

Laundry also beckoned. I snatched up my basket, swung it around, and knocked over some stuff on my dresser. God, I was clumsy. I put the basket down and cleaned up the mess. It wasn't too bad, just a can of Shaper hairspray and a small jewelry box that belonged to my mother. A few pieces of jewelry spilled on the floor. I picked up my mom's locket, and then I spied it, my wedding ring.

Seeing it was a punch to the gut. Why did I still have the ring? I sunk to the floor. My hands shook when I picked it up. It was a nice ring, a Ryan family heirloom, but to me it represented the biggest mistake of my life.

Nick Ryan came from a wealthy family in Pittsburgh. We met one night in a bar. I was with Julia and having a blast. We were about to embark on our senior year of college.

Nick noticed us right away. Two tipsy blondes were hard to miss. I had a trendy bob in college. What was I thinking? It looked terrible.

He sent over a round of drinks. We smiled and waved. He strolled over to our table with this air of confidence. I assumed he was there to talk to Julia and her voluptuous perfectness. He wasn't; he honed in on me.

He was handsome in his own way, nearly six feet, with dark hair and deep-set brown eyes. I was twenty-one, and he was twenty-seven. I wasn't looking for a boyfriend, but he wouldn't take no for an answer. He'd pop up on campus and whisk me away. My favorite thing was a good, old-fashioned family dinner. At first, Nick's family welcomed me. They appeared loving and tight-knit. It was what I longed for.

However, the relationship moved too fast. Nick was ready to settle down and I wasn't. Eventually he wore me down. We announced our engagement at Thanksgiving. Then, he changed. He was more domineering and not as attentive. I almost broke it off, but I was scared.

I had no plan after graduation. I couldn't go to LA with Julia. Dad would've flipped. He never supported any of my acting endeavors. My minor in theatre disappointed him, because it took the focus off my major, business management.

When my final semester loomed before me, I was lost. So, when Nick pressured me to get married over the winter break, I agreed. Then, he demanded I drop out of college. He said I didn't need a degree. After all, I was Mrs. Nick Ryan.

I stared at the ring and choked back tears. Why did I ever marry him? Visions of what he did during my last terrifying night in Pittsburgh invaded my brain. My entire body shuddered. I couldn't go there.

I opened one of the drawers and hurled the ring inside. I slammed it shut so hard it shook the dresser. I wrapped my arms around my legs and prayed, "Please don't let Nick ever find me." I kept repeating it. Had we done enough to keep him away from me forever? I left Pittsburgh in the middle of the night with Julia's help. I went back to being a brunette and changed my name to Nia Kelly. Mrs. Meagan Ryan was gone. As far as I was concerned, she never existed.

I picked myself up and got the hell out of there. I marched to the main house more determined than ever. I wasn't weak, scared, or vulnerable. I wasn't going to waste a single second dwelling on any man. That included, Derek Pierce!

Chapter Three

My cell rang. I was barely awake and didn't answer. I took a lot of crap for never answering my phone. In my defense, I was usually in the car or in class.

Oh, nuts! The phone woke up Coco and Sammy. I stumbled through the TV room and opened up the French doors. Even though they had a doggie door, Coco hardly used it. I checked my voice mail. It was from Brooke.

"Hey, Nia, I hope I'm not waking you. I got a message from the fitness desk, guess who requested you for a private spin tonight at seven. Derek Pierce! You must have made some impression, first the flowers and now this. Anyway, it's for two people. Call me when you get this and let me know if you're available. Talk to you soon. Bye."

Well, shit! Seeing Derek again made me anxious. Seeing him and his movie star girlfriend made me sick. I hated to say no and let Brooke down, but I couldn't do it.

I took a deep breath, and called her back so they could get someone else. I rambled for about five minutes, making no sense. Brooke was sweet. She let me off the hook.

* * * *

The day whizzed by. I finished teaching and was ready for doggie duty. I took a quick shower and threw on some shorts. The dogs and I scurried out for a walk. It was a beautiful Las Vegas evening, and we enjoyed every minute of it.

Julia and Phillip adopted Coco and Sammy from the local Humane Society shortly after I moved to town. They were about five years old. Their owners turned them in because they lost their house and couldn't keep them anymore. In a way, Julia and Phillip rescued all three of us.

Coco was a little smaller than, Sammy. She was mellow with a brownish soft coat. She was also a lab, but probably mixed with something else. We weren't sure. Sammy was the alpha dog and super protective of me. I loved them as if they were my own. It made Saturday night's benefit even more special.

The country club was hosting a fundraiser for the Humane Society. Julia was the chairperson. Brooke and I volunteered too. We were quite a team. Earlier in the year, we did an event for the women's shelter and raised a ton of cash. In fact, after the walk, I was going to work on the goody bags for Saturday night.

We made our usual loop around the neighborhood and were close to the main house. Running toward us was Larry Wall, aka Larry the Letch. He was out for a jog in short shorts and no shirt. *Ewww!* It was so disgusting! His body looked like an old bath mat that needed vacuuming. Oh hell, he saw me. I couldn't cross the street.

"Hey, Nia, you house sitting for the Dickson's again?"

"Yes. How are you, Mr. Wall?" There was no safe place to rest my eyes.

"I was just thinking. I have a house. Maybe sometime you could sit for me. I got a hot tub and a great wine cellar." The Letch lurched in my direction and Sammy barked at him.

He jumped. "Hey, what's with that dog?"

"Sorry about that, Mr. Wall. I better get them home."

We walked toward the house. Larry jogged off in the opposite direction and shouted over his shoulder. "Think about that hot tub."

Sammy bolted after Larry!

I yelled, "Sammy, no!" Sammy halted, but I went down like a bag of dirt. My knees smacked the pavement. "Motherfucker!"

"Miss Kelly, are you okay?" He was there. Derek Pierce was right behind me.

You have to be kidding me!

He offered a hand to help me up, but I declined. I was not falling under his spell.

"I'm okay, thank you, Mr. Pierce." This was a brand-new level of embarrassment. This was embarrassment's ugly cousin coming to bitch slap me in the face.

He quickly shifted his attentions to the dogs. "Well, who do we have here?"

He bent down to pet them. It warmed my heart to watch Mr. Big Strong Vampire melt into a puddle of goo. Sammy was good with him, but could not have cared less. Coco on the other hand, worked it. She wagged her tail and wiggled her butt. No female could resist his charms. He loved on her and she rewarded him with kisses. *Coco, you lucky bitch!*

"We really should be going."

He turned his attention back to me, with a look of horror.

"Sweetie, you're bleeding."

A…did he just call me sweetie? And B…what the fuck!

There was a scrape on my right knee, but my left knee bled like mad.

"Here, I have an idea." Derek peeled off his shirt. I swore the heavens opened up and the angels sung, or moaned. His chiseled abs appeared beyond perfection. He had that thing, that irresistible V-thing. I called it the panty soaker. What a glorious sight! I nearly keeled over—again.

He stooped down with his T-shirt in one hand and tended to my knee. His other hand caressed the back of my calf. Thankfully, I shaved my legs. *Good, Lord!* I could not lose control.

"Thank you, but I'm fine. I really need to get the dogs home."

Derek rose and looked at me with those enchanting blue eyes. "Please allow me to walk you home."

I hung my head. I was afraid those icy-blue eyes would evaporate my determination. I opened my mouth to say no when he tucked his finger under my chin and tilted it to meet his gaze.

"Miss Kelly, I insist."

I succumbed and off we all went. He walked Coco and Sammy, while I limped along with his T-shirt tied around my bleeding, now throbbing knee.

The closer we came to the house, the more Coco and Sammy pulled on the leashes. They were excited for their post-walk routine, diving into their water bowls and lounging on the grass.

On the front porch Derek asked, "You live here?"

"No, I'm the house sitter." Coco was going nuts. "Sorry, they're dying for a drink."

"I'd better see you in and take care of that knee."

Like an idiot, I invited him in.

When we arrived in the kitchen he asked, "Where's the first aid kit?"

"It's in the middle drawer over there. I can get it."

"I'll get it, my dear."

My dear? Oh, dear! My steely resolve acquired a crumbling crack. He led me to the kitchen chairs, sat me on one, pulled out another chair, and gently placed my legs on it. Was I in an alternative universe? What was I doing in Julia's kitchen with a bloody knee and a shirtless vampire?

He found the first aid kit. I found myself staring at every inch of him.

"Are you a doctor too?"

He cracked a devilish grin. "No, but I played one on TV. I'm sure you didn't see it."

Oh snap!

His medical skills impressed me. Wow, he had great hands. Even his hands were sexy. He lightly stroked the area around my knee. Why didn't I fall on my ass?

He glanced at me. "I was surprised to see you tonight since I called the fitness desk to schedule a private class with you. They said you were unavailable. And yet, here you are."

Crap, I forgot about that. Flustered, I didn't respond.

His tone turned slightly ominous. "I thought maybe you had a date. Are you seeing anyone, Miss Kelly? Do you have a boyfriend?"

What the what? Why did he care? For some strange reason, I channeled Jan Brady. "Yes, I do have a boyfriend. His name is George, George Glass."

"Hmm…but you're not on a date. Did something suddenly come up?" Apparently, he was a fan of the *Brady Bunch* too.

I flinched when Coco barked. She wagged her tail at the French doors.

"I need to let Coco out."

Before I could move he said, "Allow me."

He went to the TV room and opened up the doors. Back in the kitchen, he wore a satisfied smile and held a DVD case in his hand. He showed me, it was *First Bite – Season 3*.

"So, you've never seen *First Bite*? I believe people call this the 'Naked Season.'"

"Yes, I've seen it! I've watched the 'Naked Season' sixty-nine times!"

He cracked up laughing. "Why did you tell me you never saw it?"

The nervous rambler revved up. "I…um…thought, well, I didn't want you to be uncomfortable…crazy fan girl and all." I couldn't form a coherent sentence. Was he grilling me? Frustrated I sighed and said, "Where's your girlfriend?"

I regretted asking it the minute it flew out of my mouth. Derek's posture changed. "I'm sorry. I don't ever discuss my personal life. I'm very private."

"I understand. George Glass and I are very private too."

A trace of a smile appeared. "Did you get the flowers I sent?"

Oh *geez*, I forgot to thank him. "Yes, thank you so much. They're lovely. I appreciated the gesture."

"I appreciated the class. You're, really something." He sauntered toward me. Our eyes met, and once more, I felt that surge, that connection.

I replied meekly, "Thank you, Mr. Pierce."

"Please call me Derek, I insist."

He was so mesmerizing. I couldn't speak, but I had to say something before I was a goner, like, *Hey, how about those Giants?* "Hey, how about…benefit?"

Derek cocked his head, "Benefit?"

"There's a fund raiser for the Humane Society. It's this Saturday night at the club." Since I was supposed to be working on the goody bags, the pamphlets were on the kitchen table. I handed him one. Whew, good save!

"Oh yeah, I heard about this," he said with eyes back on me. "I'm in town—maybe I'll come. Will you be there?"

"Yeah, I volunteered to help out. In fact, I should be working on the goody bags."

"I should go and let you get to it," Derek approached closer. "You know, I'm just down the street."

"Really? Are you at the Manning's place?" They were on an extended European vacation.

"Yes, only now it's the Pierce's place. I bought it."

No way! My mouth gaped open.

He pinned me with those ice-blue eyes. "I really love it here. I think it's beautiful." He leaned in and caressed my face.

I peered up at him, powerless to resist. His mouth closed in on mine. My lips parted. This was it. He kissed...my forehead. Fuck!

"Take care of that knee. Do you want me to get you some ice before I go?"

Coming back to planet Earth, I murmured, "Oh, no, that's okay, let me walk you out."

"I can show myself out."

"I'm fine. I need to walk it off. Besides you could get lost in this house."

We made our way to the porch. Did I just get off a roller coaster? What was this man doing to me?

"Thank you for helping me out tonight, Mr. Pierce...I mean Derek."

He shot me his million-dollar smile. "You're very welcome."

"Damn it! I forgot to give you your shirt back. Let me go get it."

He grasped my hand. "Don't worry about it." He drew me close. "Oh, and, Miss Kelly, you have a very dirty little mouth. I like that in a girl."

Off he went, cool as a cucumber. I was like a baby carrot, ground to a pulp.

I couldn't take my eyes off him as he glided home. The way he carried himself was something to see. Derek was sex on a stick, and he was pissing me off.

One minute he looked like he was going to rip my clothes off, and the next he was angry because I brought up his girlfriend. This didn't make any sense.

The best thing to do was keep busy. I stuffed the goody bags until they were finished. Later, I remembered I hadn't checked my phone all night.

I had a voice mail from my new therapist's office. They canceled my appointment tomorrow night.

I'd been in and out of therapy since my mom died. When I got here, Steve hooked me up with a great therapist, but she moved. I couldn't connect with anyone after that. Now this one canceled on me. Frustrated by everything, I called it a night.

Coco, Sammy, and I cuddled up and I turned on the TV. I was more anxious than ever. What mindless fluff could I find? Bingo! My favorite reality show was on, *The Real Housewives*. They were one hot mess after another. Heck, my life wasn't so bad. Once the crazy one screamed at the fake one, I was asleep.

Chapter Four

When I opened my eyes, my nose practically touched Sammy's snout. I petted his head and he granted me a big, sloppy good morning smooch.

"Sammy, you're the only who gets me."

We were up and I was off to work. Thursdays were more hectic, since I traveled back and forth, from the gym on the other side of town to the country club twice. I ended the day at the club with Pilates. My last class was over, and everyone left. It was quiet while I gathered my things. Oh great, Sonya encroached toward me.

"Nia, someone wants to do a private Pilates class with you tonight, like now. Can you do it?"

Why did she sound so annoyed with me? The words tumbled out of her mouth as if she just ate a shit sandwich.

"Sure, Sonya, no problem. Send him in."

There he was, Mr. Sex on a Stick. Why did he have to be so flipping handsome?

He gave me that irresistible smile, "Well, hello, Miss Kelly."

At first, I was pissed. What was Derek doing here, playing some kind of cat and mouse game? Hmm…two could play that game. He was on my turf, and taken. What harm could come from a little innocent flirting? I was taking control of this situation. He'd better buckle up.

"Hello, Mr. Pierce. I understand you're here for Pilates. Have you ever done it before?"

"No, but I'm sure I can handle it."

I took a mat, unrolled it, and slapped it on the floor. I stared him dead in the eyes. "We'll see. Lie down. I insist."

His brow furrowed. "Where's your mat?"

"I'm not going to do the exercises with you. I'm going to watch." I stood over him, leaned in, and whispered, "I like to watch."

This was going to be fun. Such a shame we weren't doing yoga. I would love to see his downward facing dog.

I guided him through his paces and drank in his loveliness. Derek was the perfect specimen of raw masculinity. Of course, his form was impeccable. I couldn't help getting turned on by watching him obey my every command.

He performed single leg circles. Flat on his back with one leg extended on the mat, and the other one was straight in the air. Awesome; his shorts rode up. I positioned myself to get a better view.

"Miss Nia Kelly, if I didn't know better, I'd say you were trying to look up my shorts."

"Why, Derek Pierce, I would never do such a thing." I totally was.

He chuckled a little. After the single leg circles he delighted me with bridges. I sat on the floor next to him. His knees bent as he lay on his back pressing his hips up and down. Observing him thrust his pelvis was a remarkable wonder. It was almost too much, but I was in control.

"When you lift your hips, you need to squeeze your glutes. Always put your mind to the muscle. In other words, your head is in your ass."

Derek cracked up and faced me. "You think you're pretty funny, don't you?"

"Yep, I'm a freaking riot."

We laughed. Then Derek gave me a look that wasn't so funny. It was a look of desire. It happened so fast. He offered me his hand. I met him halfway. He gathered me in his arms. His lips crushed mine. My body rippled and tingled. One arm cradled me and his other hand cupped my face and traveled to my neck.

Yes, it was fierce and passionate. I've never experienced a kiss this intense. The way his hungry tongue dove into my mouth as he eased me on my back.

Holy crap, I was at work! I jerked away, breathless. "What are you doing?"

"I believe I was kissing you."

I stared at the floor. "Huh…um… I mean, why? Why were you kissing me?"

With one finger, he tilted my head and our eyes met. "Nia, isn't it obvious? You're amazing. I can't stop thinking about you."

Did I hear him right? I jumped up and retreated. I leaned my back against the mirror in the front of the room. I was as far away as I could get. "Look, I'm not even supposed to call you Derek, so I'm assuming kissing during class is frowned upon."

He rose and stalked toward me like a lion, hunting prey. "I can't explain it. I can't get you out of my head. There's something here." The back of his hand brushed my cheek. I trembled under his touch. "You feel it too, don't you?"

I whispered, "Yes."

His mouth devoured me, my lips, my neck…my God! His rock-hard body molded flush against me. This is exactly how I imagined it in my head. My pussy clenched in need. I wanted him to take me, but deep down, this was wrong. Before I lost control, I stopped. "I can't. I can't do this."

"What's wrong?"

"You have a girlfriend, don't you?" He didn't answer. "Don't you have a girlfriend?"

He mumbled. "It's complicated."

"Complicated? It's pretty much a yes or no question."

He looked away, silent.

The dawn broke. "Oh, I get it. You have your movie star girlfriend, Eden Fox in LA, and now you want someone to bang when you're in Vegas. I'm sure there are thousands of women who would line up for that job, but not me. You picked the wrong girl."

Derek stopped me. "It's not like that. Let me explain."

"Go ahead, explain. I would love to hear it."

"Here's the deal. I'm leaving tomorrow."

"You're leaving?"

"Just for the day, I have to go back to LA. I came here tonight because I wanted to see you. I needed to talk to you before the benefit Saturday night."

"Why do you need to talk to me?"

"I need to explain my situation with Eden, because —"

"Are you bringing her? Is she coming to the benefit with you?"

"I think so."

"Are you kidding me?" I fled to the door.

Derek blocked me. "Nia, please don't go."

"What is wrong with you? Why did you kiss me? Why did you say all those things when you knew she was coming to the benefit? I told you I'm going to be there. How could you do that?"

"Please let me—"

"You know what? You can fucking save it. I don't need your bag of bullshit."

I turned to leave. Derek grabbed my hand, and I shook him off. He pleaded, "Nia—"

"I've got to go!"

I bolted, ran to my car, and raced home. My emotions spiraled in anger and confusion. What was there to explain? Did he hurt me on purpose? How could I have been so stupid?

I sat in my car, completely drained. Tears threatened and I squelched them. I wasn't going to cry over some man I just met, even if it was Derek Pierce. He wouldn't derail me from moving on. I was fine. I made a mistake and lost control, but it would never happen again.

I was fine.

Chapter Five

Friday afternoon I went to Brooke's house to finalize the preparations for the benefit.

"Hey, I am dying to talk to you," Brooke said with excitement. "I heard Derek Pierce had a private class with you. You have to fill me in."

I flopped down at the kitchen table and spilled everything, the kiss, the fight, everything. She listened intently.

After I finished, Brooke smiled. "Is that it?"

"Yes, I'm afraid that's all the gory details. I hope I haven't put you in a bad position."

"No, that's nothing. I've walked in on my fair share of people getting busy in that room."

"No way. Are you serious?"

"Yep, remember the politician who did a private class with Barb? I busted them."

"Wait a minute? Wasn't that the guy who used to be a pastor before he got into politics?"

"That's the one. Barb was on her knees, but I don't think she was praying."

We burst out laughing.

Brooke continued, "Listen, I don't want you to worry about this Derek situation. If anyone saw or heard anything, I would have gotten a call first thing this morning. I'm more concerned about you. Are you okay?"

"I'm fine. I'm trying to keep busy. Enough about me. What's going on with you?"

"I've never been better, check it out."

She handed me a manila envelope addressed to Mrs. Brooke Andrews from the law offices of Schwartz, Stone & Keating. "My divorce is almost final. I just need to sign, seal, and deliver."

Brooke didn't talk much about her soon-to-be ex. She was a pillar of strength.

"Wow, good for you. You must feel relieved. Do you think you'll go back to your maiden name?"

"Are you kidding? My maiden name is Butts!"

We giggled.

"I'm keeping his name, the house, and car. And he can keep his twenty-two-year-old assistant."

"It's his loss. You are fabulous."

"You know what, you're right. We're both fabulous. But Julia will kill us if we don't get everything done."

* * * *

Saturday morning we gathered at the country club for our next task. The ballroom was fantastic with its dark wood, marble floors, and high ceilings. It was ornate without being over the top. The outer lobby, for guest check-in was decked out and taking shape.

"Hey, girls, I'm back." Julia bounced into the lobby.

"I missed you so much." I squeezed her a little too tight.

"Nia, I was only gone a few days. What's going on with Derek?"

"I don't want to talk about him. Today is about the Humane Society."

Brooke chimed in. "That's right, because our love lives have gone to the dogs."

"Julia, did you hear the news?" Sara dashed through the door.

She was the director of the Humane Society. We called her Saint Sara. She was in the trenches every day working on the animal's behalf. She was in her mid-thirties and cute as a button.

Out of breath, she huffed, "It's unbelievable. My phone has blown up."

"Sara, what is it?" Julia asked.

"I just found out that Derek Pierce and Eden Fox are coming tonight. The press is going to be here to cover our event. We are going national!"

"That's wonderful, Sara," Julia said.

"That's not all. I don't have a single ticket left. Here, I was worried we were going to have a small turnout and now...well, this is just incredible. I still have so much to do. I'll check in with you later. Thanks, girls."

Sara ran off. Once she was out of ear shot, Brooke asked me, "Are you going to be okay?"

"I'm not upset about Derek and Eden. I knew he was bringing her. I just didn't think it was going to get national attention. Maybe I should stay home."

Julia interrupted, "Please don't do that. It'll be fine."

"The place will be crawling with photographers. I don't think I should risk it."

Brooke suggested. "What if we station you in the back? You can help with the silent auction. We have all those expensive pieces of jewelry that come with their own security guards. It's right by the hallway. You can duck out if you need to."

"I think that's a great idea. You've been such a big part of this event. I don't want you to miss it," Julia added.

"Okay, I'll come. You know I don't know what I would do without you two."

Julia and Brooke were amazing, loyal friends. They understood why I couldn't have my picture in a national publication. Protecting me from Nick was priority number one. We choked up a little.

Julia piped up, "Girls, no time for tears. It's all good. Remember, in a few hours the real work begins— hair and makeup at my house!"

* * * *

Pop went the champagne. The three of us were upstairs in Julia's massive master suite. I referred to it as Julia's day spa. We donned cozy bathrobes while the hair and makeup team worked its magic. It was one of the many advantages of the Mountain Heights Country Club. Every whim was a phone call away. A car and driver could take you wherever your heart desired, or it could come to you.

The three of us had a ball. Phillip popped in to say hi, but didn't stay long. The way he rolled his soft-brown eyes said we were too much for him.

The benefit was formal attire. Since I didn't have any, Brooke lent me one of her dresses. It was a sleek black halter with a slit in the front. It was sexy. Maybe I was a little sexy too. Julia took care of me in the jewelry department. I opted for some chandelier earrings and a jeweled cuff.

I dabbed on a final swish of powder, and my ensemble was complete. I loved the way my hair and makeup turned out. For the first time in a long time, I looked pretty.

Julia, Phillip, and Brooke waited for the limo, but I drove myself.

I told Julia and Brooke if things got too intense for me, I would slip out the back and leave. I was less concerned about the media. After all, they were there for Derek and Eden. It was seeing them together.

Erasing Derek from my mind was impossible. How could I forget his laugh, his touch, and…his kiss? No one ever kissed me like that before. I was nervous. I was scared, and if I was honest, my heart broke in two.

Chapter Six

The benefit was in full swing. The ballroom overflowed with guests, which meant more money for The Humane Society. I was in the back with all the high-end jewelry for the silent auction. Every piece was divine, but a pair of emerald drop earrings snagged my attention. I didn't dare touch them since my new friends, Frank and Mac, the security guards, kept a close watch.

The band warmed up and the bar was packed. Servers bustled about with champagne and hors d'oeuvres. The room hummed with excitement. From the back, I had a view of the lobby. The media types caught the arrivals outside. Sara managed a last minute red carpet.

Brooke stopped by with a glass of champagne for me. I gulped it down and willed it to settle my nerves. She told me Sara talked to Derek and Eden's publicist. They were only staying a half hour. I probably wouldn't talk to him. Perhaps it was for the best.

A huge commotion erupted from the lobby. I assumed it was Derek and Eden making their grand entrance. My stomach churned. The crowd noise swelled and the band quit playing.

Their lead singer approached the microphone and said, "Ladies and gentlemen on behalf of the Mountain Heights Country Club and the Las Vegas Humane Society please welcome your favorite vampire from *First Bite*, Derek Pierce."

Applause filled the air and the cameras flashed. I braced myself and snuck a peek at Derek. He was alone.

My heart skipped a beat. Where was Eden? The photographers backed off. I took in a full view of Derek in his tuxedo. Now my heart raced. It was like 007 meets a prince and a super hero—a spectacular combination and utterly delectable.

All of the women, and some of the men, swarmed him, like bees to honey. His head bobbed about the room until our eyes met. Immediately tears pooled. I ducked into the hallway.

Brooke was there with another glass of champagne. "Hey, I thought you'd be thrilled his girlfriend isn't coming."

"I don't think it means anything. Is Sara upset Eden isn't here?"

"Actually, she's thrilled. Derek told her he'd stay for the whole event instead of a half hour."

"Really?"

"Yes, really, so you and I are going to down this champagne and go have some fun."

Brooke and I threw back our champagne and went to the auction table. She stayed and jollied me up. I pointed out the emerald earrings I liked.

She picked them up, and held them to my face. "Hey, Frank, if these earrings go missing, what's the worst that could happen?"

Frank was not amused.

Julia and Phillip were out on the dance floor with Steve and Scott and the chorus girls from spin class. The Petersons danced too. Mrs. Peterson crushed it. Was she trying to get Derek's attention?

Derek danced with everyone. He worked the room like a true charmer.

The other auction table was across the room by the bar. "Madame Scowl-A-Lot" was over there. Although I must admit, when not sporting her camel-toe mom jeans, Sonya cleaned up well. She even smiled.

The band took their first break. The crowd dispersed, and then it happened again. Those ice-blue eyes met mine.

Brooke grabbed my hand. "Derek's headed this way. He's so handsome, it's ridiculous." She giggled while I quaked in my heels.

Derek landed in front of us. "Ms. Andrews, I was wondering if I might have a moment alone with Nia, in private."

Brooke glanced at me, and I nodded. "Sure, give me a second."

We stood in awkward stillness. Derek broke the silence. "Nia, you took my breath away when I saw you. You look stunning."

I stared at the ground and quietly said, "Thank you."

Brooke returned with her enormous key ring. It probably weighed more than she did. There were hundreds of keys on there, but since Brooke was like me, tiny little labels identified each one. She had a key to every lock on the property.

She said, "This is the key to the private dining room. It's down the hall and to the left."

"Thank you, I promise to bring her right back."

Once we turned the corner, Derek planted his hand on the small of my exposed back. My body shuddered on impact.

"I really like you in this dress."

I didn't utter a word.

Once inside the private dining room, I moved away from him. With arms folded, I gathered my strength and asked, "Where's Eden? Why isn't she with you?"

"I asked her not to come."

"Why would you do that?"

He let out a heavy sigh. "I need to tell you something, but before I do, please know I'm taking a huge risk here. I need to know I can trust you."

"Trust me? I don't get it. What are you trying to say?"

He approached me and placed his hands on my shoulders. He was so serious. "What I'm about to tell you can't leave this room, understand?"

"Yes, you can trust me."

"The truth is, Eden and I are just friends."

Was he making this up? "What?"

"It's a publicity thing. We have an arrangement."

"Why? I don't understand."

"It's one of those things. It's hard to explain. I'm begging you. You can't tell anyone."

"I won't. I won't tell anyone."

Relief washed over him. "Thank you."

"Why do I get the feeling you're not telling me everything?"

"There is something I'm not telling you, but it's not for me to say. Nia, please trust me. Eden and I are good friends, and that's it."

"Why didn't you tell me this the other night?"

"I was trying to. Look, this is my fault. I should've told you this before I kissed you. In my defense, you were impossible to resist."

I smiled. "Well, right back at you, Mr. Pierce."

He drew me into his strong arms. I basked in the sweetness of him. Maybe I was making a mistake, but I trusted him. There was this undeniable, powerful connection between us. Maybe it was worth the risk.

He released me. His hands traveled to my face and his warm lips gently met mine. "I'm sorry. I know you were really upset Thursday night."

I peeked up at him. "I'm sorry I said I didn't need your bag of bullshit."

He grinned. "Oh, that dirty little mouth, Miss Kelly."

His hand caught the nape of my neck and he graced me with a kiss that went from delicate to decadent. Derek tasted like champagne. He was delicious. His beautiful hands pressed against my naked back and produced a trickle of wetness between my thighs.

A knock on the door startled us. *Damn it!* Brooke poked her head in. "Hey, I'm sorry to interrupt, but Sara is asking for Derek."

"You go ahead. I'm going to wait here for a little while."

Derek held my hand. "I'm staying for the whole event, so I'll see you later, okay?"

I nodded. He squeezed my hand and headed out with Brooke. She looked back, gave me two thumbs up, and followed Derek out.

I floated back to the auction table, light as feather. Although my elation waned when I observed Derek interact with the guests. If I could trust him and he wasn't a player or a liar, wouldn't it make him perfect? What could this perfect man possibly see in me? He didn't know anything about me, and if he did, what then?

"Hey, Nia," Julia said, "I haven't seen you all night. You look upset. What's going on?"

"Oh nothing, I'm fine." I changed the subject. "Hey, what time do you guys leave tomorrow?"

"Not until the afternoon. By the way, I don't know what's going on with Derek, but he hasn't taken his eyes off you all night. I think he's totally in to you."

I skirted the issue. "It's a long story. When you get back, I'll fill you in."

"Yeah, we need a girl's night so we can get caught up. I'd better go. It looks like Sara needs me."

I relaxed and watched the evening unfold. Derek did keep an eye on me the entire night.

All the photographers left except for one man hanging out in the lobby. The doors opened and he snapped a photo of Larry the Letch. What was he doing here? Where was Mrs. Wall?

He traipsed to the bar, downed a cocktail, and hit on Sonya. She giggled like a preteen. I found it disturbing. Like one of those Lifetime movies, you shouldn't watch, but you couldn't help yourself.

Throughout the evening, students from various classes visited the auction table to chat or bid on the jewelry. Steve and Scott plied me with champagne and shrimp on toast.

I was happy behind the table and out of the spotlight. In fact, when it was time to announce the winners from the auction, I excused myself and went to the ladies' room.

After a bit, I popped my head into the hallway. Sara gave a short speech to thank Julia for being chairperson and Derek for coming. The Humane Society broke a fundraising record. She said the band would play its last set and everyone should dance the night away.

The crowd thinned out when I returned. I stayed behind the table with Frank and Mac. It proved to be an excellent decision since Larry Wall lumbered toward me. That douche looked hammered.

"Hey, Nia, did you save me a dance? I got the moves like Mick Jagger." He had the moves like a turtle in heat.

"Sorry, Mr. Wall, I can't, it's against the rules."

"Whatever," he replied. He actually was peeved at my rejection as he stumbled away.

The lights of the limos pulled up outside and guests filed out. The band announced it was time for their final song. Julia and Phillip were the last couple standing. Derek danced with every woman in the place. He was off the hook.

He hightailed to the band and said something to the keyboard player. Then he went to talk to Brooke. She looked at me and nodded.

With a gleam in his eye, Derek strolled in my direction and extended his hand. "Nia, may I have this dance?"

"I don't think I can. It's against the rules." I glanced at Brooke and she gestured it was okay.

Derek shot me a bewitching smile. "Miss Kelly, I insist."

I placed my hand in his. "I think that was the last song."

He nodded at the band and they played "Unforgettable."

I folded into his arms and we swayed.

Then he stopped. "Nia, are you going to let me lead?"

I laughed, "Oh, sorry."

He glided me across the dance floor with grace and ease. I rested my head on his chest and took in his scent. He smelled like a man, clean and fresh, like the air in the Red Rock mountains.

I spied Larry Wall fumbling about in the lobby. Was he watching us, or looking for a ride home? It was hard to tell. Sonya hurried in his direction, but Sara intercepted her. I kept my eye on Larry until his drunk ass nearly fell out the door.

Derek asked, "Is everything all right?"

"I think so." I peered up at him. "I don't want the song to end."

"Just because the song ends doesn't mean the night has to."

"Really, Mr. Pierce, what did you have in mind?"

Before he could answer, the photographer charged the room. He snapped pictures of us and he hollered, "Derek, where's Eden? Did you break up? Why isn't Eden here?"

Everything happened so fast. I buried my face in Derek's chest. Derek yelled, "Get him out of here."

Frank and Mac were there in flash. I lifted my head, and saw them drag the photographer down the hall.

I freaked out!

Derek held me by the shoulders. "Are you okay?"

I panicked. "I've got to go!" I took off and got the hell out of there. Did he get my picture? Would it be in a tabloid? What would I say to Derek?

I ran until I reached my car in the back of the parking lot. I couldn't drive away. I didn't have my keys or purse. I leaned against the car with my hands over my face.

"Nia Kelly, you fucking bitch!" It was Larry Wall. He was enraged.

"Mr. Wall, you should turn around and go home." He lumbered toward me, smashed out of his mind.

He yelled back, mocking me. "Oh, Mr. Wall, I can't dance with you it's against the rules. You're nothing but a little cock tease."

"Please, you're drunk. You don't know what you're doing. Go back to the club house and someone will take you home."

"Fuck the club house. Fuck you too!"

I made a run for it, but he lunged and caught me by my wrists.

"Let me go, please stop it."

We struggled. In the distance, I heard Derek, "Nia!"

Derek was there in an instant. He ripped Larry off me. "Let her go!" He punched him so hard Larry smacked the pavement.

"Get the hell out of here," Derek yelled as he pulled Larry up and shoved him away.

Larry stumbled back to the clubhouse. "This ain't over! You're going to be sorry, both of you!"

Everything grew dark. I slumped toward the ground. It was the last thing I remembered.

When my eyes fluttered opened, Derek's arms nestled around me. He was on the curb by car. The back of his hand stroked my cheek.

My brain was fuzzy. "What...um...am I...what happened?"

"Sweetie, you fainted."

"I did? How long have I...I'm sorry."

"Hey, it's okay. I have you. Do you want to go to the hospital, just to be safe?"

"No, I'm fine," I squirmed to stand. Derek picked me up and set me on my feet.

"I have to get my purse. I want to go home."

Derek picked it up off the ground. "Here, Brooke gave it to me. You ran out of there so fast. What was that about anyway?"

There it was. The question I couldn't answer. I couldn't be with any man, especially one in the spotlight. Nick would find me. I had to protect myself. I had to protect Derek too.

With a lump in my throat I said, "I'm sorry, I can't. I can't tell you."

"What do you mean?"

Tears welled up. "I mean, I can't do this, I have to go."

Derek gripped my shoulders. "Please, tell me what's wrong."

"I just want to go home."

"Okay, let me take you home. I don't think you should be alone."

My voice shook. "Derek, please, I have to go."

He backed away. "God damn it, just talk to me."

"I can't. Please leave me alone. You don't even know me."

"I'm trying to get to know you, and you're making it impossible. What is it? Why do you keep running away from me? What's wrong?"

"Nothing's wrong! *I'm fine! I'm fine!*"

I lost control. Tears poured out of me like a river. I sobbed so hard I could barely breathe.

Derek cloaked me in his arms and held me close. "Nia, it's okay. Let it out."

He gave me his handkerchief, and I kept on crying. Once the dam broke, that was it. It was too late to put the genie back in the bottle.

After what seemed like an eternity, Derek said in calm tone. "This is what we're going to do. We're going to get in the car, and I'm going to drive you home. I'm going to stay with you, but I'll sleep on the couch, okay?"

All cried out, my voice quivered as if I had the hiccups. "Do…you…insist?"

"Yes, sweetie, I insist."

* * * *

We entered the guesthouse through the patio doors. I slunk down on the bed. I could tell Derek was surprised I lived here, but he wasn't about to ask me any more questions. He hung his tuxedo jacket on the chair close to the bed, bent down and took off my shoes.

"Now listen, I know you feel like there is something you can't tell me. You're right. We don't know each other very well, but you can trust me. I won't pry. Whatever it is, you can tell me when you're ready. Did you text Brooke and Julia? They were worried about you."

I nodded. He stood up. "Which way is the kitchen?"

I pointed him in the right direction. "It's through that door, why?"

"I'm going to get you some water while you get ready for bed."

He went to the kitchen while I grabbed up my T-shirt and boxers and padded to the bathroom. I fantasized about spending the night with Derek Pierce a million times, but not like this. My eyes were red and puffy from crying. I was so embarrassed I lost control and broke down. Why didn't I have something sexier to wear to bed?

I laid out a fresh towel and a new toothbrush for him. Then I trucked to the linen closet for some sheets and a blanket. Six-feet four inches of Derek would never fit on my couch, but I put the sheets down on it anyway and got him a pillow.

I made my way back to the bedroom, and we were both in T-shirts and boxers. His shirt and pants were on the chair with his jacket. Of course, he was sexy as hell. I looked like a dork.

I said, "The bathroom is all yours, and I made up the couch for you."

"Thanks, I'll be right back to tuck you in."

Tuck me in? Now he saw me as a child or some pathetic girl he had to take care of. I suppose it was for the best. The relationship was over before it began, if you could even call it that. I sat on the side of the bed. After a few minutes, he returned to "tuck me in."

"You know the couch is going to be really uncomfortable. If you want to, you could sleep here, with me."

"I don't think that's a very good idea." He was right, but it still hurt.

He pulled the covers back, and I lay down. He covered me up and kissed my forehead. "I'm right down the hall if you need me. Get some sleep."

He turned out the light and left. His kiss on the forehead spoke volumes. I was no longer the girl he couldn't resist.

Chapter Seven

A luminous beam of light streamed through the doorway of the black room. A shadowy figure approached. It was Nick. His eyes seared me with hate. He grabbed the empty suitcase and swung. It pummeled me in the head and nearly knocked me out. Pain ripped through me. I fell on the bed in the fetal position and wept. He taunted me, but his garbled words eluded me. The room spun. He pulled me by my hair. I pleaded with him to stop. His hands drew near my throat. I screamed, "No, please, *nooo!*"

"Nia, wake up."

Someone gripped me and I shrieked in fear.

"Nia, it's me."

I flung open my eyes and Derek was there.

"Sweetie, you were having a bad dream."

I threw my arms around his neck.

He rubbed my back. "Hey, you're okay. You're safe. I'm not going anywhere."

He held me, and in his arms, I was safe.

He smoothed the hair off my face. "Do you want to talk about it?"

I shook my head no.

"Here, drink some water." He handed me the water bottle.

I took a swig. "I'm so sorry."

"Sorry? Sorry for what?"

"For everything, I'm sorry for ruining your night."

"You didn't ruin anything."

"I'm sure you didn't think this was how your night was going to end up."

Derek smiled. "No, but you've been through hell tonight. Lay back down for me. You need some sleep." He gave me a platonic smooch on the cheek and rose.

I reached for him and tugged him back to the bed. "Please don't go. Stay with me?"

His hand caressed my cheek and my entire body flushed. I glanced up and his lips adorned me with a soft kiss. A heavy breath expelled from both of us.

Derek sat on the bed and rested his forehead on mine. "Sweetie, I can't stay in this bed and not touch you. I don't trust myself. I want you too much."

I offered him my mouth and he slid his tongue inside. I didn't trust myself either. Our connection crackled and fizzed.

I couldn't deny it any longer. "Derek, I want you too. I do. I want you so much."

With a penetrating stare, he moved to his knees and extended his hands to mine.

My pulse quickened. We touched and every tiny hair stood on end. There was no turning back, nor any desire to. Derek Pierce was in my bed.

He drew me to him. His hands cupped my face. His mouth came down on mine. We melded into tender, needy kisses that dizzied my stomach. A low, appreciative hum sounded from his throat.

His hands shifted to my back, sealing our bodies together. My erect nipples puckered against the fabric of my T-shirt. My fingers gripped his hair urging him to take my mouth harder. His soft, sweet tongue entwined with mine, sent warm twinges coursing through me. I expelled little mewls and murmurs as Derek's lips fell on my neck. The smell of his skin and the way he feasted on my neck, stirred every cell in my body.

Heaving and breathless, Derek stopped and stripped off his T-shirt. I touched my fingertips to my lips, swollen from his kisses. My gaze floated over his rippled flawlessness.

His fingers skimmed the hem of my T-shirt. "I want to see you."

I nodded. He wasted no time whipping it off. My breasts were perky, but small. I covered myself. Maybe he would be disappointed.

Derek caught my hands. "Don't. They're perfect."

He palmed my breasts and I exhaled. His mouth descended on one of my nipples. He suckled the pert bud between his lips. My sex clutched, causing me to groan. His tongue circled and teased my nipple while his hand tended to my other breast. I gripped his head, holding it to my elongated, sensitive teat. Soft whimpers released under his masterful touch.

His mouth withdrew from my breast. He grasped my face. "I need to see all of you."

Derek's boxer shorts were still on, but as he guided me onto my back, he slid mine off and tossed them to the side. I trembled as his eyes drank in my naked body.

With his gaze locked on mine, he whispered. "You're beautiful. You're so beautiful."

In that moment, I wanted to be his.

He lay down next to me and worshiped me with his mouth. Moisture pooled between my thighs. My pussy ached in a way I never experienced before. He lashed his tongue over both of my nipples and rolled my taut nubs between his thumb and finger. More juices seeped forth. I closed my eyes and moaned. His hand slid over my stomach to my landing strip of pubic hair. I was embarrassed I was already so wet. I pressed my legs together.

Derek removed his hand. "Do you want me to stop?"

"No, I don't, I just, uh."

He grinned. "You're wet, aren't you?"

How did he know that? I heaved. "Yes."

"Well, then I need to make you come. Spread your legs for me. Let me take care of you."

Derek held me in one arm, his other hand traveled to my sex. I opened up for him and his fingers explored my now soaked pussy.

"You really are wet for me. You're a very good girl."

My body was pure sensation responding to his touch. I groaned and grinded into his hand.

Derek pressed his lips to mine. One of his long, exquisite fingers delved into me. It probed and searched inside. The pad of his curious digit brushed the top of my...*Oh fuck!*

He discovered my G-spot. He was the Christopher Columbus of cunts. Until this moment, I swore the G-spot was an urban labia legend.

My body jerked and I cried out. I had zero control. My shoulders rose in tension.

Derek held me tighter. "Relax, sweetie, and let go. Come on my hand."

Two fingers fucked my willing hole. They stretched and stroked me. Steady swift thrusts pushed me higher and higher. He picked up speed. His thumb rubbed my clit and I pressed my arousal into him. I was so close.

"That's it, just let go."

Derek's fingers rode me through a quivering climax.

I screamed, "Oh my God, ah, ah, Derek, *yes!*" I let go. I truly let go. I'd never come so hard in my life. Was that my first real orgasm?

Derek planted light kisses on neck. I peeked at him, still breathless. "You're really good at that. You should get like a trophy or something."

He chuckled. "You haven't seen anything yet." He hopped off the bed, reached in his tuxedo pants, pulled out three condoms, and tossed them on the nightstand.

Sassy in my post-orgasmic glow I said, "Why, Mr. Pierce, someone must've been feeling pretty cocky!"

"Miss Kelly, you have no idea."

I rose in bed and Derek slid off his boxer shorts. There he was in his naked, erect glory. *Yippee-ki-yay!* It was the mother lode!

I wasn't exactly a penis connoisseur, but I was certain this was the biggest cock in the northern hemisphere. I regretted every Kegel I ever did. What a work of art! It belonged in a museum. The museum of hard cocks!

Derek must have seen my eyes pop out of my head, because he asked, "Is everything all right?"

I answered back in a devilish tone. "Sure, I was just curious if that had a name, or perhaps its own zip code?"

He laughed and sat down next to me. The mood shifted as he swept my hair off my face. "We don't have to do anything. I'd be happy to hold you all night."

Sweet merciful heavens! I was powerless to resist this man and his giant penis. I looked him square in the eyes. "I…I want you to make love to me."

Derek drew my hand to his lips. "I've wanted to make love to you since the second I laid eyes on you. This thing between us…this connection I feel with you…this is something I've never felt before."

I felt it too, but what if he really knew me, what if he knew my secrets? My brain twirled like a top.

Derek cupped my face in his hands. "Nia, don't think, just feel."

I nodded. He eased me on my back and climbed on top of me. Our naked bodies pressed together like velvet hot perfection. His mouth ravaged me. My sex dripped in anticipation of him being inside me. I was ready. I parted my legs. Derek grabbed a condom and rolled it down his throbbing shaft. The head rested at my slit.

"Nia, look at me. I'm going to be gentle with you. I promise. Keep your eyes on mine." Derek took his time sliding his tip in and out of my slippery pussy. I was too small for his ample girth. I pressed against him, willing him further inside. It didn't budge and my body stiffened. I squeezed my eyes shut.

"Hey, sweetie, give me your eyes. You have to relax for me. Just breathe. It's all good. We don't need to rush. I've got you."

Like a laser, I focused on those crystal-blue eyes. I breathed with him and relaxed. He brought his lips down on mine. "That's it, sweetie."

My arms clung to his broad shoulders and he sunk further inside. Our bodies moved together in slow easy strokes. Each one stretched and pulled me open for him.

He pushed in deeper and I gasped.

"Are you okay? Did I hurt you?"

"No, you feel amazing."

"That's a good girl, no thinking, just feeling. Feel me, Nia."

I spread myself wider and he pressed further inside my tight hole. This was everything I ever dreamed. Derek was on top of me with his dick buried inside. Our connection flourished in fierce heat. I released a lung full of air and relinquished all control. My body surrendered to his.

The entire length of his shaft nudged inside. We moaned into each other's mouth.

Derek grunted, "God, you're so tight."

He took me with long, luxurious strokes that escalated our passion into overdrive. My sopping pussy clenched on his cock. My hands flew to his ass and gripped it tight. The pressure inside me built. Our pace frenzied, propelling me to the fringe.

He pounded on me full force and hit me in my newly discovered twat spot. I threw my head back in ecstasy, gasping and groaning.

Derek's mouth embraced mine. "Look at me, Nia. I want you to come for me. Come for me, sweetie."

I wailed in pleasure. "I'm coming, ah. Oh God, I'm coming."

I burst into a shattering orgasm that thrashed my body. Derek let out a deep moan and came. He practically collapsed on top of me. We laid there shuddering in our post-coital haze.

He pulled out of me slowly, rolled to his side, and rested his head on his hand. He'd rendered me immobile. The back of his fingertips brushed my cheek.

Little flickers of euphoria spiked through me. "Wow!"

"I take it the lady is pleased."

Still unable to speak in full sentences, I answered, "Very!"

"Me too, and may I just say, you might be small, but you're very loud."

I covered my face with my hands.

Derek peeled them away. "I like it." He granted me a quick peck, and headed to the bathroom.

My eyelids grew heavy. When he returned, he climbed in bed and draped his arms around me. My head relaxed on his bare chest. Derek kissed me good night and held me close. "Get some sleep, you need your rest."

"That's right, because I totally want to do that again."

We snuggled up and drifted off.

* * * *

The sun crashed through the windows and lulled me out of my peaceful slumber. When I opened my eyes, I faced away from Derek. What a relief since I drooled on my pillow. How could any woman not drool with Derek in their bed? Was I really waking up next to him? I rolled over to face him. He was still asleep. What a magnificent sight! So perfect in every way and I was the opposite.

Before my anxiety and self-doubt crept in, the sexiest man alive opened his gorgeous eyes. "Good morning, sweet girl.

Go figure, he even woke up perfect. I answered back softly, "Hi."

He grazed his fingertips over my arm. "Did you sleep okay?"

I murmured, "Yes."

"Me too."

He was so hot with his sleepy face and messy hair, while I was a hot mess and had to pee. I scampered to the bathroom and brushed my teeth.

Still naked, I examined my reflection in the mirror. What did he see in me? He could have any woman in the world. I didn't possess sexy curves. I was barely a B-cup. I wasn't tall or skinny like a model, and my dark eyes were nothing special. People described me as the cute girl with the nice smile. My mind drifted to the gorgeous women at the benefit, and the equally stunning women Derek encountered in Hollywood. Overcome with insecurity, I convinced myself this was a mistake. It couldn't mean as much to him as it did to me. I grabbed my robe and covered myself.

Back in the bedroom I said, "I'm going to jump in the shower. I have a class at noon. So, if you need to leave or anything, that's okay."

He popped up in bed. "Is everything all right?"

"Sure, I thought you probably had stuff do, so if you want to leave, that's cool."

"Nia, come here."

I hesitated. Then he shot me that "I insist" look, so I sat on the bed.

"Do you really want me to go?"

I stared at the ground. "No, but I thought maybe you wanted to."

He took my hands in his. "Of course I don't. Why would you think that?"

I shrugged my shoulders.

"Are you upset we made love last night?"

"No, it's just that, well, you could be with any woman you wanted. I mean, have you seen you? I'm just, me."

His finger tipped my head to meet his gaze. "Nia, you are so beautiful. I am completely captivated by you." His lips pressed softly to mine. "Now, did you say something about a shower?"

I nodded yes.

"I think I'll join you."

I smiled. "Okay."

We scurried to my bathroom. He brushed his teeth while I fastened my hair in a clip. The mood lightened. Even though we were doing something ordinary, the heat between us was palpable. I wore my robe, but Derek stood there in the most delightful naked way. I was already aroused.

"Thank you for the toothbrush by the way."

"No problem. I like to be prepared, like a girl scout."

He sauntered to me. "A naughty girl scout who uses very salty language."

"Son of a bitch, you are so right."

His arms snaked around my waist. "You are such a bad girl, what am I going to do with you?"

My body burned for his. Who knew what came over me. I stepped back and flung my robe to the ground. "I was kind of hoping you'd fuck me."

A look of shock and excitement crossed his face. "Well, Miss Kelly, if you insist."

"I insist!"

He pulled me into his arms. His mouth took mine with an urgent passion. The fresh taste of mint on his tongue invaded my senses. *Yes, please fuck me!*

His hands traveled to my ass and he smacked it in a playful manner. "First we shower, and then we fuck." I was surprised I didn't come on the spot.

It was impossible for us to keep our hands off one another in the shower. I ran my fingers over his panty-soaking V-thing. It was like a road map to heaven.

He picked up the body wash and smelled it. "Oh, is this why you always smell so good?"

My aromatherapy body wash was a mild blend of jasmine and vanilla. It wasn't overpowering or flowery; it was just right.

"You like the way I smell?"

He squirted the body wash in his hand. "I do. I wish I could bottle it."

"It's just that. Body wash and me. I'm allergic to perfume."

"Trust me, sweetie, you do not need perfume. You smell amazing."

"I like the way you smell too."

He grinned. "Turn around for me, let me get your back."

I turned around. His exquisite hands slathered me in soothing body wash, first my shoulders; then my back. He arrived at my bottom and that dizzy feeling circulated in my stomach and headed south.

His hands ran across my hips. He tugged me to him and whispered in my ear, "I need to wash your front, but I'm tempted to fuck you right here. You're driving me crazy."

I spun around and he trapped me in a heated gaze. I shrugged. "I'm good with that."

He chuckled. "Are you sore?"

I exhaled. "Only a little."

He pressed his lips to my forehead. "Then I better stick to my plan for you."

"There's a plan? Does it include fucking me in the shower?"

He clasped me to him. "It will, someday. We'll get there, I promise."

"We're not there yet?"

"No, I need to be careful with you. We need to go slow."

"Did I disappoint you?"

"Of course not. You were exceptional. I want more."

His words left me stunned, speechless, and super horny. *Let's get the hell out of this shower, ASAP.*

He washed me at breakneck speed. I did the same to him. Before he turned off the shower, he grabbed a washcloth and cleansed my tingly sex. My heart rate spiked, and for a second I considered humping that washcloth.

Derek turned off the water and toweled us off. We hurried to the bedroom. "I'm glad your class isn't until noon. It gives us plenty of time."

He removed the clip and my hair cascaded down my back. His eyes floated over me. He smiled in appreciation. "Absolutely exceptional." He picked me up and laid me on the bed.

God, he was so strong, it was as if I weighed nothing.

He hovered over me with that look. "I want to show you how captivated I am by you. I'm going to kiss every inch of you."

Yes, I was in! The dampness rushed between my legs and he hadn't even touched me yet.

His lips set sail on their adventure, destination, me. My earlobes were the first port of call. His tongue danced and tickled. I giggled and his teeth nibbled my spongy treasure. My body glowed in warmth.

Next, he traveled to my neck and delivered raindrop-like kisses. I wriggled under the prowess of his mouth. I yearned for him to take this journey to the main attraction. My hands dug into his shoulders and steered him south.

"You really are a bad girl. You just can't wait, can you?"

He reached between my legs and surveyed my wet folds.

I gasped. "Do you really have to kiss me everywhere?"

"Trust me. Your patience will be rewarded."

He toured my breasts and my nipples stiffened beneath his expertise. I was in agony. This party ship required dropping anchor on my pussy, stat.

The voyage continued to my stomach while he fondled my breasts. His succulent lips were like feathers on my skin. My legs separated. He landed.

Then he stopped.

I whimpered. "Derek, please."

"Good things come to this those who wait."

He sucked my big toe. It sent a scorching sensation to my sex. I was a throbbing puddle of need. He roamed up my inner thigh. I spread myself wider and begged to be pirated.

I looked down at him. "Please don't stop."

His nostrils flared as he glared into my waiting pussy. He inhaled. "Hmm...you are very enticing. You smell so sweet."

The vibration of his voice caused me to squirm. I was ready. *Pillage me!*

He ventured to my other foot and peppered light kisses on my instep. My juices flowed. His lips coiled up my inner thigh. My body was ripe and ready. He slid his hands under me, on my ass.

Yes! His tongue circled my clit. I expelled a grateful moan.

"You taste even better than I imagined."

No one ever said anything like that to me. It was so freaking hot. When he gently sucked my pulsing nub in his mouth, my body convulsed in pleasure. Derek removed his hands from my ass. His fingers peeled back my lips. My clit protruded like it was on parade. He ran his tongue up and down the layers of my pussy's flesh, causing my juices to leak. His skillful tongue stroked and flicked me, bounding me to the lido deck of orgasms. My slit was drenched. Derek lapped up every drop, even the drippings that trickled into my taint. I nearly levitated off the bed. "Ah, oh my God!"

His tongue resumed his assault on my clit. He drew it into his mouth and fed on me. Two fingers plunged inside and worked my hole until my release sailed through me. My body flailed. "I'm coming, ah, I'm coming!" *Anchors away!* My body was limp and sated.

Derek, on the other hand, was not limp at all. His hand wiped my juices from his mouth. He grabbed a condom, and slid it down his straining erection. With our flesh melded together, he grinned. "You are delicious."

"You're like really good at…stuff." Wow what an epic fail.

Derek's grin widened, "Sweetie, we were made for each other."

What did he say? I didn't have a chance to process it before the tip of his cock performed its magic below. I tilted my hips, and he thrust deeper inside.

He whispered, "I love the way you feel." His hands drifted underneath my back and he scooped me up.

The sudden intense shift of Derek's cock inside me provoked a loud groan.

He slowed down. "Are you okay?"

"Yes, everything you do to me feels incredible."

"Good girl. Hold on to me, let me take you."

Face-to-face, our bodies intertwined as one. His hands cradled my head and my bottom, coaxing me up and down. He clutched me close. Our lips came together. The smell of my sex hit my nose. My lips parted and he thrust his tongue into my mouth. My taste buds were alive with the flavor of my sweet syrup on his tongue. I closed my eyes and exhaled a shaky breath.

His hands caressed my face. "Sweetie, eyes on me. I want to see you when we come."

With my gaze fixed on his beautiful ice-blue eyes, our intense connection accelerated our pace. He shunted me hard and fast. My body quickly reeled to the edge. My pussy contracted on Derek's hard cock. With just a few more sharp thrusts, I let out a shriek and came before Derek's eruption of groans followed.

The air filled with the sound of our weighted breaths. Quiet, Derek guided me on my back and pulled out.

My cell beeped. "God, I hate the phone." I checked it. "It's a text from Brooke. She's letting me know she'll be at the club today filling in for Sonya. Sometimes she takes Sunday off."

"You need to her tell about Larry Wall."

"I will. You don't think he'd have the nerve to show up in my class today?"

"He better not. I should come to your class just to be safe."

"You would do that?"

"Of course. I gave you a workout. It's only fair I let you return the favor."

I giggled. "That's true, but your workout is much more fun."

"What are you teaching?"

I teased. "Spin, so saddle up, it's going to be a rough ride!"

"I enjoy a rough ride with a beautiful girl."

"I think I want to stay here."

He pressed his lips to mine. "Me too." A sudden smirk crossed his face. "But since we can't, who's a guy got to fuck around here to get a cup of coffee?"

"Well, Mr. Pierce, you are in luck. You just fucked the right girl. Please follow me into the kitchen for the best coffee you've ever had."

* * * *

I donned my bathrobe and Derek was in his boxers and T-shirt at my kitchen table. I rustled up coffee, juice, and egg white omelets. It was so comfortable, as if we'd breakfasted together a hundred times.

Derek said, "You're right, this is the best cup of coffee I've ever had. So, what are you doing after your class?"

"Well, I'm on dog duty. Julia and Phillip are flying to California in a couple of hours. That's about it. Why?"

"I was thinking about going to Mount Charleston. I haven't been up there yet. Do you want to go with me? We could take the dogs."

"Sure, Coco and Sammy love it up there."

"Then tonight you could come to my place if you want."

"Really?"

"I want to spend time with you before I head back to LA tomorrow."

Reality sunk in. I almost forgot he was a celebrity while we were in our little sex bubble. We came from two different worlds, equally as complicated. Common sense told me to protect myself and not succumb any deeper. I padded to the sink and pondered his request.

"I don't know if I should since I have to look after the dogs."

He came to me and snaked his arms around my waist. "You can bring them to my house. I just want to be with you."

Derek lips found my neck, and he rested his forehead on mine. "I loved waking up next to you. I'd like to do that in my bed."

Common sense was overrated. Dinner and a sleepover at Derek's—what more could a girl want?

Derek poured himself another cup of coffee and sat down at the kitchen table. I rinsed off the dishes and loaded them in the dishwasher.

"Hey, by the way," he said. "What do you want for dinner? I could have something delivered."

I made a sour face. "Like takeout?" Restaurant food and I were not friends. It either made my stomach upset, bloated, and occasionally gassy. I wasn't taking any chances.

"I can have anything delivered. What would you like?"

I sat at the table. "Would it be okay if I went to the grocery store and made dinner?" I wasn't a great cook, but I preferred to make everything myself. That way I maintained total control.

"Of course, whatever you want to do, but you don't have to go to the store. Make a list and I'll have the groceries delivered."

"I would feel better if I went to the store and picked it out myself." In exasperation, I let out a heavy sigh. "I have a few control issues."

In a playful yet sarcastic tone, he replied, "Really? I hadn't noticed."

I rose and poised my lip next to his. "Bite me."

He laughed, pulled me on his lap and nuzzled my neck. "Gladly, Miss Kelly.

* * * *

It was an hour before my spin class. I dropped Derek off at his place so he wouldn't have to do the walk of shame in his tuxedo. Then I drove to the club, floating on a cloud. The last twenty-four hours were a whirlwind. The next twenty-four, promised to be even better.

There was one glitch, Larry Wall. If it weren't for Derek, Larry's attack would've thrown me into a tailspin.

"Hey, Brooke, do you have a minute? I need to talk to you."

"Sure, I have a million questions for you too. Thanks for your text. I'm glad you're okay, but what the heck happened last night?"

I relayed the entire awful incident with Larry. She was dumbfounded. "I'm so sorry. I can't believe he did that to you."

"I can't believe how drunk he was."

"You know people have been complaining about him for years. Female members and employees want him out of here. I'm going to tell our managing director. Maybe there's something that can be done."

"What can they do? He lives here. Do you think he'll come to my classes?"

"No, don't worry. You will never have to see him at work again. I'll make sure of it. Actually, it would be great if they could revoke all of his privileges. Think about it, if he's banned from the sports club and the clubhouse, maybe he'll move."

"That would be great. Well, I better set up for class. Thank you so much."

Brooke stopped me in my tracks. "Wait a minute, not so fast."

I sheepishly asked, "What?"

"You didn't tell me what happened with Derek last night. The way you two danced, I'd swear you were in love."

"I don't know about in love, but definitely in lust."

"I'm afraid I'm going to need more information. What about his girlfriend?"

"It's a little complicated. I promised I wouldn't tell anyone. I can tell you this, Derek is amazing, and I'm not sure if I'm going to be able to sit on my bike seat today."

"Oh, you are so bad."

"So I've been told. Actually, he's coming to class today, and afterward we're taking Coco and Sammy up to Mount Charleston."

"Really? That's great."

"And I'm making dinner for us tonight at his place."

"I'm so happy for you."

"Thanks, I should get set up."

"Hey, when you get back from Mount Charleston drop the dogs off at my place. They can spend the night with Aunt Brooke."

"You don't have to do that."

"I want to, and in exchange, I will need copious details about everything. Have a great class."

I only wheeled out a few bikes and mats after I considered the alcohol consumption of last night. Steve and Scott socked back enough champagne for Times Square on New Year's Eve. Without a doubt, they were fast asleep.

The class was at noon for a reason. No one was interested in an early spin on Sunday mornings. After the last charity event, only two people showed. We referred to Sunday's class as the Church of Perpetual Spin. Everyone repented for Saturday night's sins.

I was happy to see the Petersons and the chorus girls. They hopped on their bikes and warmed up. Before I hit the music, I wheeled out another bike.

Derek sauntered in with all his charm. The women gasped.

I said to the group, "Hey, guys, Mr. Pierce is joining us today."

Mrs. Peterson gushed, "Oh, it's so nice to see you again."

Mr. Peterson rolled his eyes.

All three women flushed a lovely crimson shade. It was a community hot flash.

Poor Derek; the girls eyed him as if he was a juicy man-steak.

I hit the music and off we peddled. Sitting on the bike seat resulted in sheer torment for my junk. Derek did give me quite a workout. I shifted gears and did more drills out of the seat.

Derek's eyes fixed on me the entire class. It was difficult to focus. Everyone appeared oblivious, except Mrs. Peterson. Her head bobbed and darted as if she was watching a ping-pong match.

When the class was almost over I said, "Okay, last song. Bring it up out of the seat."

Derek downed his water and Mrs. Peterson piped up, "Is it just me, or did we do a lot of stuff out of the seat today?"

Derek nearly did a spit take. Now I flushed crimson. Was it possible they knew Derek thoroughly fucked me, and my naughty bits ached?

Between my sore business and my longing to be alone with Derek, this was the longest hour of my life. We had an entire day and night together. Maybe I was letting go a little. Maybe I could open up. Maybe he was the man I could trust with my heart.

Chapter Eight

Mount Charleston was superb. It was about sixty-five degrees, no clouds, and no wind. I could still see some snowcaps at the higher elevations. For March, it was warmer up here than usual.

Derek walked Coco, and I took Sammy. I was having the time of my life. It was so peaceful, barely a soul around.

Both of us talked nonstop. He told me about his family. His mother was an actor. Valerie Bennett was the "It Girl" in her day. My mom was one of her biggest fans. Valerie was married to Charles Pierce, a well-known Hollywood producer. They were legends and happily married after forty years. Derek also told me about his sister, Dina who lived in Chicago. She was a teacher and married with two girls. He spoke about them with such love. His childhood was ideal, despite growing up in the Hollywood spotlight.

I hated to be a Debbie Downer, but it was my turn to share. "Well, I had an amazing childhood until I was twelve. My mom died in a car accident."

"I'm so sorry. I can't imagine how hard that must have been for you."

I choked up a little. "It's still hard. I miss her so much."

"Of course you do, sweetie. Are you and your dad close?"

"Not really, he remarried the wicked witch of the east. She had two daughters. I didn't fit in. I couldn't wait to graduate high school and go away to college. That's where I met Julia. We've been best friends ever since."

I wasn't ready to divulge anything else. I asked him questions about *First Bite*, and his career.

Derek explained he worked non-stop since the show started five years ago. He spent half the year filming the series and the other half on movie sets. His goal was to strike while the iron was hot. Once the show ended, he wanted to work less and return to what he enjoyed most, theatre. He loved the work and hated the fame aspect of his career.

His show wrapped in a couple of weeks and two movies premiered this summer. For the first time he wasn't going to work until the show filmed in the fall. It was a revelation to hear him say he was lonely, another thing we had in common.

"I felt like my life was moving so fast, and I wasn't really living. I decided to take a break and see what happens."

"What made you want a house in Vegas?"

"It wasn't that I wanted to live in Vegas. I wanted a place that was private. The Manning's are old friends of my parents. They used to rave about the club, so when they decided to sell, I jumped at the chance." He smiled. "Plus, the club has this gorgeous fitness instructor with a foul mouth. I can't get enough of her."

"Well, she is a very naughty girl."

We cuddled on a picnic table and his mouth caught mine in a heart-stopping kiss. I was dying to rip off his clothes and do it, provided a park ranger wouldn't arrest us.

Instead, I said, "I did some theatre in college."

"You did?"

"Yep, Julia and I were in the chorus of *Guys & Dolls* when we were sophomores. We were hot-box girls."

He grinned in that devilish way. "That is quite a hot box you have there."

"It's a little bit of a sore box now."

He tugged me onto his lap. "I'm sorry. I was afraid of that. I promise to take care of it later." Then he graced my lips with another steamy treat.

"I think it's feeling better already."

"That's what I was hoping to hear." He draped his arms around me. "Was that the only play you were in?"

"No, I played a few small roles. My big claim to fame was junior year. I played Ado Annie in *Oklahoma*."

"Isn't that the girl who 'Cain't Say No?'"

"Yeah, it was typecasting. I did a lot of stupid things in college." I paused for a moment and confessed, "I guess you could say I was a walking country song, 'Lookin' for Love in All the Wrong Places.'" Embarrassed I opened my big mouth and shared too much, I climbed off Derek's lap and pet Sammy.

Sammy yawned. "Are you ready to go, Sammy? Are we boring you?" He licked my face. I laughed. "That means yes."

"You're so good with them. Did you have dogs growing up?"

"I did, a black cocker spaniel mix named Sadie. My stepmother claimed she was allergic, so my dad got rid of her."

"I'm sorry."

"It's okay. Sadie got a better deal. She didn't have to live in that house anymore."

Coco rolled on her back, beckoning Derek's attention. She begged for a belly rub like a canine hussy.

"Derek, Coco is flirting with you."

He bent down and loved on her belly. He was so cute with her. It lulled me out of my momentary funk.

"Look at Coco. She is giving it up for Derek Pierce. She gets that from me."

Derek cracked up. We gathered our things, and strolled back to the car hand in hand.

* * * *

I dropped Derek off at his house, and then I was on a mission. First, I deposited Coco and Sammy with Aunt Brooke. Then I hit the grocery store. I asked Derek what he was in the mood for and he said, "Surprise me." Why couldn't I be easygoing like him?

I settled on prawns in my homemade citrus marinade, plus a salad with mango, red pepper, and cilantro with a little avocado on the side.

I journeyed to my favorite part of the store. There it was—my one weakness besides Derek—cheese. I wasn't sure if an addiction to cheese was a real thing, but if it was, I was a cheese-aholic. I grabbed up some Havarti, Brie, and Gouda. Normally I steered clear of the tempting homemade baguettes, but Derek might enjoy, so why not?

He instructed me not to pick up wine since he stocked up, but I bought a Sauvignon Blanc and strawberries for dessert.

Beyond excited, I drove home to change for our evening together. Derek also said not to bother with an overnight bag. He would take care of it. I planned to bring a few things anyway. How could he be acquainted every toiletry a girl required for a sleepover? I wouldn't give up control of certain things, but in the bedroom with Derek, it was practically effortless. I couldn't explain it. Maybe it was our powerful connection or that Derek was an expert lover. Whatever it was, I let myself go with him.

* * * *

"Come in," Derek said. His eyes lit up. He looked so yummy in his casual shorts and tank.

He helped me with the grocery bags and showed me to the kitchen. The layout resembled Julia's house. His bare walls and sparse furniture told me he hadn't lived here long.

"I like your house."

"Thanks, it needs a lot of work. I bought some of the Manning's furniture, but I haven't had time to do much." He rifled through the grocery bags and pulled out the wine. "I see you really listened to me about the wine."

"I'm sorry. You know I'm a very bad girl."

"One of the many things I enjoy about you."

Derek gave me a quick peck on the cheek and dashed upstairs. I mixed my marinade and fixed the salad.

Was I for real in Derek Pierce's house, cooking us dinner? In my head, I imagined Derek to be as beautiful on the inside as he was on the outside. I was spot on. My affection for him grew with every look, every touch. Every simple sweet moment with Derek was special.

When I finished my preparations, Derek returned.

I said, "We're all set. We just need to let the shrimp marinate a little longer."

He had that look. "Come with me, I have a surprise for you."

"Oh wait, I want to grab my bag."

He cocked his head. His expression confused me. Was he mad?

"Is that the overnight bag I said you didn't need?"

Crap, I should have listened to what he said. I panicked, fumbled through my purse, and produced my birth control pills.

"I'm sorry, but you didn't know about these." I laid my pack on the counter.

"You didn't tell me you were on the pill."

"I know. I was kind of dreading the whole conversation."

Derek softened and asked, "Why?"

I exhaled. "Because it's so freaking uncomfortable. What was I supposed to say—hi, I'm Nia, I'm on the pill, and I'm clean as a whistle."

He smiled. "You should put that on a poster." He closed the gap between us. "I'm clean as a whistle too."

"I'm sorry I didn't listen to you about the wine and everything. Are you mad?"

"No, come here, sweetie." He held me. "I'm not mad. That's not it at all. It's that I had a plan to surprise you."

I peered up at him. "You had a plan?" He nodded. I flung my arms around his neck. "I love a good plan. I'm all yours."

The mood brightened. He hoisted me in his arms and carried me upstairs.

Derek set me on my feet in his bedroom. His master suite blew me away. Julia would totally crap her pants if she saw it. It was way bigger than hers.

On the bed laid the cutest pajama ensemble. It was black and the material was cottony soft. It came complete with a short robe, little tank, shorts and panties. It was something I would have picked out. I usually wore black. In fact, I had on a black sundress, probably not for long.

"Derek, I love it. Thank you so much."

"Wait, there's more." He ushered me into the master bathroom. It contained a huge roman tub with separate shower. A chaise longue matched perfectly with the slate tile. On the oversized double sinks were all of my toiletries, everything down to my body wash and lotion. He lit candles, and with the champagne chilling, filled the tub with bubbles. The smell of jasmine and vanilla permeated the air.

I ogled in shock. "How did you…you did all this for me?"

He replied, "Of course."

"Why?"

He shrugged with a warm smile. "Nothing but the best for my girl!"

Did he really say that? I clutched his shirt and yanked him to my mouth. We ripped each other's clothes off. Then he stopped and left me breathless.

"Sweetie, you said you were sore. I want you to get in tub first. We have all night."

He hung up our clothes, led me into the tub, and poured us champagne. He was right. This was the best. Maybe I really was his girl. I wanted to be, and I wanted this night to last forever.

We faced each other, drank champagne, and exchanged soft kisses.

I said, "You know, I've been meaning to tell you something."

"What's that?"

"I really like it when you call me sweetie."

At first, sweetie sounded a little corny or old-fashioned. The way he said it was endearing and kind of sexy.

A devilish twinkle sparked his eyes. "I've been meaning to tell you something too. I really like it when you announce your arrival."

"What, my arrival? I don't get it."

He chuckled. "I'm coming! I'm coming!"

"I don't do that! Do I?" He nodded and I remembered. "Oh no, I totally do." I shifted to my knees and splashed him.

He grabbed me and crushed his lips to mine. "Nia, I can't wait to be inside you."

He toweled my body with care. Then placed a dry towel between the two sinks and sat me on top.

"Open your legs for me and lean back. I've been dying taste you again."

I unfolded myself and granted him my arousal. The man ate pussy like he was born to it! His delectable tongue nearly sent me to the edge. A little sprinkle of juices trickled on the towel.

A subtle finger dipped inside. "Good girl, you feel ready for me."

I was more than ready. He penetrated me with his eyes. "Do you want me to use a condom?"

I shook my head and there was that look. "Wrap your legs around me, sweetie."

He slowly impaled me with his rock-hard cock. Oh yes, it was skin on skin. It was totally fucking hot!

"Nia, I can really feel you, God, it's so good." His firm, even strokes pushed me higher and higher. Derek growled, "Hang on." He swept me up and slammed against the wall.

I cried out, "Yes, ah, Derek, yes!"

He was in me deeper than ever before. "Are you okay, is it too much?"

"Oh God, no! Fuck me!"

He hammered away at me and I loved it. My back skidded up and down the rough wall. I held onto his shoulders as he trounced me. The friction of our bodies set off a blazing fervor. My orgasm neared and his thrusts quieted.

"Derek, don't stop. Please, don't stop."

He held me with one arm and his other hand grabbed a towel. He whisked me to the chaise longue.

He threw the towel on it and eased me on my back without coming out of me.

"I want you to come for me, Nia. I want us to come together." I curved my legs around his waist. He pumped my pussy with vigor. His cock was unyielding. It pummeled my hot spot and flew me toward my impending release. I gripped his shoulders and shut my eyes tight. I couldn't hold on another second.

I gasped in pleasure, "I'm going to come! Ah, I'm going to come!"

"Your eyes, Nia, I need your eyes." With that, we climaxed, locked in each other's gaze. I felt his hot cum flood inside me. It was freaking phenomenal.

The second he pulled out, I missed him inside me. My head rested on his chest and I was in heaven.

This was by far the most extraordinary thing I ever experienced. "That was amazing."

"Nia, you're amazing. You take my breath away."

"I've never done that before." I paused and asked, "Is it always like this?"

"What do you mean?"

I mumbled. "Is sex always like this?"

"Didn't you tell me you did all those stupid things in college?"

"Yeah, no I'm sorry. I did, I mean, I've had sex before, but it's never been like this. My sexual encounters can be summed up in two words—selfish and quick."

He chuckled, but it was true. I never understood what the fuss was all about, until Derek.

The back of his hand brushed my cheek. "I think the sex is this good because it's with you."

I looked away. "Sometimes I feel like I don't know what I'm doing."

"Sweetie, look at me, you're incredible. I can't get enough of you."

When Derek tucked me in for a kiss, I melted. He was the incredible one. I was like the luckiest girl in the world.

He released me, and the mood shifted to playful.

He pulled me onto his lap. "You know, since you said you felt like you didn't know what you're doing, maybe it's time for the teacher to become the student."

"I don't know. I'm a tough teacher. I'm not sure I'd be a good student."

"If you're not, maybe I'll spank you."

"Don't you mean if I'm good, you'll spank me?"

"I like the way you think."

His mouth was on mine and just like that, we were at it again. Whatever brewed in his devious head could commence right now.

"Can class be in session?"

"I like a girl who is so eager. But no, it can't."

"Why not?"

"Because you better eat first, you're going to need your strength."

We dressed and returned to the kitchen. While Derek grilled the prawns, I retrieved the cheese, wine, and salad and placed them on the island. I found his plates and set the table by the window. His dining room table was formal. I liked how cozy it was in the kitchen. Besides, it had a great view of the mountains.

Derek came inside with the prawns and asked, "Do you want me to set these on the table?"

"Sure, do you have any foil so I can cover them?"

Derek opened a drawer and handed me the foil. "Here, but I think they'll stay hot."

"It's not just for the heat. When I pull something off the grill I always cover it in foil, and let it sit for a bit, so the juices can redistribute."

"So the juices can redistribute?"

I trotted to the table and covered the dish with foil. "You never heard of juices redistributing?" I sauntered to Derek. "My juices are redistributing right now."

He threw his head back and laughed. I loved how I could crack his ass up.

He snaked his arms around my waist. "While you're redistributing, do you mind telling me something?"

I draped my arms around his neck. "Not at all."

"What's with all the cheese?"

"I have a little problem. I'm addicted to cheese, and I hope you like it too, because it's a deal breaker."

"I love cheese. I'm actually glad you like it. You're so little; it's probably the only thing holding you together."

"I'm not little. I'm just compact. I'm very tough. I could kick your ass right now."

"Yes, sorry, you are very tough. What I meant to say is, your body is perfect." He rubbed my ass. "Hmm…this is perfect." One hand traveled north and cupped my breast. "These are perfect."

"You're right about my boobs. They are little."

He had that look. "No, they're perfect. God, Nia, I love your body." He pressed me up against the kitchen island and took my mouth in a sultry way. He exhaled. "We better eat before I take you right here on the island."

"You can. I'll move the cheese."

He chuckled. "No, we better eat. I think all the juices are redistributed now."

"My teacher is so hard."

"My student is so right."

My food was a hit. Derek gobbled it up. We chatted up a storm. We talked about our workout regimes and the gyms he installed in both of his houses.

My stomach knotted when he asked me how long I lived in Vegas and why I moved here. I said I was in limbo, and Julia suggested the change and helped me out. In a way, it was true. Could I ever tell him everything?

I changed the subject and asked him more questions about his two movies and *First Bite*. I found it fascinating. I liked the way his face beamed when he talked about his craft. As we cleared the table I asked, "What time does your flight leave tomorrow?"

"My call time on set is six o'clock tomorrow night. I'll probably leave early afternoon, whenever."

"You didn't book your flight? Do you need to?"

He hesitated. "I don't have to book a flight because I have my own plane."

"You have your own plane!"

He nodded.

I blurted, "You do know your show is on cable?"

Derek shook his head. "Oh, Miss Kelly, what am I going to do with you?"

The kitchen was clean, the food put away, and Derek escorted me upstairs. My heart skipped in excited anticipation. Just what did he have in store for me? I stood by the bed. Derek disappeared for a moment and returned with a towel and massage oil.

I asked, "Is that the same scent as my body wash?"

"Yeah, since you said were sore, I thought I'd treat you to a massage. I want to massage all of you."

He threw the towel at the foot of the bed and set oil down on the nightstand. He stripped off his clothes and I admired his nakedness. He peeled off my easy access black sundress. I was wet and hungry for him.

His hands traveled to my ass and he whispered. "Oh, how I love this ass." He tugged at my panties. "I don't think you're going to need these."

Derek knelt and slowly slid them off. He grazed one hand up my inner thigh and his fingers disappeared inside. I panted. His lips danced on my stomach as he toyed with my hole. I trembled under his probing spell.

Derek rose and spread the towel. In a quiet commanding tone he said, "Lay on the bed for me, on your stomach."

Holy shit! Who knew what was coming. I hoped it would be me. I reclined on my tummy. Derek reached for the oil and knelt on the bed beside me. He smoothed my hair over to one side and leaned in close.

"School is in session, Miss Kelly."

Son of a bitch, this was double fabulous.

He lubed oil on his hands before massaging my back and leisurely working his way to my ass. Derek's hands made me purr like a kitten. He descended, moving the delicious rubs down one leg and moseying up the other. He arrived at my bottom. He slid his hand between my legs and skimmed it against my impatient pussy. I exhaled in arousal, opened my legs, and raised my hips a little.

"That's it, good girl." He petted my clit. A lurid, blistering sensation waved over my body. It was different in this position, like bad girl different.

I lifted my hips to him. Derek gained access to all of me. His kneading hand granted my engorged nub the perfect amount of friction. I writhed in ecstasy. Two fingers dove into me and I bucked on his hand like a naughty, wanton, schoolgirl. "Fuck yes!"

I was on my hands and knees climbing to the edge. That now familiar pressure flourished inside. It was so intense, I cried out in delirious pleasure.

One of Derek's fingers coated in massage oil touched my anus, testing me, as any good teacher would. I liked it. I screamed, "I'm going to come, ah fuck, give it to me." He pushed the tip of his finger inside and my orgasm shot through me like a bullet! I collapsed face down with my head in the pillow. For a moment, I lay still, while my body shivered in awesomeness.

He kissed my shoulder. "Was that okay?"

I rolled on my side. "If we're keeping a list, can you put that on the top?"

"Of course. I love how responsive your body is. It makes me want you more."

I craved him so much. It frightened me. This gorgeous, incredible man opened up an entire new world to me. It was exhilarating, but scary. I was falling for him. I was lost in him, and I wanted him inside me.

"I want you right now."

"Well, if you insist."

"Teacher, I insist."

He possessed a look in his eyes. A look that said he was so going to be fucking me. He kissed me hard, and he was hard. It was this stiff, rigid, salacious situation.

In a sexy growl he said, "Lay back down on your stomach."

Hell yes! This might be my new favorite position.

"Lift your hips, sweetie."

He readied my pussy with his fingers and planted soft kisses on my ass. His hands roamed to my hips. Derek's thick erection invaded me from behind and stretched me further. He took his time with patient thrusts. It made my pussy weep around him.

He growled, "You're even tighter like this. Do you want more?"

I panted. "Ah, yes."

I pushed back and he squirreled in deeper. His hands fondled and teased my cheeks. He steadied while I adjusted to his concrete cock pushing inside. A spasm rocked my walls as Derek built back up to a steady pace.

He hissed, "Are you ready, do you want all of it?"

"Yes, I want all of it."

He rammed me with the entire length of his shaft. It robbed me of my breath. I could barely hold myself up. He gripped my hips and slammed me into me even harder. Oh God, this was *fuck-tastic!* Derek wrapped one arm around my waist and his other hand circled my clit.

I was close, just a few more swift strokes. He slowed. "Nia, don't come yet."

Was he freaking kidding? He pulled out. "Turn over for me. I want to see you when you come." I rolled over. He gazed down at me. "Sweetie, I don't just want to fuck you. I want to make love to you too."

I practically came right there. I spread my legs to him, and he enveloped me. We didn't take our eyes off each other. It was passionate, it was gentle, and when we came together, it was like, love.

Tears welled up. Too many emotions ran through me at once. I covered my face with my hands and hid my threatening tears.

Derek took my hands in his. "Nia, are you okay? Did I hurt you?" He meant physically, but he could crush me emotionally and shatter my heart.

"No, I'm okay."

"You look like you're going to cry."

I sighed. "This has been the best day ever, thank you."

A couple of tears spilled down my cheeks, Derek wiped them away with the pad of his thumb. My head rested on his chest and his arms wound around me. We were silent.

Derek kissed the top of my head. "You know, it looks like I might have a short week on set. If all goes well I could be back in Vegas by Thursday."

I popped up. "Really?"

"I wasn't planning on coming back until we wrapped for the year, but I think I might miss you too much."

I would miss him too, but instead I teased, "Well, if you're here next week I will do my best to pencil you in."

He gave my bottom a playful swat. "Young lady, I think you need to get some rest. What time do you need to get up tomorrow?"

"Oh, I don't know. I have to get Coco and Sammy settled before my first class, seven would be good."

Derek set the alarm. "I'm going to get us some water while you get ready for bed." Somehow, he made the simplest things sound sexy.

He threw on his shorts and headed downstairs. I trucked to the bathroom and did my thing. I was sitting on the side of the bed when Derek strolled in with our water.

He placed one on each nightstand, handed me his phone and asked, "Can you program your number in there for me?"

He hit the bathroom and I plugged my number in his phone. I was tempted to send Eden Fox a text and tell her to vamoose, but better judgment prevailed—this time.

Derek returned to bed, all adorable and naked with his freshly fucked hair. I gave him his phone. "You now have my number. I put it under Bad Girl."

"Your phone was on the island, so I programmed all my numbers in there."

"Did you list them under Giant Penis? Sorry teacher, I call 'em as I see 'em."

Derek climbed in bed and gathered me close. "Speaking of your phone, did you want me to get it for you?"

"No, that's okay. I kind of hate the phone in general." Sometimes a ringing phone was nothing but bad news coming my way.

"Why do you hate the phone?"

I shrugged and changed the subject. "How come you don't have a TV in here?"

"You want to watch TV? It's after midnight."

"No, not right now, but don't you ever watch TV before bed? I usually fall asleep with the TV on."

"You know, they say that's not good for you. But, if it's a deal breaker, like you and your cheese, I'll get a TV."

I kissed his cheek. "Thank you."

He flicked off the light. "Something tells me when I get the TV; you're never going to let me touch the remote control."

"You're probably right."

He delighted me with a quick peck. "Goodnight, my sweet girl."

Chapter Nine

When I opened my eyes, Derek and I faced each other. He kissed my forehead. "Good morning, beautiful."

Beautiful was not how I looked in the morning. On the other hand, Derek and his ice-blue eyes were something I'd like to look at every day.

I cuddled close. "What time is it?"

"It's a little before seven. I turned off the alarm. I thought it might be nicer to wake up like this."

He pressed his erection into my naked flesh. In the past, I was never a fan of morning sex. In college, I fled the scene of the crime before the sun came up. However, there was no way to resist this hot, handsome man. My desire for him produced a trickle of moisture between my thighs.

I helped myself to his rigid cock and teased, "Wow! You're really awake."

He slid his hand over my breasts, past my stomach and delved inside. He smiled. "You're really awake too."

I rested my leg on his hip and he slipped inside. We were still face-to-face. Something else I had never done before. Derek took total control. I moaned with every tender thrust. God, everything he did was so sensual, so right.

"Nia, I want you so much." He rolled me on my back and our hips moved in perfect sync. "That's it, sweetie. God, you're amazing." He penetrated me with greater force. This quickie had me on the cusp.

His mouth was all over me, as our fiery passion raged. We were about to detonate. I arched my back and met him thrust for thrust. My legs opened wide and coiled around him. My hands flew to his ass. Our bodies heaved and we clung to one another.

He grunted. "Come for me, Nia."

"Yes, I'll come for you. Oh God!" My pussy clenched and squeezed his cock. It rocked us to a violent release.

Stillness permeated the room. Was he really coming back on Thursday? Would he miss me? Derek gathered me up and held me to his chest. I clutched him tight. I didn't want to let go, ever. My world flipped upside down.

Derek smoothed my hair. "I'm going to see you on Thursday, okay?"

Unfortunately, work beckoned. "Is it okay if I hop in your shower before I take off?"

He caressed my cheek. "Of course, I'll get us some coffee."

I hit the shower and dressed. Hmm... Clothes... also overrated.

When I returned to the bedroom, Derek was on his balcony. The view was stunning, Derek and the Red Rock mountains.

On the table, I spied a breakfast tray with coffee, juice, and the strawberries I bought for dessert.

I gleamed and curled my arms around his waist. "This is so nice. I think you're spoiling me."

"Good, that's what I was going for. Are you warm enough?"

Yes, I was warm enough. I glowed from the inside out. Somehow, the morning sun shined brighter and coffee tasted more robust after our night of primal sex and lovemaking. Derek was so freaking sexy with his messy hair and a little bit of stubble. Why couldn't time stand still?

We finished our breakfast, I grabbed up my things, and Derek walked me to the door. He grew a little quiet. It was hard to read him. I wasn't sure what to say.

Eventually I said, "Be safe traveling." Gosh, that was lame.

"You too, the drivers in Vegas are almost as bad as California."

I lightened a bit. "Julia says that too." Then my newly discovered bad girl sailed to my rescue. "I hope I remember everything I need to do for my classes today. You pretty much fucked my brains out."

Derek cracked up. "I'm going to miss that dirty little mouth of yours. Come here." He pulled me in for a heart-stirring kiss. "Thursday, okay. I'll call you."

With that, we said goodbye.

* * * *

I was off. I picked up the dogs. Of course, Brooke requested a full Derek report, but I told her we'd have to catch up later. I settled them in at the main house and ran to the guesthouse to change for classes. First up was Body Sculpt and Pilates back-to-back at the country club. Then I had a little break and a private spin at noon with Nancy Simmons, one of the chorus girls. She was leaving town and squeezed in one more workout before her trip.

Sonya wasn't scowling like usual. She was quiet, which I preferred.

Afterward, I checked on the dogs, grabbed a bite, and changed for my next class. The day whizzed by. I focused on work so I wouldn't miss Derek, but I wasn't successful. How could I not miss everything about him? I just experienced the most amazing weekend with this incredible man. I already missed his laugh, his touch, his voice. Absolutely everything—even the way he smelled.

When my final class was over, I checked my phone. Derek didn't call or text. I wasn't expecting to hear from him, but my heart sank a little.

Last week at this time, I was on the phone with Julia discussing my anniversary celebration. Brooke left me the message about Derek's private spin. So much had happened in only one week.

Before I got in the car, a brilliant idea crossed my mind. Right down the street was a salon that did the best bikini waxes in town. I'd never done it before, but Julia bragged Brazilian was the way to go. She said Phillip loved it.

Would Derek love it too? There was only one way to find out.

I hopped in the car and drove to the salon. I was in luck—no waiting, they took me back right away. As I stripped down, I wondered if it would hurt. I shrugged it off. I could take it.

Holy fucking shit balls! What was I thinking? Brazilian wax was a big, fat fucking mistake. I suppose there were more painful things in life, like giving birth to an elephant or having a building fall on you, but to me this was the worst pain ever!

I paid them good money to torture my lady parts. How did women do this on a regular basis? Was their business made of stone? Maybe the wax was too hot. When I sat in the car, my pussy was on fire, and not in a good way.

I was going to walk the dogs, but instead I grabbed a bag of frozen peas to cool my area. I was lying on Julia's couch watching TV with Coco and Sammy. I heard a beep. I checked my cell. Yea, it was a text from Derek. "I made it back to LA, and I'm on set. I'm shooting all night. I will give you a call tomorrow, Derek."

I was disappointed it was so formal. I texted him back. "Thanks for letting me know. Have a great night, Nia."

There, I could be formal too. I was inclined to write, "Hey, dumbass, I got a Brazilian wax for your pleasure. Now my goddamn crotch is burned and you didn't bother to say you miss me," but I didn't."

It was only nine-thirty when exhaustion set in. I let the dogs out, got a fresh bag of frozen peas and conked out.

* * * *

Where was I? I was supposed to be in the fitness room at the country club, but this was an old bowling alley. How could I teach spin here? My iPod was frozen. I was so frustrated I searched for the exit. A man in a black leather jacket and jeans sauntered toward me. It was Derek Pierce. Why would he come to spin class in that outfit? I didn't care what he wore. I wanted him. He reached for me. Yes, I longed to touch my lips to his. A cool breeze flowed over my exposed privates. I was naked from the waist down. Where were my pants? Why didn't I have any pants on?

I cried out, "Son of a bitch!" Oh, it was just a dream. Great, I scared the dogs and the frozen peas melted. I stumbled to the kitchen for some water and camped out in the living room with Coco and Sammy. I flicked on the TV and fell asleep.

* * * *

I woke up with a jolt because the TV was too loud. Sammy rested his head on the remote. I grabbed it, to turn it down and froze. Please tell me this wasn't happening.

The blonde entertainment reporter on a morning "news" show said, "Say it isn't so! Are Hollywood heavy hitters Eden Fox and Derek Pierce calling it quits? Sources say Pierce was spotted in Las Vegas over the weekend with a mystery woman."

It was a picture of Derek dancing with me at the benefit.

The reporter continued, "Pierce and Fox have been dating for two years and their publicists could not be reached for comment. However, a source said Pierce appeared rather cozy with this Las Vegas woman at a fundraiser for the Las Vegas Humane Society. Stay tuned for more as this story develops."

Frantic, I checked my phone. I didn't have any messages from Derek. Should I call him? Before a panic attack erupted, Julia called.

"Julia, did you see what I saw?"

"I know you're freaking out, but you're fine. You can't see your face in the photo, and they don't know your name, so that's a good thing."

"I guess you're right, but I'm still freaking out."

"Those slime balls that spin ridiculous stories won't be able to set foot on the country club."

"Actually, it's not a story."

"What do you mean?"

"Look, I have a lot to tell you, and it's really complicated."

After a brief silence, Julia took control in her Julia way. "This is what I want you to do. Tell Brooke everything. She can talk to security and make sure no one comes sniffing around trying to find out who you are. I also want you to steer clear of Derek."

"That should be pretty easy since he went back to LA."

"Is he coming back to Vegas? I don't think he should."

"He said he was coming back Thursday, but I haven't heard from him."

"Tell him to stay put until this blows over."

"Maybe it won't be a big deal. In the next ten minutes, a celebrity could announce a divorce and this will just be a blip on the radar."

"Promise me you will be extra careful. I couldn't bear it if anything else happened to you."

"I'll be fine, I promise."

The minute I hung up the phone, my cell beeped. It was a text from Brooke. "I saw the picture of you and Derek on TV. I'm going to meet with security right now. I don't want you to worry. I'm on it. BTW, I don't know all the deets, but I heard Larry Wall moved to CA. Please call me later. I want to make sure you're okay."

At least Larry Wall was one less thing to worry about. I threw on my clothes and dashed to the other side of town.

When I arrived at the gym, I checked my phone and there was still nothing from Derek.

I drove back to Julia's after class. Everything was normal when I pulled through the country club gates. Perhaps I was upset over nothing.

I checked on the dogs, changed, and breathed a little easier. Then my phone rang. It was Derek.

"Hey, how are you?"

He sounded angry. "Not good."

"Why, because of our picture? I saw it on the news."

He raised his voice. "Yes, because of the picture. Eden is pissed. This is a huge mess. You haven't talked to a reporter or anything, have you?"

"No, I would never do that. Why are you yelling at me?"

"I'm not yelling. I'm just mad."

"Are you mad at me?"

"No, I'm not mad at you, but if you hadn't freaked out when that guy took our picture this probably wouldn't have happened. You made it look like we had something to hide. And the frustrating thing is you are hiding something from me, and you won't tell me what the fuck it is."

A lump formed in my throat. "I'm sorry."

"So now I'm worried about you. Eden flipped out, our managers and publicists have a huge mess to clean up. Plus, I've got to be back on set in an hour when I was there all night."

"I don't know what to say."

Derek snapped. "Don't say anything to anyone."

My voice cracked. "Please stop yelling at me."

He softened. "I'm sorry. There's so much you don't understand." He paused. "I don't think I'll be back in Vegas for a while. I have to stay here and do damage control."

Now I was mad. "You have to do damage control for your fake relationship? Is it really a publicity thing or is it something you said so I would sleep with you?"

"You know I would never do that."

"No, I don't know that. The only thing I know is your fake-ass relationship with Eden is more important than the real relationship I thought was happening with us."

"I have to go but I'm going to call you later. I think we both need to calm down. Are you going to be home tonight?"

"I don't know."

"Nia, my manager is calling. I have to take this. I'll call you later."

I should hurl my phone through the window. Yesterday I woke up in Derek's arms and now this. He sounded like a different person. My walls flew back up.

Our relationship would never have worked anyway. His world was so different. I had to protect myself and not be part of it.

An image of Derek making love to me flashed through my head. *Damn it!* I exhaled and pulled myself together. Spin class at the country club neared.

My heart wasn't the only thing hurting. After my waxing debacle, the bike seat would hurt too. Talk about adding insult to injury. Perhaps it was the universe's way of telling me I made two huge mistakes.

When I walked in the club, Sonya wouldn't make eye contact. She'd gone from scowling to quiet, to pretending I didn't exist. I had no time for her crap.

I wheeled out the bikes while my students entered the room, until there were none left. We only had ten bikes, and I had ten students. I relinquished my bike to a new student, Carrie Rodgers. From that day on, I called her my Carrie God Mother. She magically rescued my sore snatch from the bike seat.

I hit the music and guided the class through their drills and hills. Sometimes it was fun to teach off the bike. The room overflowed with positive energy. Sue Peterson sang along with Sharon Gill, since the other chorus girl, Nancy, was out of town. Then the entire class joined in.

Afterward, I hopped in the car and drove to the grocery store. Even though my head remained steadfast in forgetting about Derek, my heart wasn't ready to let go. I checked my phone a hundred times. For once, it was silent.

As I rolled my grocery cart to the car, I spotted Sue Peterson in the parking lot. I called to her. "Hey, Mrs. Peterson."

"Hi, Nia, I do wish you would call me Sue. We aren't at the club, and I think it's a silly rule anyway. Class was so much fun tonight. I felt bad you didn't get a bike, though."

"That's okay. I needed a break."

Her expression turned serious. "Can I ask you something? Did something happen with you and Larry Wall Saturday night?"

"Yeah, something happened. He was drunk and things got ugly. I heard he moved to California."

"I heard his wife got sick of his shenanigans and threw him out."

"What? Where is Mrs. Wall anyway? I've never laid eyes on her."

"Oh, it's so sad. Her parents back East have been ill, and she's been taking care of them."

"How do you know all this?"

"Well, I'm not one for gossip, but I play tennis with the Wall's neighbor, Stephanie. She filled me in. You know Mrs. Wall is the one with all the money. Larry's been unemployed for years. She's been supporting them."

"I feel so bad for her."

"I do too. I'm glad when he harassed you, the club called her and not Larry. It was the last straw. You will never have to see him again. He is in California, sleeping on his brother's couch."

"That is a huge relief."

"I'm sorry you had to go through that." She embraced me. Sue was nurturing and bubbly. She reminded me of my mom.

"Thank you so much for saying that. I feel a lot better."

"Good and you know if you ever need anything, say the word. Jeff and I adore you."

* * * *

Back at Julia's, I chilled out on the sofa with the dogs. I tuned into one of those Entertainment Access Gossip shows. Were they still talking about Derek and Eden or was it old news?

Our photo flashed on the screen. The male reporter with the bad hair said, "Does this mean trouble in paradise for Derek Pierce and Eden Fox? Not so, says the couple's publicist, 'The photo is from a benefit in Las Vegas. Both Fox and Pierce planned to attend, but Fox canceled due to illness. The woman in the photo is nothing more than an overzealous fan wanting her fifteen minutes of fame.'"

I changed the channel. How could Derek allow them to say that? I was such an idiot. I cradled my head in my hands. I couldn't fight back the tears anymore. I curled up on the couch in the fetal position and sobbed.

The phone rang. It was Derek. What did he want? Hasn't he hurt me enough for one day? I didn't answer. We were so over. There was nothing to say.

* * * *

I cried myself to sleep. When I opened my swollen eyes, my head and my heart ached. In a fog, I checked Derek's voicemail. It was short and curt.

"Nia, it's Derek, I really need to talk to you. Call me back if you get this in the next hour. I'm working all night. Bye."

What could he say to the "overzealous fan" that would change a thing?

I deleted his message and fought my way through the day. I had trouble focusing in my zombie-like state.

After my classes, I checked in with Brooke and touched based with Steve and Scott.

Slumped on Julia's sofa, I tuned into a different entertainment gossip show. Perhaps a new celebrity scandal broke. Then they would stop airing the picture of Derek and me.

No such luck; things grew worse. They rolled footage of Derek and Eden all over Hollywood with their relationship on display. This was disgusting. They went to celebrity hot spots to be seen holding hands and having lunch. There was a picture of Derek kissing Eden on her forehead.

Another gossip show ran a video of them embracing. I turned it off. Was this what he meant by damage control? If they really aren't together, why was this so important to him? Without a doubt, I was duped and dumped.

I wandered to the kitchen and checked my phone. I had a voicemail from my dad.

"Hey, kid, it's your dad. I wanted to see how you're doing. Give me a call if you get this message in the next hour or so. I'm up by myself, watching the news. Bye now."

I did want to talk to him. Our relationship had improved since I moved to Vegas. At first, he was furious I left the East Coast without telling him. I didn't understand that. All communication between us ceased after I married Nick.

The first few times we spoke, I blocked my number. I wasn't sure I could trust him. Something changed along the way. I never went into a lot of detail about what Nick did to me, but Dad knew he abused me and I was afraid. The second time we talked, I divulged more details.

The third time I phoned him, Dad confessed my stepmother badgered him about my situation and needled him for information. He told her there had been abuse, and she said, "Well, she brought it on herself. She's always been so difficult and stubborn." He said she was wrong and it wasn't my fault. It was our turning point.

I didn't give him my phone number, but I gave him my post office box. About a week later, he mailed me my mom's old jewelry box, her locket, and some pictures. It meant the world to me. He never spoke of Mom after he remarried. Perhaps it was to appease step-mommy dearest.

When I called Dad the fourth time to thank him for the package, I gave him my number and he said he would never share it with anyone, not even her. That was right before Christmas.

I loved how he called me "kid" now. I wasn't comfortable with my old name Meagan, and he wasn't comfortable calling me Nia. That was fine by me. I was happy to hear from him.

Since he said he was alone, I called him back.

"Dad, it's me."

His voice sounded excited. "Well, hey there, kid, how are you?"

"I'm good. What's up?"

"I wanted to see if you could come for a visit soon?"

"I would love to see you. But, I don't think your wife would like it."

He sighed. "I understand."

"Are you okay?"

"Sure, I'm fine. You know, this summer Evelyn and the girls will take their trip to the Mall of America. I'll have the place to myself. Could you visit then, my treat?"

"I think so. I'm sorry I can't come sooner. I hate that I always disappoint you."

"You don't disappoint me. I'm disappointed in myself. I feel like I failed you. I keep thinking if I'd been there for you and done things differently, you wouldn't have gotten mixed up with a guy like Nick."

My voice shook. "Dad, it's not your fault."

"I want you to know I still love your mother. I miss her. I know now I didn't do right by you, but your mom and I are proud of how strong you are."

Tears burned my eyes. "I miss Mom every day. I miss you too."

"Well, then it's settled, I'll see you this summer. I love you, kid."

"I love you too."

"Give your Aunt Mary Jane a call when you can."

Wow, what a breakthrough, it was the first time Dad mentioned Mom since he remarried. He still missed and loved her every bit as much as I did.

He even told me to call Aunt Mary Jane. I missed her too. She was my mom's best friend and dad's sister.

Her husband, Uncle Bill, was an engineer and received a job offer in Wichita when I was nine. When they moved, I was devastated. I spent a couple of summer vacations there, but when Dad remarried, they had a huge falling out. Aunt Mary Jane didn't get on with my stepmother either.

She and Uncle Bill were retired. I hadn't seen her in years, but we kept in touch. She and Dad were the only people from my past who had my phone number. She was always there for me. I would call her now if it wasn't so late in Kansas.

My cell beeped with a text from Derek. "I tried to call you. I need to talk to you. When are you free?"

I deleted it immediately. I wasn't going to let him bring me down. My dad told me he loved me. He said I was strong. He was right. I'd been through worse and I would get through this too. I was fine.

Chapter Ten

Even though I didn't sleep much, I woke up renewed. I vowed to focus on all the good things in my life and forget the rest. I was excited to teach my classes with sharper focus than yesterday. This was going to be a good day.

I couldn't wait to hang out with Julia tonight. Phillip wouldn't be home until Saturday, so I had her all to myself.

The day cruised by. Before my last class, I got a text from Julia.

"Text me when you're done for the day. The gang is coming over to binge watch *Will & Grace*. We won't start until you get here."

What a perfect plan. I texted and said I was in, hundred percent.

When I arrived at Julia's, Brooke was already there, but Steve and Scott weren't. I filled them in on the latest. I told them about the break through with my Dad. Then I did my best to explain what happened with Derek.

"I'm completely confused by all this," Julia said.

"Well, that makes two of us. He yelled at me on the phone, and now I have to see them splashed all over the

TV. Oh, and get this, he called and texted. He wants to talk to me."

Brooke asked, "About what?"

"I have no idea, because I haven't responded. I figure, what's the point? I don't think I could handle being with someone like Derek anyway. He probably has women throwing themselves at him all day long. Plus, he's not the man I thought he was."

Julia responded with a cheeky grin. "You're better off. But I have to ask, how was he in the sack?"

We all giggled and I quipped, "Pretty freaking great! I will miss that fantastic giant penis."

The girls laughed so loud I almost didn't hear my cell. I checked it and was stunned. Derek called again.

"Well, speaking of giant penis, it's Derek."

Brooke and Julia broke out in a chorus of, don't you dare answer your phone.

I shoved the phone back in my purse. "Don't worry. I'm not going to answer. Julia is right, I'm better off. Oh, and by the way, I got a Brazilian wax."

Julia piped up. "Isn't it fabulous?"

"No, not fabulous. I feel like my lady parts have been violated."

They thought it was funny, but my nether regions were not amused.

Steve and Scott arrived and we had a blast. We drank wine, ate cheese, and laughed our heads off. While everyone headed home, Julia asked if we were free Friday night for an evening out on the Vegas strip.

Steve and Scott already had plans. I thought it would be us girls, but Brooke declined too. She was evasive and it made me curious if she had a date. There was a new tennis pro at the club named Tom Hyland. Every time she mentioned him, her eyes lit up.

After everyone left Julia said, "Looks like it's only you and me tomorrow night. It'll be just like college."

"I hope it's not exactly like college, because it means one of us will be throwing up by the end of the night."

"It was usually me. I better behave."

"Girls gone wild, the Vegas edition!"

I padded down to the guesthouse and got ready for bed. I shouldn't have, but I checked my phone to see if Derek left a message. He didn't, but there were three more missed calls from him. It was frustrating. If he would leave me alone, this would be so much easier. My mind wandered to the last time we made love and how we clung to each other.

Before I shed a tear, there was a familiar scratch at the door. It was Sammy. I opened the door, and he jumped in bed. I didn't turn on the TV. I didn't want to take any chances. For all I knew Derek and Eden would be on the eleven o'clock news making out. Sammy and I called it a night.

* * * *

The workday was over, and the party was about to commence. Julia went all out for our girls' night. The same hair and makeup people from Saturday night's benefit arrived to glam us up. She also arranged for a car and driver.

It was a good thing Phillip was still out of town because he wouldn't have approved of our outfits. Julia wore a plunging, deep-purple dress. Her tits and long legs looked spectacular. I donned a short, black, form-fitting number and added some killer heels.

The driver dropped us off at the Bellagio. They had two cocktail lounges that were our favorites. They were the best place to people watch.

We settled into a great spot and within minutes, a group of men at the next table offered to buy us a drink. It was one of the many advantages hanging out with a beauty like Julia. The girl never bought her own drinks. If I were along for the ride, I would reap the benefits.

Normally, I drank wine, but on a special night like this, I branched out and chose a vodka cocktail. They had a signature drink called the Bellisimo Delight. I wasn't exactly sure what was in it, but it was yummy.

Julia asked, "Have you heard from Derek today?"

"No, but I haven't checked my phone."

"What else is new? Do it."

I retrieved my phone. I had a text from him and read it to Julia.

"Sweetie, will you please answer your phone? I need to talk to you."

"He calls you sweetie?" Julia pondered that notion for a moment. "That's, actually kind of charming, and you know, sweet."

"It was sweet before he decided to stay in LA and make out with his girlfriend."

"I think you should talk to him. I know that last night I said you're better off, but maybe you should give him a chance to explain, and if nothing else, it could give you some closure."

I set the phone on the table. "Maybe I'll call him back tomorrow. Tonight is about us. In fact, you've got to see what's coming our way."

It was a bachelorette party. A pack of girls drunk off their asses, one stumbled along not noticing her left boob flopped out. I got the attention of the guys who bought our drinks and told them to take a gander. They high-fived me and bought us another round. In reality, I was a jerk for doing that. When the girls approached, I flagged down the bride-to-be, and she helped her friend wrestle the stray boob to safety.

After many more rounds, the effects of the Bellisimo Delight took hold.

Julia ranted about one of her Vegas pet peeves. "Why would you bother to get all dressed up with a fabulous new black dress and shoes, and then carry your giant, brown, mom purse? It doesn't make any sense."

I spied a cute couple holding hands. He towered over her by at least a foot. They were so into each other.

That could've been Derek and I if things had worked out differently.

Another round of drinks appeared from our new friends. The guys were harmless and didn't hit on us. They were married and in town for a convention.

My cocktail haze turned me into Julia spring break drunk, which was not so much. I was about to tell her we should go home when my phone rang. It was Derek.

I slurred my words a little. "Julia, it's Derek, he's calling again."

"Don't answer it."

I didn't listen. I answered it. "What? What do you want?"

"Nia, thank God I've been worried about you. Are you okay?"

My cocktails did all the talking. "What do you care?"

Derek's voice turned stern. "Have you been drinking?"

"You know what, yes, a smidge."

"Where are you? Are you with Julia?"

I held out the phone and shouted to my new table of male friends, "Hey, he wants to know who I'm with."

The guys chimed in. "She's partying with us. Is that your boyfriend?"

I slurred into the phone. "The guys want to know if you're my boyfriend." I said to them, "He's not my boyfriend. He fucked me and went back to his girlfriend in LA. Now he won't quit calling."

My new male friends booed him. Julia waved her arms and told me to get off the phone, but it was too late. The crazy train had already left the station.

"Nia, please, I want you to go home," shouted Derek.

"You are so bossy."

"You're not driving, are you?"

"No, and another thing, what do you care anyway?"

"Sweetie, of course I care."

"Don't call me that. I'm an over jealous...I'm a zealous...I'm just a fan. Stop calling me!" I hung up and put the phone on the table. "Well, that ought to do it."

"Yep, I don't think you're going to hear from him again."

I shook my head. "Nope."

Julia got up. "We should go."

"Julia, I'm drank...drunk, oh, I'm so drunk."

I either passed out or fell asleep in the car on the way home. Julia helped me get ready for bed. This was a role reversal. She was the one placing a cold cloth and water on the nightstand. She also laid out a T-shirt and boxers. Then put the trash can by the bed in case I hurled. I did manage to brush my teeth and take off my makeup.

As I crawled in bed, Julia handed me some ibuprofen. "I texted Brooke, she's going to teach your classes in the morning."

"I can do it."

"No, Nia, you can't. I'll make sure Sammy doesn't come down here tonight."

"I should've never answered the phone."

Julia giggled. "You think? I tried to stop you. Do you feel like you're going to throw up?"

"Not right now. Maybe I'll sleep it off."

"Text me if you need anything. Everything will seem better in the morning."

I passed right out. When I opened my eyes, it was still dark. I had a splitting headache, which was no surprise. I replayed my drunken Derek phone call again in my mind. Why did I answer the phone? My mouth felt like a giant cotton ball. I drank some water and brushed my teeth again. I was restless, but eventually drifted off into a deep sleep.

* * * *

My doorbell rang. Nobody ever rang my bell. I didn't even get a stray Jehovah's Witness or *FedEx* package. I pulled the covers over my head. It had to be my imagination. The doorbell continued its assault. I heaved myself out of bed to tell who ever it was to kiss my hungover ass. I looked out the peephole and nearly died. It was Derek.

Fuck me! What was he doing here? This must've been payback for pointing out some drunken girl's runaway boob last night.

I opened the door and Derek barged in. "Good morning, sunshine. How's your hangover?"

Derek strolled into my small living room, but I kept my distance by the door. So many emotions ran through me at once. I was angry and hurt, but our connection was still there. I could stay strong as long as I didn't look him in eye.

I folded my arms and stared at the floor.

He had the nerve to lecture me. "Nia, do you want to tell me why the only time you answered your phone was when you were drunk?"

I said quietly, "No."

"Do you want to talk about that conversation?"

I shook my head.

"Do you have any idea how worried I've been about you?"

I shrugged my shoulders.

"Do you realize that you're acting like a child right now?"

"Maybe I'm not acting like a child, maybe you're acting like you're in your early hundreds." That sounded much better in my head. Perhaps I was still drunk.

"Maybe I'm going to take you across my knee and give you a good spanking."

His comment was a total curve ball. I lifted my head and looked into those ice-blue eyes. I didn't utter a word. I also didn't understand why he was mad at me.

Derek paced and yelled. "Do you have any idea the hell I've been through this week?"

I yelled right back. "The hell you've been through? You have to be fucking kidding me. I saw your week on TV. You were having the time of your life with Eden."

"I told you we're not together. When are you going to get that through your head?"

I covered my face and choked back tears. "Please stop yelling at me."

Derek came to me. "I'm sorry."

"Why do you think I didn't answer the phone? The first time you called, you were yelling. Then I saw the official comment you told your publicist to say. You said I was just a fan."

He placed his hands on my shoulders gingerly. "I didn't say that. I didn't approve it either. That's why I wanted to talk to you."

"The next day you and Eden were all over the TV holding hands and kissing. It was too much."

He pulled me into his arms and rubbed my back. "I'm sorry, but you didn't give me a chance to explain."

My voice shook. "But you said you couldn't tell me everything."

"I know, but Eden can. She came to Vegas so she could talk to you."

I stepped away from him. "She… What now? You brought her *here*?"

I was about to go postal when Derek interrupted. "Just hear me out. She's at my house and came to see you, because I asked her to."

"Are you high? I don't want to talk to her."

"Nia, listen to me. This is what we're going to do. You're getting in the shower, and I'm going to make you some breakfast. Then I'm going to send a car to get Eden and bring her here."

"I do not see that happening. You got a plan B?"

Derek smiled. "I will pick you up and put you in the shower myself. Please, sweetie, trust me."

Damn him and his freaking sweetie! I gazed into his eyes and was a complete goner. "Okay, fine. Has anyone ever told you, you're super bossy?"

He caressed my face. "It's been mentioned." He swatted my bottom. "Go get in the shower, young lady. I insist!"

I stomped off. "Okay, Mr. Pierce."

While I was in the shower, I couldn't wrap my brain around Eden Fox coming to my humble little abode that wasn't even mine. What would she say? What should I wear?

After I toweled off, I checked myself in the mirror. Gross, I looked like hell. I slapped on a little makeup, but it didn't make much difference. I cringed at the idea of Derek seeing Eden and I side by side.

Those two looked like they belonged together. She was like a sexy, blonde Snow White, and I was more like Dopey.

I threw on one of my many black, little sundresses and went to the kitchen. Derek made me toast and coffee. We sat at the kitchen table.

He asked, "How are you feeling?"

"Not great, but okay. I'm sorry I didn't answer my phone."

The bell rang. "That's Eden. She's here." He offered his hand and led me to the door.

I opened the door, and there she was, the breathtaking Eden Fox. She was a goddess wrapped in a super model.

She extended her hand. "You must be Nia. I'm so happy to meet you."

Even though I didn't want to talk to her, I found myself star struck. She was very charming.

Eden and I sat in the living room. Derek said he'd be in my bedroom. This was surreal. I was so nervous in her presence I couldn't form a sentence.

Which was fine, Eden did most of the talking. "I know this must be odd for you, but Derek asked me to come, and I'm glad he did. I wanted to apologize to you."

"Apologize to me, what for?"

"I overreacted to the picture of you and Derek. I had no idea he was seeing anyone, so it caught me off guard. It was my idea to say you were just a fan. I'm truly sorry."

"Oh, I didn't know that."

"Derek and I have the same publicist and management team, so they assumed he approved it."

"Can I ask you something? Are you in love with him?"

"No, but we've been good friends for years. Nia, you mean a lot to Derek. He trusts you, so I'm going to trust you too. Please know what I'm about to tell you can't leave this room."

Eden leaned in. "I'm gay."

My mouth gaped open. I whispered, "Shut up." I did not see that coming. I collected myself. "I mean... I'm sorry. Are you sure?"

"Yes, I'm sure. I've been sure since I was five years old."

Eden relayed how awful it was to live a lie, but it wasn't only about her. It was also about the people who worked for her too. Eden was a modern day Marilyn Monroe. Her manager said if she came out, it would ruin her career and her brand. It was fine with her to leave the business, but she was responsible for the livelihoods of many people.

Derek had a few people, but Eden had an army. It couldn't be an easy way to live. However, there was still one piece of the puzzle I didn't understand.

"I get why you needed a fake boyfriend, but why did Derek agree to it?"

"He doesn't like to talk about it, but when he landed the show, he dated Gisela, you know, the redheaded vampire, Victoria."

I rolled my eyes. "Oh, her."

Eden laughed. "Yes, and she is vile. Anyway, the relationship fizzled because Derek was never that interested in her. After he broke it off, Gisela raked him over coals in the tabloids. She said Derek had a different girl outside his trailer every day to service him on his breaks. It was humiliating, not true, and she wouldn't stop."

"That's awful. I do remember hearing those rumors about him."

"See, people believe that stuff. Anyway, I started seeing someone. My partner and I were being followed everywhere. I was under pressure from my team to have a relationship with a man, for the cameras, like red carpets and that kind of thing. Derek agreed, and Gisela backed off."

"Why didn't Derek just date someone?"

"Until recently I don't think he's had an entire day off in five years. When he came to one of my movie premieres, he'd leave right after we walked the carpet, because he was so busy. The only women he meets on a regular basis are actors. After Gisela, he'd probably never date another person in show business again. We can be a bit much."

"I can be a bit much too."

She smiled. "I don't think so. If Derek hasn't told you yet, he's crazy about you. You're all he talked about the entire way here. He was so worried when he couldn't get a hold of you."

"Really? You know, I'm not a red carpet kind of girl, so if you find yourself in a red carpet situation, Derek is all yours."

"He told me there's something you can't tell him. What I'm about to say makes me a hypocrite, but you should come out with it. You can trust him. We've known each other a long time. He's one of the most caring people you'll ever meet."

She was right. It wasn't fair to Derek.

I hugged Eden, thanked her for coming and trusting me with her secret. Derek came out of the bedroom. They said their goodbyes and Eden left.

I stood at the door lost in his eyes. Yes, I'd fallen for this man, hook, line, and sinker. I was ready to trust him with my heart, but what about my secret? I should tell him. I should tell him right now.

My voice quivered. "Derek, I want to tell you. I want to tell you everything."

He had that look. "You can tell me later. Right now, I have to have you. I need to make love to you."

He crushed his mouth to mine and we erupted like a volcano. He devoured me with such intensity. It nearly knocked me off my feet. The sound of our aching need filled the air. His scent washed over me, making my skin break out in goose bumps.

Derek was like a stripping ninja. He tore my dress off in a flash and his T-shirt and jeans hit the floor in record time. Naked, Derek backed me into the living room. He grabbed the blanket off the back of the couch and spread it out on the floor. Kneeling on the blanket, he was a man with a plan—a sex picnic.

He offered his hand and I joined him on my knees. "Someone still has too many clothes on."

He slid down the straps and unhooked my bra. He caressed one of my breasts with his skillful hand while he suckled my other nipple. How I missed his touch and the way my body responded to him. My nipples puckered. The fizzy ripples in my stomach ebbed and flowed, settling in my sex.

His hands gripped my ass and I grasped his hair, pulling his delicious mouth to mine.

He whispered, "Lay down." His body was on top of mine with his steely cock digging into my flesh. He placed a pillow under my head and tugged on my thong. "I must free you from these." He slid his hand toward my panties.

Oh no, the Brazilian wax off. I sat up like a shot. "No, wait!"

"What's wrong?"

My face flushed. "I did something stupid." My lady bits quit hurting two days ago. The redness disappeared and revealed they ripped off the first layer of skin at the top of my business. It was not pretty.

"What did you do?" I turned away. Derek took his finger and turned my face back to him. "Nia, you can tell me anything."

"This is really Julia's fault. She said it would be fabulous. I tried it. And guess what? Not even fabulous adjacent. It was horrible." I covered my face with my hands and confessed. "I got a Brazilian wax."

"Is that all? Did it hurt?"

"Yes, it hurt like a motherfucker!"

Derek laughed.

"Seriously, are you laughing at me?"

He stifled himself mid chuckle. "I'm not laughing. I swear I'm not." He pulled my hands away from my face, leaned against the back of the couch, and scooped me onto his lap. "Come here. My poor girl, does it still hurt?"

"No, but it kind of went awry."

The back of his hand brush my cheek. "Sweetie, you didn't need to do that for me. You're perfect the way you are. Can I see?"

I shook my head. "It's too embarrassing."

"Don't be embarrassed. I'm not going to take your panties off. I'm just going have a look, okay?"

He pulled my thong down and revealed my bared mound. The red mark was the size of a nickel. His finger traced over the area. "Does it hurt when I do that?"

I exhaled. "No, it feels good."

He grinned. "Hmm…excellent." He patted my bottom. "Let's get these off you." I shimmied out of my thong and he laid me on the blanket. "I need to have a taste."

How did he do that? I went from embarrassed to wet in one sentence. I lay on the blanket and we resumed our sex picnic. I spread myself for the debut of my Brazilian pussy.

He looked at my naked, sensitive flesh in wonder. His fingers slid over my smooth outer lips. "You feel like satin. I love it."

Yes, this was a great picnic, because I was on the menu. His lips blazed a trail up my inner thighs. He licked his way to my delicate folds. His enticing tongue surrounded my clit, sampling the first course. He indulged me with liberal licks and sucks, and my juices oozed. I peered down at him, reveling in the sight of his hungry mouth eating me out.

A finger pressed and rubbed my clit in a circle. His tongue rested at my slit. He pushed it inside, and I broke out in quiet whimpers. He tongue fucked me with forceful strokes.

My body sizzled in heat. I hooked my arms around my knees and drew them to my chest. Beads of sweat formed on my brow.

I rocked into him and he replaced his tongue with two fingers. They banged my hot spot.

He glanced up at me. "I love your pussy like this." Then he brought his mouth down on my clit, slurping and driving me to orgasm.

I shrieked, "Oh God, yes, Derek, yes! I'm going to come!" He thrust into me with vigor. I came unhinged and my release slashed through me. My body hummed in pleasure.

My arms reached for him. As amazing as that was I needed him to fill me. "Derek, I missed you."

He gathered me to him. "I missed you more than you can imagine. Come here, my beautiful girl."

His back leaned against the couch, and I straddled him. He guided his cock inside. "God, Nia, you feel incredible."

Maybe the Brazilian wasn't such a bad idea after all. I felt him more. It was more intense. I dug it. His dick sheathed my longing walls. His hands were on my ass tilting my hips up and down. He was slow and gentle. He was always careful with me, but I craved every inch of him, and bore down harder. A sudden exhale expelled from both of us.

"Are you okay? Is it too much?"

I shook my head and grinned. "I have to have all of you."

He drew his lips to mine and bit my lip. I released an achy murmur.

"Are you sure you want all of me?"

I whispered, "Yes."

"Then I'm going to give it to you." He gripped my hips and thrashed me with ferocious strokes.

Our bodies heaved and ramped together as one. He burrowed balls deep inside my grinding cunt. It hurled me to threshold at lightning speed. I barred my teeth and bit his shoulder, it amped up his relentless thrusts. Then it hit me like a tidal wave. "Ah, Derek, I'm coming!"

"Yes, fucking come for me."

I let go and one orgasm rolled into another. He clutched me tight and rode out each forceful release. *Holy fuck!* I just kept coming.

Then Derek's climax surged inside, setting off one final explosion that tore me to shreds. My head collapsed on his chest in exhaustion. He held me as our breath calmed and bodies quieted.

I showered his chest with soft kisses, lifted my head, and joked. "If this is make-up sex, we should fight a lot more."

Derek didn't find it funny. "No, Nia, no more fighting. I feel like you're always running away from me."

All this time I worried about protecting myself from getting hurt. It never occurred to me he was hurting too.

"I'm sorry. I do that when I get scared. I know it's not right, but it's my way of trying to control everything."

Derek lifted me off him and sat me down his legs. "But you can't control everything. Things are going to happen. I need to know you'll answer the phone, so we can work it out. It's all part of being in a relationship."

"We're in a relationship?"

"I'm afraid so."

"Eden told me you were crazy about me."

"Oh, did she?"

I nodded, and a sly grin came across his face.

"Yes, Miss Nia Kelly, I am crazy about you."

"I thought I was just driving you crazy."

Derek chuckled. "Well, that too. So what's your plan for today? I know you have one."

"Actually, before you got here, the only thing I planned on doing was calling you."

Derek was surprised. "Really?"

"Yep, it was Julia's idea. I read her the text you sent. She said I should give you a chance to explain."

"First the Brazilian and now this? That Julia is okay in my book."

Derek played with my hair. "Well, what would my girl like to do today?"

I loved it when he called me his girl. I just had the best sex of my life with this beautiful man. I wanted to stay in his arms all day and I was exhausted. I had the perfect plan. "Would it be okay if we took a nap? I haven't slept much since, well, since I spent the night at your house."

Derek kissed my forehead. "I haven't either. Taking a nap with my girl sounds perfect."

I sent a quick text to Brooke and Julia to let them know I was okay. I also mentioned Derek was here, and we worked things out.

Then we cuddled up naked in my bed. It was pure bliss. I tucked myself under his arm and rested my head on his chest. I was so relaxed, even though I hadn't come clean about my past. Maybe it would be too much for him, but for now, I drifted off to sleep.

I stirred while Derek nuzzled my neck. We were spooning.

He said softly, "Hey sleepy head, it's after six."

I rolled over and ran my fingertips over his chest. Still groggy saying, "I must've really conked out. Were you asleep the whole time too?"

Derek stroked my back. "I woke up about ten minutes ago. You're so cute when you sleep, especially when you snore."

I jolted up. "I don't snore."

"You sound like Shemp from the Three Stooges."

I scrunched up my face. "Who are the Three Stooges?"

"You don't know who the Three Stooges are? Young lady, exactly how old are you?"

"I'll be twenty-five next month. How old are you?"

"I'll be thirty-three in September."

"Wow, you're like old!" I found myself hilarious.

Derek shook his head. "You are such a bad girl. I should've spanked you."

The way he said the word spank intrigued me. "Were you really going to do that?"

He responded in a playful tone, "Only if you didn't behave."

I faced him, on my knees. "I almost never do."

He granted me a light tap on my bottom.

I whispered, "I kind of like it."

I parted my lips and he graced my mouth with an urgent kiss, a loving kiss that took on a life of its own. Our bodies radiated with heat as Derek laid me on my back. My head was at the foot of the bed. He pressed his entire weight into mine and claimed me in one seamless motion.

His eyes met mine. "Nia, I was so worried I was going to lose you."

In that moment, it was clear. I was in love with him. I finally admitted it to myself. I loved Derek so much.

"Derek I..." I couldn't say it, and I shouldn't say it. It was too soon. I couldn't say anything. Tears spilled down my cheeks with zero control. What was wrong with me?

He brushed the tears away and whispered, "Don't cry, my sweet girl. It's okay. I know. I do too."

There was no longer a single doubt. I was his.

Chapter Eleven

"I'm starving!" It was after seven. We hadn't eaten since this morning.

Derek retrieved our clothes from the living room, and asked, "What would you like?"

"Pizza."

"You eat pizza?"

"Of course, there's cheese on it, but it has to be from Grimaldi's, and I only like red peppers and mushrooms."

"And there it is. Whatever my little control freak wants, sounds good to me."

When the pizza arrived, we sat in the kitchen, ate, and talked. Well, I talked. I barely let Derek get a word in edgewise. I told him about Larry Wall's wife kicking him out. He was relieved Larry was in California living with his brother. I also told him about my conversation with my dad, and my plan to go visit this summer.

Then, it was time; time to tell him everything. I gathered the courage to broach the subject when Derek's phone rang.

He sounded angry. It wasn't a long conversation. Derek's tone was clipped and irritated.

"Is everything okay? You look upset."

He let out a sigh. "That was my agent."

"Does your agent always call you on Saturday night?"

"My team has been told if I'm in Vegas they aren't supposed to call me at all. It's non-stop when I'm in LA."

"That must suck."

"It does suck. All of them are pissed at me because I turned down a big blockbuster shooting this summer. I passed on it a while ago. But it's a lot of money, so they tried one more time to get me to sign on."

"You don't want to do it?"

"No, I don't need more money. I need a break. I have two movies coming out this summer. That's already going to be a lot of traveling. I'm sorry. I don't want to bother you with this."

"It's not a bother. It sounds exciting. Isn't it fun to travel?"

Derek got up from the table, kissed my forehead. "It would be, if you came with me."

Was he serious? It would be a dream come true to travel with Derek. But I made the mistake of dropping my life for someone else once; I would never do it again. He cleaned up the dishes and threw away the pizza box.

Finally I said, "I would love to, but I have a lot of classes. I have to keep working."

"Of course, I meant if you could get away for a weekend once in a while and come with me. I would love that."

"I would too."

Derek sat back down at the table. "Have you traveled much?"

"Nope, I've only been to New York once on a school trip and to Kansas. I don't even have a passport."

"Nia, come here." He sat me on his lap. "It's no big deal. You'll get a passport and when you can, come with me. Is there any place you'd dreamed of going?"

"I never thought about it much. Well, there is something I've always wanted to do, but you might think it's kind of silly."

"I promise I won't, tell me."

"When I lived in Pittsburgh, I had this great bike. I loved riding outside. I thought it would be fun to go to Napa for wine tasting and bike riding, but maybe not at the same time, because I'd probably fall off the bike."

Derek nuzzled my neck. "I think that sounds like a great plan."

"Did you just say plan? If you're trying to turn me on it's totally working." I flung my arms around his neck

Derek stood up, and abruptly took me by the hand.

"Where are we going?"

"You're coming with me. We're going to have a shower and then bed."

I stopped. "But I wanted to talk to you. I still haven't told you everything."

Derek caressed my cheek. "I know. Tomorrow, okay?"

He was irresistible. My body flushed from his penetrating gaze. I had to have him. Our kisses ramped up in the kitchen, and we left a trail of clothes on our way to the shower. There was no way we'd make it to the bedroom. While the water rained down us, Derek gave me that look.

He whispered, "I think you're ready. Turn around for me. Put your hands on the wall to steady yourself. I'm going to fuck you from behind."

Hell yes! I was so in! He clenched my hips and went to town on me. It was so rough and raw. The sound of our bodies slapping together, and the grunts and groans of our needy lust, unleashed the bad girl within me. This was pure and simple fucking. *Mama like!*

He rammed me with abandonment. His dominant thrusts were out of this world.

He growled, "Nia, I'm close. If you want to come, get there, touch yourself."

He pounded my cunt so hard, I was afraid if I moved my hand, I'd slip.

He gripped me tighter. "I've got you. You won't fall."

My fingers touched my clit. I worked myself into a frothy daze while Derek slowed.

Then his cock pulled out all the way. "Derek, don't stop, I'm right there."

"No chance in hell I'm stopping."

He speared my hole and fucked me at maximum speed. My orgasm seized me. A squeal flew out of mouth that only dogs could hear.

Derek spewed his punishing load inside me. After one final spasm, he spun me around and I fell into his arms. He never let go as he cleaned me up.

My legs were weak and spongy. "I feel like such a bad girl."

"Hmm…You're my bad girl."

His lips captured mine and I savored his sweet kiss. After I told him everything, would I still be his?

* * * *

We faced each other snuggled up in bed.

Derek took my hand. "I wanted to ask you something."

"What? Did I do something wrong?"

"Of course not. I wanted to see if you could come to LA this week."

I popped up. "Really?"

"Yeah. I shoot my last scene of the season on Thursday night. Then Friday night there's a big wrap party at the executive producer's house. Do you think you could take some time off?"

"What about Eden? Won't people ask a lot of questions or take pictures?"

"Not at the party. No phones allowed. Some people party too much. Nobody wants to end up on *Facebook* or *Instagram*. Just think about it. I have to go back on Monday, and you can come out whenever you want. Would you like to come to set with me on Thursday?"

"They'd let me do that?"

"Sure, but you would have to sign a confidentiality agreement. You can't tell anyone about the finale."

"I would love it."

His fingers brushed my cheek. "Me too. Maybe you could come out Wednesday night. I'm supposed to be done a little early. You could stay for the weekend. When's the last time you had a little vacation?"

"I don't even remember. Oh, wait, what about Gisela if you're with me and not Eden…I mean…does she still have a thing for you?"

"I don't think she'll be a problem."

"Why? What happened?"

Derek teased. "I can't tell you."

I flew to my knees. "I'm begging you. Please tell me. I won't tell anybody. I promise. Do they kill her off?

Derek relented. "Yes, and they shot it last week."

"I knew it! Who bumps her off?"

"I can't tell you anything else. I'm serious. You can't tell anyone what I told you, okay?"

"I can't even tell Julia?"

"Not a soul, but Gisela is pissed they killed her off, so I don't think she'll be at the party."

"I'm too excited to sleep now."

Derek pulled back the covers. "Just try, for me. Come here."

Who could resist that? I cuddled next to him. Derek turned out the light, and kissed me good night.

I was silent, for a hot second. "Who kills Gisela?"

"I can't tell you."

"It's you, isn't it?"

"Nia, go to sleep."

"Okay."

"Try not to snore."

* * * *

The sun was up. When I opened my eyes, Derek was still asleep. I lay quiet, taking in his lovely face. A part of me still didn't understand what he saw in me. Besides not resembling the girls in Hollywood, I could be kind of a pill. He, on the other hand, was perfect, a little bossy, but perfect. I dreaded having to tell him about my past. It could change everything. Why couldn't we stay in our little bubble forever?

Derek's eyes fluttered open. He was even sexier in the morning. "Hey, how's my sweet girl? Did you sleep?"

"I slept great."

"Me too." He gave me a quick peck and headed to the bathroom. It was a wonderful view of his magnificent ass.

When I sat up, my head throbbed. I didn't see the ibuprofen on either nightstand, so I assumed I left it in the bathroom. Derek returned as I climbed out of bed. He drew me close and his hands went right to my ass. He planted soft kisses on my neck. Of course, he turned me on, but I had to pee.

Remembering what he said last week, I backed away. "Good things come to those who wait."

I hightailed to the bathroom and brushed my teeth, but the ibuprofen was MIA. I opened the bathroom door and shouted to Derek, "Can you look in the top drawer of my nightstand, I can't find the ibuprofen?"

"Do you feel okay?"

"I'm fine, just a little headache."

Derek's voice sounded funny. "Oh... I found...it."

When I returned, he was on the edge of the bed with his hands behind his back, a devious grin on his face and a giant erect penis.

"I thought you said you found it."

"I definitely found it."

He produced the ibuprofen in one hand. Then with a gleam in his eyes said, "I also found this."

Holy crap! It was my vibrator! My hands shot to my face. "Um, I guess I forgot it was in there, because it was a gag gift and I don't ever use it." I was such a bad liar. Even I didn't believe me.

He sauntered toward me. "Please don't be embarrassed. I think it's hot."

I stared at his hard cock. "Yes, I can see that."

Derek took my hand, led me back to the bed. "Lie down." He handed me the vibrator. "I want you to show me how you make yourself come."

I flushed. I was somehow aroused and embarrassed at the same time. I peeked up at him and then looked away.

"Do you want me to do it?" I nodded. His smile widened. "Good, because I love to make you come."

Derek turned on the vibrator and maneuvered it over my breasts. His soft lips were on mine and his tongue sunk inside my mouth. It was minty fresh and rimmed along my teeth.

He trailed the vibrator down my stomach and placed it on my wanting clit. My good friend Buzz never disappointed. He awakened every nerve ending. This was delightfully sinful. It wet my appetite and my pussy.

He turned it off. I was about to object, when he whispered, "Turn over."

Heck, yeah! Why didn't I think of that? I flipped to my stomach with my hips in the air. Derek turned the vibrator back on and eased it inside.

I exhaled. "Oh, yes."

Easy, small thrusts caused my sex to dribble on the comforter. I lurched back on Buzz, pushing him further into my hole, like a naughty deviant. Maybe I should get a spanking!

Derek growled, "You are a bad girl. You love this, don't you?"

I groaned, "Yes, ah, yes."

"You want more?"

I cried, "Yes, ah, ah, fuck, yes."

He amped up Buzz's rippling power. Pulsing waves of pleasure jarred me to the brink. Oh my God, this was awesome! Derek held it firm and steady. I thrashed myself, hard. I was about to explode. He pulled it out and slid it across my burning clit until I couldn't hold back any longer.

"Oh fuck, I'm going to come."

He thrust two fingers inside me, and my orgasm raced through me like a runaway train. I face planted on the bed, reduced to a post orgasmic pile of vibrating flesh.

When I managed to turn on my side, Derek and I faced each other.

I said breathless, "Thank you."

"It was my pleasure."

"I believe the pleasure was all mine and my headache is gone."

"I'll have to write you a prescription."

He drew me close and gave me that look. We smoldered with need. As his lips touched mine it hit me, this could be the last time we made love. What if my past was too much for him and ripped us apart? Derek rolled me on my back. My connection to him overwhelmed me.

He entered me and whispered, "I love being inside you."

I loved him. I clung to what little control I had left. "I love…I love it too. I want you so much."

"Hey, sweetie, you have me. I'm all yours."

Derek moved with sensual, deliberate strokes. I relished every thrust as if I was my last. I rocked my hips and we found our special rhythm. We moved together perfectly. I arched my back and he slipped deeper inside my slick channel.

Derek's mouth fondled my erect nipples. His tongue circled and sucked them, fueling a fiery tingle deep inside.

His strokes grew urgent. I writhed in pleasure and spread myself wider. He crashed into my hot spot luring my orgasm forward. I threw my head back.

"Sweetie, look at me. Are you ready to come for me?"

"Yes, I want to come with you."

"Good girl. Eyes on me, sweetie."

He curled his hand around the top of my head, shoring me close. I held his beautiful face, lost in his eyes. Our sweet release flowed through us like soft clouds rolling through the sky.

Still inside me, Derek gathered me up. I buried my face in his chest and expelled a heavy sigh.

"Hey, I don't want you to be scared. You can tell me anything."

I lifted my head and glanced up at him.

His lips brushed against my cheek. "I meant what I said. I'm all yours. I'm not going anywhere."

I clung to him. Maybe it would be okay. Maybe Derek and I had a future together. Maybe he was really mine.

* * * *

When I walked into the club for class, no one was at the fitness desk. The place was empty, which was typical for a Sunday if there weren't any tennis or golf tournaments. What wasn't typical was the noise from Brooke's office. Raised voices erupted behind the closed door.

I came early to talk to her, but I set up for class first. When I finished, I peeked my head out of the door to see if Brooke was available.

Sonya left Brooke's office in a huff. Their heads snapped in my direction.

Before Sonya tromped off, she said in a rude tone to Brooke, "I'm going to need your keys. Maintenance is coming and they'll need access to our supply room."

She handed off her big key ring and Sonya marched past me.

I hurried to Brooke. "What was that all about?"

"Let's go outside, we need to talk."

Brooke shut the door to her office, but she couldn't lock it because Sonya had the keys.

Once outside I asked, "What's wrong? You look upset."

"I am upset, with Sonya. She wants me to fire you."

"Why? What did I do?"

"Remember when Derek came to take a private Pilates class with you? Turns out she heard the whole thing."

"Oh no, I'm sorry. I've put you in an awful position."

"There's more. She told me she knows you and I are friends, so if I don't fire you she's going to throw me under the bus too."

"What is her problem? Look, maybe I should quit. I can teach anywhere. I don't want you putting your job at risk for me."

"Are you kidding? I can't lose my best instructor. Everyone here loves you and she knows it. I'll figure something out."

"I don't know if this helps, but I was going to ask you if I could take some time off. Derek wants me to come to LA on Wednesday and stay the weekend."

"What about Eden?"

I filled her in as much as I could. I made a promise not to tell anyone Eden's secret and I kept it. I also confessed I'd fallen for Derek, and I was going to share my secrets with him tonight.

Brooke suggested I take the entire week off. Maybe the Sonya situation would blow over. Before I knew it, a half hour had gone by, and it was time for class.

I must admit I wasn't as focused on teaching as I should've been. My mind was like a laser on Derek. Would he understand why I did what I did? It was painful for me to live with everything that happened. Was it wrong to expect someone else to?

After class, I jumped in the shower. Then I received a text from my other fitness coordinator. Substitutes were in place for my classes, so I could go to LA. I sent Derek a text to let him know I could fly out on Wednesday night.

He wrote back. "You've made me the happiest man in the world."

My heart soared. Could this really work out? Was someone like me going to be with a man like Derek?

I texted him back. "I'm happy too. I was about to head to your place in fifteen minutes. Is that okay?"

He replied. "Yes. I insist."

I took a deep breath. This was it.

Chapter Twelve

I pulled my Honda into Derek's driveway. I wore my favorite pair of skinny jeans and a long-sleeved top. The little mini heat wave in Vegas was over. It was only about sixty degrees and a little cloudy. My heart raced and my mouth felt dry. I'd never been more nervous in my life.

I rang the bell and Derek opened the door right away. He was on the phone. He motioned for me to come in, took my hand in his, and led me back to the kitchen. He wore jeans and a long-sleeved, dark, fitted T-shirt. It clung to his body in the most delightful way. There was no finer, sexier man on earth. It would be difficult to keep my hands off him.

He was about to wrap up his call. He pulled out a barstool at the kitchen island and I sat down. He granted me a quick kiss on the forehead as he continued the conversation. He strolled to the refrigerator and grabbed some wine and cheese.

He said into the phone, "Okay, sounds great." He paused, looked at me, and added, "That's right, I said my girlfriend, Nia Kelly. I can't wait for you to meet her. Thanks for everything, bye."

My girlfriend, Nia Kelly, was the best sentence ever. I grinned from ear to ear. "What did you say?"

"Thanks for everything?"

Oh, he was totally messing with me. It was so cute. "No before that."

"You mean, okay, sounds great?"

I shook my head.

His hands caressed my face. "My girlfriend, Nia Kelly."

"Yeah, that part. I like it."

I hopped off the barstool, threw my arms around his neck and kissed him. Derek hoisted me on top of the kitchen island and I wrapped my legs around his waist. It was so easy to get lost in him, but I stopped. "I think we should talk first."

"You're so hard to resist. I love the way your ass looks in these jeans."

"I love the way your ass looks every day, but I still think we should talk."

Derek conceded, gave me a quick peck, and poured us some wine. We sat on the sofa in the TV room. He grasped my hand. "Remember, you have nothing to be afraid of. It's just me."

He listened as I reminded him how rough it was at home with my dad and stepmother. How miserable I was in that house. I told him I freaked out my senior year because Julia was taking off for LA. I had no plans and no idea what I was going to do after graduation.

I swallowed. "What you don't know is, I started dating someone at the beginning of my senior year, and we got married."

Derek appeared startled by my revelation. After a brief silence he asked, "When did you get married, after you graduated?"

"I'm ashamed to admit this, but I didn't graduate. I married Nick in January and he made me drop out. I was only twenty-one. It was a huge mistake. If I could go back and change it, I would."

"Hey, it's okay. We all make mistakes. Look at me with Gisela. She was huge mistake too. Am I right to assume it wasn't a happy marriage?"

"It was a nightmare. Nick had a temper. Every time we argued, he got more angry and volatile. He isolated me from everyone. I didn't have any friends. Even Julia and I weren't speaking. I suspected he was cheating on me. I mean, he was hardly ever home. One night I questioned him about Melissa Baker, this woman he worked with and he blew up at me. After that, I suggested we separate for a while. He twisted my arm behind my back and said, 'No separation, you got that?'"

"You must have been so scared."

"I was scared. Scared and alone. I didn't have anyone to turn to. I mentioned going to counseling and it caused another fight."

"What did you do?"

"For a while I didn't do anything. I just existed. It was a horrible way to live. Then, one afternoon Melissa called me and told me flat out, they were having an affair. She said I was selfish to stand in the way of Nick's happiness. I figured, great, this is my chance. Maybe he wants a divorce. I didn't have anywhere to go, but I was going to get some money out of the checking account and leave."

My voice quaked. "I threw a suitcase on the bed and ran to my closet. I had to get out of there before Nick got home, but he caught me. When Nick saw the suitcase on the bed, he screamed, 'What the hell do you think you're doing?' I shouldn't have, but I yelled back, 'Your whore called me today, I'm leaving.' That was it. Nick picked up the suitcase and hit me in the head. He pushed me on the bed and cracked me across the face. I begged him to stop, but he didn't. He choked his hands around my throat and told me if I ever left him, he would kill me."

Tears poured down my cheeks. Derek held me and rubbed my back. "Oh, sweetie, don't cry. I'm sorry."

"Can I please have a tissue?"

Derek left for a minute while I collected myself. He handed me the box of tissues. "Listen, you don't need to tell me anything else. You've been through so much. I don't need to know everything."

"Derek, I have to. If I don't tell you now, I never will."

"Can I ask you something? Have you ever been to therapy?"

Some people saw therapy as a sign of weakness, so I put the question back on him, "Have you?"

"Nia, I live in LA, it's probably required by law. I think therapy is a good thing."

"I started going when my mom died, but during college I stopped. When Nick wouldn't go to counseling, I wanted to go back to therapy. He wouldn't let me. I guess I'm still a work in progress."

"Sweetie, we all are. Are you sure you don't want something to eat, maybe some more wine?"

I shook my head. "I need to tell you the rest."

He took my hand and listened.

"After Nick threatened me, he took off. He didn't come home until after midnight. I was in bed, but I wasn't sleeping. I was scared to death. I heard him climb the stairs, and when he got to the bedroom, he was crying. He actually apologized. He even promised to go to counseling."

"Did he?"

"No, but for a little while things were better. He said he broke it off with Melissa and he wanted to start a family. Part of me thought it would help things, and within a few months I was pregnant."

Derek let go of my hands. "You were pregnant?"

"Yeah, and at first, Nick was nicer, but it didn't last long. Right after my first trimester, I got another phone call from Melissa. She told me if I thought having a baby would keep her and Nick apart I was crazy. I felt like such a fool. I slammed the phone down and curled up on the bed.

"When Nick came home, he was drunk and started to pick at me. I know I shouldn't have, but I confronted him about Melissa. He went ballistic. He told me I was the most ungrateful wife, how I didn't ever want for anything, and I should shut the fuck up. I was terrified. I had to get out the bedroom. I stood up to leave and he yanked me by the arm and...he punched me in the face."

"He punched you? That bastard! What did you do?"

"I screamed, 'Nick, no, the baby.' I didn't care what happened to me, but I wanted to protect the baby. I ran down the hall and got to the top of the steps when Nick grabbed me. I begged him to let me go. We struggled and I fell. I fell down the stairs."

I broke down sobbing.

"And you lost the baby?"

I nodded yes and a flood of tears flowed. "Oh, sweetie, come here." Derek cloaked me in his arms.

"Nick took me to the hospital, but it was too late. I was bleeding and in so much pain."

I couldn't sit anymore, and began pacing the floor. "You know the entire way to the hospital Nick yelled, 'This all your fault, you should've shut the fuck up.' Maybe he was right. Maybe it was my fault. I shouldn't have said anything. I didn't do enough to protect my baby."

Derek came to me. "Nia, it wasn't your fault. None of this is your fault. I hate that you're reliving this because of me."

"You have a right to know. I need to tell you everything."

He embraced me tight. "You don't need to, not if it's going to cause you this much pain."

I looked up at him. "Please, it's important."

Derek agreed and led me back to the couch. "What happened next?"

"At the hospital Nick acted like a doting husband. He told the staff, I fell down the stairs and that's why I had a black eye. They admitted me and did a bunch of tests. Later the doctor told us I lost the baby. Nick didn't take it well. He screamed at the doctor. I guess I was in shock. I didn't say a word.

"Then I noticed a nurse who never left my room. Her name was Gail. She was in her forties, I think. Tall and self-assured. The kind of woman you wouldn't want to mess with. After the doctor left, she told Nick I would be spending the night for observation, and he should go because I needed to rest. She stayed in the room when Nick said goodbye. He leaned in close to my face. From the back it probably looked like he was giving me a kiss good night but he whispered, 'I'm not finished with you yet.'"

"What did you do?"

"Nothing, I was numb, but thankful I didn't have to go home with him. Gail also told Nick I was running a fever and he should wait until the nurses' station called before coming back to the hospital."

"You were running a fever?"

"Actually, I wasn't. Nick left, and Gail came to my bed and said, 'Darling, I've been around long enough to know your black eye didn't come from falling down the stairs. Do you need to call someone?' She handed me her cell phone and I called Julia."

"I thought you and Julia weren't speaking."

"We weren't, but when I got pregnant I called her. We started talking on the phone again. I told her what happened and Julia did what she always does. She took charge of the situation. She was in Pittsburgh, at the hospital, by noon the next day."

"Did you ever see Nick again?"

"Nope. I left the hospital. Julia and I checked into a hotel by the airport until our flight left that night. I didn't even have any clean clothes, but Julia took care of everything. I'll never forget how she cried when she saw my face. It was bad."

"Thank God for Julia and that nurse."

"They were like my guardian angels."

"What would you have done?"

"I don't like to think about it. The way he looked at me when he said goodbye, it was as if he had gone mad. That's why I had to leave. I pray every day he'll never find me."

"How long ago was this?

"I moved into Julia's guesthouse a little over a year ago. Actually, the night we met was my one year anniversary of living in Las Vegas."

Lightening the mood Derek leaned in and kissed me. "Best day of my life."

"Do you still feel that way?"

"Of course, but I'm still trying to wrap my head around all this. Wouldn't it have been easy for him to find you or Julia?"

"As far as Nick knew, Julia Dickson was still Julia Burns and lived in an apartment in LA. Plus, I never told him we reconnected." I exhaled. "And I changed my name."

"What? Nia's not you're real name?"

My stomach turned in knots. "I prefer to think Nia is my real name. It's helped put the past behind me."

"Okay, I get it." He kissed my forehead and went to the kitchen to get us water. He handed me the bottle. "Now I understand why you freaked out about the photographer at the benefit. I'm sorry I put you in that position."

"I put myself in that position, and I shouldn't have. I still feel like I'm in danger. Maybe he moved on, but I don't know."

Derek brushed my cheek with the back of his hand. "Well, I think we've talked about your ex enough for one night. Let's get you upstairs, we'll soak in a hot bath and wash this all away."

He scooped me up to whisk me upstairs. My heart raced. "Derek wait."

"Sweetie, nothing you told me tonight changes anything. In fact, it helps me understand you better. I'm so sorry for everything you went through, but I'm going to do everything in my power to protect you and keep you safe."

He leaned in to kiss me. I backed away. "Nia, what is it?"

His phone rang and he released me. He hurried to the kitchen and turned it off. Back in the TV room he said, "Oh, I almost forgot. If Nick doesn't know where you are, or that you changed your name, how did you get divorced?"

I steadied myself. "Derek, I'm still married."

The words "I'm still married" hung in the air like a thick dark cloud. Derek's pained expression broke my heart.

"You're still married?"

I swallowed hard. "Yes."

Derek gritted his teeth. "When you told me everything, I assumed you were talking about an ex-husband."

"I know. You have to believe me, Nick is not my husband. He never really was. The day I left, I put that life behind me. I want to divorce him, but how do I do that without him coming after me?"

Derek's silence said it all. I picked my purse. "I think I should go."

That pissed him off. "Are you serious? Is that your answer for everything?"

"What's that supposed to mean? Do you think I should've stayed in Pittsburgh and let Nick beat the crap out of me?"

"No, of course not. I was talking about us. The minute things get tough you bolt."

"I don't know what else to do."

I crept to the door and Derek shouted after me, "You don't want to talk about it? You want to drop this little bomb and then leave?"

I spun around to face him. "What's there to talk about?"

"First of all, you might give me five minutes to adjust to the fact that you're married before running out the door."

I halted. "Okay, you're right."

"Do you have any idea the hell you put me through because of Eden. I felt like the biggest asshole and this whole time you're married."

My voice shook. "I know. I don't know what to say."

Derek rubbed his forehead. "I don't know what to say either."

"Just know when I left, my only plan was getting away from Nick. Beyond that, I really didn't know what I was going to do. I never planned on getting involved with anyone."

"Is that why you kept running away from me?"

"Yes, in my own way I was trying to protect you. I know what it's like to live with my past. You shouldn't have to."

"I guess you've given me a lot to think about."

The look of anguish on Derek's face destroyed me. This wasn't fair to him. I had to let him go.

The realization sent a fresh wave of tears. "I should go."

"Nia, I didn't mean, please don't go."

"I know, but I have to. I can't do this anymore."

"Can't do what anymore?"

"Us. I can't do this. I'm sorry." I ran to the door.

Derek came after me and pleaded. "Nia, please stay. We'll try to work it out."

I turned to him and sobbed, "I can't. Derek, I'm broken, and you can't fix me. Please let me go."

I flew to my car and took off like a shot. My cell rang. I ignored it and drove back to the guesthouse. I threw myself on the bed and bawled my eyes out. I loved Derek so much, and hated what my past had done to us. I'd hurt him, and that was the worst part.

I grabbed for more tissues and checked my phone. It wasn't Derek, it was Aunt Mary Jane, but she didn't leave a message. Before I could call her back, she was calling me again.

She didn't give me a chance to say hello.

"Nia, I need to tell you something."

She sounded terrible. "What's wrong? Are you and Uncle Bill okay?"

"We're fine. It's your dad."

"I just talked to Dad. In fact, he told me to call you. What's going on?"

Her voice cracked. "I don't know how to tell you this. Your dad had a heart attack yesterday and…"

"What? Is he okay?"

She wept. "Nia, he's gone. I'm so sorry."

We broke down and cried together. "I don't understand. What happened?"

"He actually passed yesterday. Your stepmother just called me."

"Did she ask about me?"

"No, she didn't. What a miserable bitch. I know I shouldn't say that, but I can't help it. The funeral is at Holy Family on Tuesday. There's a graveside service right after. I can't go. I'm having a…procedure. I can't change it."

"A procedure? What kind of a procedure?"

"It's nothing. I'm just sorry I can't be there for you. I love you, dear."

"I love you too."

Oh, my poor dad, was this why he wanted me to come home? Did he know something was wrong with his heart?

I saw lights on at the main house and ran to Julia.

"Nia, what's wrong? Have you been crying?"

Tears burned my eyes. "It's my dad. He had a heart attack."

"Is he okay?"

I shook my head and cried. "He's gone."

"Oh my God, I'm sorry."

Julia calmed me down and took control. For as much as I loved to plan everything, I wasn't good in a crisis. I was far too emotional. This was Julia's forte.

An hour later, my bag was packed, and I was on my way to the airport. I texted Brooke and my other coordinator to let them know what happened. Phillip took care of my travel and rental car. I was scheduled on a red-eye from Vegas to Chicago and then to Harrisburg. I had a long layover in Chicago on the way out, and would touch down in Harrisburg on Monday night.

Once I arrived, I could sort out everything else. Like not coming face-to-face with my stepmother, since she waited an entire day to call Aunt Mary Jane and didn't even mention me.

On the way to the airport Julia asked, "How are you holding up?"

"I'll be fine. Thank you so much for helping me. I know I say this all the time, but it's true. I don't know what I'd do without you. You've always been there for me. You're like my sister."

"Now you're going to make me cry. Hey, what happened with Derek? I got your text yesterday. You said it was going great."

"It was, but then I told him everything. He got upset when he found out I was still married to Nick. I mean, I don't blame him for feeling that way."

"Maybe he needs some time to adjust. I'm sure he was shocked."

"That's weird, that's kind of what he said. It didn't end well."

"What did you do?"

"Well, I broke up with him and left."

"I think you could've worked it out if you gave him a chance."

Looks like I really blew it, but I couldn't take that in right now. Dad was foremost on my mind.

Julia dropped me off and said goodbye. She also made me promise to text her when I arrived in Harrisburg.

The plane boarded and I picked up my phone to turn it off. Derek was calling. I didn't answer. I was afraid I'd fall apart.

I closed my eyes, but couldn't sleep. I was the only person awake when the drink cart came around. I drank some water, but my churning stomach couldn't handle anything else.

When the plane touched down in Chicago, I checked my phone. I had two voicemails, one from Derek, and one from Julia.

Derek's said, "Sweetie, it's me. Julia told me about your dad. I'm so sorry. Please call me, I'm worried about you."

Julia's said, "Nia, Derek was looking for you. I told him about your dad. I hope that was okay. Please call him. He was so worried about you. Text me when you get to Harrisburg. I'm thinking about you."

I stared at my phone and debated if I should call Derek back. Why was he looking for me? I shoved the phone in my purse. I wasn't strong enough to deal with another breakdown.

The flight to Harrisburg was full. It was a much smaller plane. I sat on the aisle. The sweet woman in the middle seat was very chatty. She was about my dad's age and off to visit her first grandchild. Her name was Beth. She was so excited and talked my ear off. I appreciated the diversion.

I climbed in my rental car and drove to a nearby hotel. It wasn't fancy, but I didn't care. It was clean and had a nice warm bed. It was only eight o'clock, and I was exhausted. I checked my phone again.

I had a text from Derek. "Please contact me. I understand if you don't want to talk, but I need to know you're okay."

I wrote back. "I'm sorry I worried you. I'm okay. I made it to Harrisburg. The funeral is tomorrow. Can we talk when I get back to Vegas?"

Derek texted back immediately. "Of course, sweetie. Be safe."

I was glad to hear from him, but it didn't change anything. The image of his face when I told him I was married to Nick haunted my mind. It was too much for him. It was too much for anyone.

I texted Julia, showered, and formed a game plan for tomorrow. It included hiding in the back of the church and going to Dad's grave later in the afternoon. I could be alone with him and Mom too.

When I was teenager and couldn't stand to be around my stepmother a minute longer, I would hop on my bike, ride to the cemetery, sit at Mom's grave, and talk to her. As sad as I was about Dad, I took comfort in my last conversation with him. He missed Mom. He still loved her. Now they were together. They were at peace.

Chapter Thirteen

Why did I bother to set an alarm? I didn't sleep a wink. Not even my favorite reruns helped. I was a ball of anxiety.

I sat in my rental car across the street and watched the mourners file in the church. It was so incredibly sad. I was my father's only child, and yet I wasn't welcome. I also couldn't make my presence known because of Nick.

The hearse pulled up and out came my stepmother and sisters. For a second my heart broke for them. The way they clutched onto each other in their grief, they were devastated.

I wasn't emotionally prepared to see my father's coffin. My lips quivered, but I had to stay strong. I had to be invisible and draw no attention.

I snuck in the side door. There was a memorial with pictures of Dad through the years. There wasn't a single photo of me. I shouldn't be surprised, but it still cut like a knife.

It was standing room only. I took a spot by two people I'd never seen before. I scanned the church and only recognized a few faces.

I imagined my stepmother would spin a tale about how awful I was for not coming. She wouldn't mention she made no effort to contact me. Although, Dad knew I was here. He told me he loved me the last time we talked. I focused on that and forgot the rest.

When the service ended, I slipped out the back and drove to a florist for flowers to bring to the cemetery later.

I picked out two bouquets of yellow roses. They were Mom's favorite. The sales woman said I was lucky to get them. She had many requests for yellow roses this week.

When I returned to the hotel, I had a text from Julia. "Wanted to know how you're doing. Call me if you want to talk."

I texted back. "I'm fine. I will see you tomorrow afternoon. Thanks for picking me up. My flight gets in at four."

I changed my clothes, curled up on the bed and fell asleep for a bit. When I woke, it was after three. I drove to the cemetery with my yellow roses.

I parked close to Mom's headstone, but Dad wasn't next to her. When Mom died, Dad bought three plots so we could all be together. I spotted a canopy far away at the top of the hill; step-mommy dearest strikes again. I knelt, had a good visit with Mom and my anxiety fell away. I told her I loved her, left her one of the bouquets, and trucked up the hill to Dad.

I was surprised to find a huge spray of yellow roses in one of the corners of the canopy. It stood upright. There was no way my stepmother would've ordered it. She knew it was Mom's favorite flower.

I sat my small bouquet down and my emotions bubbled to the surface. "Dad, I'm sorry I disappointed you. I can't believe you're gone. I was coming to see you this summer."

My stepmother's voice echoed in my head. "She's nothing but trouble, her and that smart mouth."

I shook it off. "I love you, Dad."

The wind blew and the card tucked in the yellow roses toppled to the ground. I picked it up. My knees buckled. It read:

With deepest sympathies.
Mr. and Mrs. Nick Ryan.

Oh my God, how did he know about my dad?

My heart was in my throat. The way Nick signed the card—he was sending me a message. He hadn't moved on at all. He was still looking for me. He knew yellow roses were my mom's favorite. They were in my wedding bouquet. Was he here? Did he have me followed? I ran to the car and sped off.

Back at the hotel, I panicked. I called the airline to change my flight, but I couldn't. The next flight out was the one I was already on.

My cell phone startled me. Thank God, it was Aunt Mary Jane.

"I've been thinking about you all day. Are you okay?

"I'm fine, dear. Don't worry about me. How was the funeral?"

"It was nice, the church was packed. I didn't have to come face-to-face with you know who."

"Well, that's good news. I wish I could've been there with you."

"I do too. Did your procedure go okay?"

"It was fine. I will tell you all about it when I see you. Let's make that soon."

"Yes, I will see you soon. I love you."

* * * *

It was six o'clock in the morning. I'd stayed awake all night on purpose. I was afraid I'd have a nightmare about Nick.

I looked awful. I hadn't worked out for three days, and barely ate or slept. My body appeared frail and my skin was pale.

I checked my phone. I hadn't heard from Derek since his text on Monday night. I wasn't going to LA and all classes in Vegas were covered. What was I going to do with myself?

The trip home was quick and easy. One short layover in Chicago and everything was on time.

Julia rolled through and picked me up curbside.

What a welcome sight. "I'm so glad to see you."

"How was the funeral?"

"It was tough, but I'm glad I went. Please tell me you're not leaving town. I have five days free without a thing to do."

"I'm not leaving town, but I'm really busy, just like, crazy busy. Did you see your stepmom?"

"No, but she must have called Nick and told him about my dad."

"How do you know that?"

"He sent flowers, yellow roses, signed Mr. and Mrs. Nick Ryan."

"No offense, but I've always hated your stepmom."

"None taken. I'm right there with you."

We pulled through the gates and Julia drove down to the guesthouse.

"You don't have to park down here. I want to come in and say hi to Coco and Sammy. Pull in your driveway. I can carry my bag down later."

She smiled. "I'm afraid I can't do that. I have strict orders."

"What are you talking about?"

"You'll see."

Julia hopped out of the car, ran to the patio doors, and flung them open.

She scampered back to me. "Close your eyes."

"What's going on? You know, I don't like surprises."

"The entire world knows that, Miss Control Freak."

Just this once, I relented. Julia led me by the hand.

When I opened my eyes, my jaw hit the ground. The bedroom was a virtual greenhouse. Gorgeous spring flowers were everywhere. On the bed was a beautiful black cocktail dress, with shoes and a bag. "Julia, what is all this?"

She handed me a card. "Nia, please come to LA. We can work this out. I can't lose you. Love, Derek."

"I don't understand. I haven't heard from him since Monday. How did he…? Did you know?"

"I may have known a little something. When Derek came to our house on Sunday night, we told him about your dad, and that you were already gone. He was crushed."

"But I didn't think…"

"Nia, Derek is in love with you."

"I don't think so."

"He is. I know it. Please go to LA. You'll regret it if you don't."

I scanned the room, taking in the flowers. Then I smiled at Julia. "You're right. I'm going."

Julia squealed with delight. "I was hoping you'd say that. I took the liberty of packing you a bag. Let's do this."

We were like two silly teenagers. I freshened up and changed, while Julia placed my new ensemble from Derek in a garment bag.

"Julia, do you really think this is the right decision? I just got home from my dad's funeral. Am I being disrespectful?"

Julia paused and pondered. "You paid your respects to your dad in your own way. The chapter of your life in Harrisburg is closed. Derek could be a new chapter. He could be your future. You deserve a chance to be happy."

"Thank you, I've always felt like I was less than. I thought I screwed everything up so much that I didn't deserve to be happy."

"I don't think there's anyone who deserves it more. Now come on, we've got to get this show on the road."

We hurried to the car. "Are we going back to McCarran?"

"No, we're going to the Henderson Executive Terminal. It's an airport for private planes. When you get there, make sure you text Derek, so he knows you're on your way."

"Wow, you two must have been in cahoots while I've been gone."

Julia laughed. "Perhaps a smidge. Trust me when I tell you, the man is in love."

After I ran away from Derek on Sunday, I was sure we were through, even though I didn't want it to be true. Now I was bound for LA on his plane. Could he really be in love with me?

It took an hour to get the Henderson Executive Terminal. Henderson was right outside Las Vegas, and we lived on the opposite side of town. I had never even flown first-class before, so I didn't know what to expect.

Julia pulled into the parking lot about six-thirty. The airport was small and was a nice change from the big, busy crowds at McCarran.

Derek's pilot, Brett, greeted us. He picked up my bags and delivered them to the plane.

Julia peered out the window to check out Derek's plane. "Oh, look, Nia, it's a Cessna Citation. It's really nice."

I had no clue what that meant, but Julia had flown private a few times and she was impressed.

She squeezed me tight. "Text me when you land. Have the time of your life. I love you."

"I love you too. Thanks for everything. I'll give you a full report when I get back."

Julia left, and Brett escorted me to the plane.

This was awesome sauce! It was so plush and much fancier than a first-class cabin or my Barbie Dream Plane. It had four oversized captain's chairs. Two faced front and two faced the other way. Behind the captain's chairs were a sofa on one side and a bar on the other. The interior was neutral and very crisp looking.

Brett said, "Miss Kelly, we will be leaving shortly. I'm supposed to remind you to text Mr. Pierce."

"Thanks, I almost forgot." It tickled me even Brett, the pilot, knew I was bad with the phone.

I slid in to one of the luxurious captain's chairs and texted Derek. "I'm on my way. I can't wait to see you. Thank you. I'm speechless."

He texted me back. "My girl is speechless? I didn't think I'd ever see the day! LOL! I'm counting the minutes. See you soon."

His text made me beam.

Brett appeared from the cockpit. "We're about to take off, Miss Kelly, can I get you anything?"

"No, I'm fine, thank you."

"It won't be a long flight. Once we get to our cruising altitude, I'll radio and let you know. Mr. Pierce requested some wine and cheese for you. Please help yourself."

How sweet was that? Derek thought of everything. For the first time in three days, I was hungry. When Brett said it was okay, I raided the refrigerator.

"Miss Kelly, we're about to touch down. Please put your seat belt back on."

Brett's voice startled me. I dozed off. Before I put on my seat belt, I grabbed my purse and touched up my makeup. I couldn't wait to see Derek. Yes, we were on the ground.

I spied out the window. Derek stood next to a big black car. Butterflies swirled in my stomach. The kindest, most amazing man in the world awaited me. I loved him so much.

Chapter Fourteen

I flew down the stairs to Derek. Our connection sizzled with electricity. His hands captured the nape of my neck and he kissed me as if his life depended on it. Tears streamed down my face.

"Hey, I'm right here. Please don't cry."

"I'm sorry. I don't know why I'm crying. It's just everything. I didn't think I was ever going to see you again."

Derek pressed his lips to my forehead. "Nia, nothing could be further from the truth."

His mouth came down on mine. I was completely lost in him, swept away by our passion.

Brett interrupted, "Excuse me, Mr. Pierce, Miss Kelly's bags are in the trunk. I'm going to take off."

Derek thanked him and said we'd see him Sunday. I climbed in the big black car while Derek conferred with his driver, Bernie. Then he slid in the back seat next to me.

He didn't waste a moment getting back to his bossy self. "Young lady, put your seat belt on."

"I'd rather sit on your lap."

"I'm afraid I'm going to have to insist. Besides, we need to have a talk."

"I suppose you're right. I do need to tell you something. When I left your house on Sunday night, it wasn't because I wanted to. It was because I thought I was doing the right thing for you. I know it hurt you. I'm sorry."

"No, I'm sorry. I can't believe what you went through. I'm sorry for the way I reacted when you told me you were still married to Nick. I feel terrible for raising my voice after you opened up to me. Then it hit me, you were so worried I couldn't accept your past, I never stopped to think if you'd be willing to accept my present."

"I don't understand."

"When I went to the guesthouse and you weren't there, it destroyed me. Then Julia told me about your dad, and, well, I just knew. I knew I needed to be with you. I almost got on my plane and headed to Harrisburg to be by your side."

"But if you were with me, it would have drawn a lot of attention."

"That's what I'm talking about." Derek grabbed my hands. "Nia, being with me isn't going to be easy either. It won't be a normal life."

"I know. I just flew on a private plane."

"That's right, and I travel all the time. Even though I want to spend every minute with you, it just can't be that way. My life gets out of control, and it's a lot to ask someone to be a part of it. It might be too much."

"Do you not want to be with me?"

"No, sweetie, that's not it at all. I'm trying to say we both have stuff we have to get past so we can be together. When I came to find you on Sunday night and you weren't there, it made me realize I want to do whatever it takes to be with you. I can't lose you."

He leaned in to kiss me but it was difficult because of the darn seat belts. "Can I please take my seat belt off?"

He undid it for me. "Of course, come here."

He tugged me onto his lap and kissed me. I was in heaven. I loved him so much. I wanted to shout it from the rooftops, but I didn't dare.

Instead, I said, "Thank you so much for the flowers and the dress. I feel so spoiled."

A sly grin crossed his face. "That reminds me, there's something missing from your ensemble."

"I don't think so. There was a dress, shoes, and a bag."

He reached into a side pocket on the door, and pulled out a black square velvet box. It was about the size of a CD case.

"What is it?"

He smiled. "Open it."

No way! It was the emerald drop earrings. The ones I liked from the silent auction at the benefit.

I stammered. "How did you know?"

"A little bird told me. Do you like them?"

Did I like them? I loved them! That was what I totally meant to say.

Instead I blurted out, "I love you!" *No!* There was nowhere to hide. I scurried off his lap to the other side of the car. "Derek, I meant I love them, the earrings. Please don't freak out, I love the earrings, that's it."

He suppressed a chuckle. "Are you through?" I nodded and braced myself. He unbuckled his seat belt and slid to me. "Sweetie, it's okay, I love you too."

"You do?"

He cupped my face in his hands. "Of course I do. Nia Kelly, I have fallen madly in love with you."

Derek pulled me in for the most romantic kiss ever. Our connection surged higher with just three little words.

I whispered, "Can you say it again?"

"I love you. I think I've loved you ever since you said, 'son of a bitch.'"

"I love you too. I think I've loved you since, well, the naked season."

We chuckled and then it was on, until Derek's stupid phone rang.

"I'm sorry, I have to take this."

Derek was all business and blunt on the phone. I fired off a text to Julia to let her know I arrived safe. I also told her Derek said he loved me. She texted back. "See, I told you so. I'm so happy for you."

That made me smile. Julia was always right.

Derek's serious tone told me this would be a long conversation. I cuddled up next to him and shut my eyes.

I zonked out. Derek kissed my forehead. "Nia, we're here. Wake up, my sweet girl."

"I'm sorry. I haven't slept much."

"That's okay. Let me take you to bed."

Derek's voice had a magical, direct line to my pussy. It was awake and so was I. My entire body perked up. "I'm not sleepy anymore."

"That's what I hoped you'd say."

Derek's lips engulfed me. How in the hell would we ever make it out of the car? He hoisted me in his arms. The next thing I knew, I ascended a grand staircase. I felt just like Scarlett O'Hara, minus the Civil War and dress made out of curtains.

His bedroom door flung open and he deposited me on my feet. First he peeled off my shirt and then his own.

His fingers traced my jawline and traveled to the strap on my bra. "I want to see you. Take it off."

His forceful tone caused my nipples to pebble. I did as he requested. He palmed my breasts. His mouth voyaged to my erect nipples. He pleased them with slippery sucks. Derek blew a cold stream of air on each one and treated them to a randy pinch.

I expelled a shaky gasp. Everything below the waist dizzied.

His fingertips danced across my breast. "Did you like that?"

"Yes, now I have to see you. Take off your pants, please."

Ninja style, Derek was naked in two seconds. It was my turn for chest kisses. I pampered him with my mouth and stroked his straining erection. I delighted in this striptease torture. He moaned under my spell, releasing a dollop of pre-cum.

He grasped my wrists and took control. "Turn around, slide your jeans off."

His command made moisture pool between my legs. I peeled off my jeans. His hot, sweet breath on my neck prickled my skin in goose bumps. "Are you wet for me?"

"Yes, I'm wet for you."

"Let me see. Take your panties off and bend over."

I was in agony, desperate for him to touch me. I did what he said, dripping in anticipation. His fingers skimmed over my ass and found their way inside. I sucked in a heavy breath of relief.

"You are wet, so very wet for me." His fingers glided in and out of my dewy cunt.

My arms wilted beneath me, forcing my ass further in the air. I was ripe for the taking. "Oh, Derek, please, please fuck me."

He stopped. "Come here." He angled me in his arms. "As tempting as you are, we have plenty of time for fucking. I need to hold you and kiss this beautiful face.

Our mouths joined in our aching desire. "I can't wait a second longer. I have to be inside you."

I gazed up at him. "Yes."

His body was on top of mine with his eyes burrowed into me. "I love you, my sweet girl. I love you so much.

"I love you too."

With one smooth thrust, Derek sank himself deep inside me. He looked in to my eyes. "We're so perfect together."

He was right. We were perfect together. His sensuous strokes sent my body reeling. My walls convulsed around him. Our bodies hummed together in harmony. His hands dove beneath me scooping me up to face him.

He clasped me close to his chest. His hands splayed on my back, guiding me in small, gentle rocks.

I embraced his scent. He smelled like heaven. "Derek, I missed you."

"I missed you too, but we're good, we're solid. Nothing can come between us. I won't let it."

His finger tipped my head to meet his eyes. "Are you ready to come together?"

"I'm ready, take me."

He cradled my head and my bottom, floating me up and down. I held on tight, with my legs snaked around him. He submerged me deep and fully. My pussy luxuriated and liquefied on his cock.

His luscious strokes grew more fervent. A fierce rumbling overtook my body, catapulting me to the edge. My grip on him intensified. "Ah! Oh! I'm going to come."

Derek panted. "Come with me, sweetie."

Our orgasm cascaded and then tore through us. It was so powerful, so amazing. Only Derek could do this to me.

We quaked in the aftershocks. He hugged me close. We stayed like that for a while, lost in one another. Then more tears threatened. What was wrong with me? I never used to cry. Now I couldn't control myself. A soft sob escaped from my throat.

He rubbed my back. "Nia, are you crying?

I left my head in his chest and responded in a muffled tone, "No."

He lifted my chin. "I'm afraid you're not a very good liar. What's wrong, my girl?"

"I guess I've always thought, I was so damaged, no one would ever love me."

"You don't see what I see. You're so special in every way. I've never felt like this before."

"I've never felt like this before either."

His words meant everything to me, but I didn't make it easy for him. "I'm sorry."

"Sorry, for what?"

"For everything. I feel like I drive you nuts."

"You can be quite a handful, but I like it. For the most part, everyone in my world is on my payroll, so I'm used to people doing exactly what I say."

"Is that why you're so bossy?"

He chuckled a bit. "Yes, I suppose so."

"Do you want me to keep driving you nuts?"

"Not on purpose."

Derek gently lifted me off him. He smoothed the hair off my face. "Nia, can I ask you something?"

I nodded.

"I know you have control issues, but when we're together like this you're different."

"I know. It's hard to explain... The first night we were together...the way you looked at me...I felt like... I was yours." I put my head down and exhaled. "Did that sound totally stupid?"

"Of course not, I felt it too. You are mine and I am yours. We belong together, I love you."

Wow! I straddled him, in appreciation, ready for round two.

Derek stopped. "Before we get carried away, I want you to come with me."

"Where are we going?"

"I thought we could get dressed and head downstairs. You must be starving?"

"I'm not really hungry for food."

"Have you eaten much the past few days?"

I shook my head.

"Do you think you could come downstairs with me anyway, in case you change your mind?"

It was sweet the way he looked out for me. I didn't want to be a pill about it, so I relented and got dressed.

When Derek turned the lights on full blast in his master suite, I noticed it was even more luxurious than the one in Vegas.

He showed me to my bags in the walk-in closet. "My trainer Joe is coming tomorrow. You can workout with us if you want."

"That would be great. I hoped Julia packed my workout clothes."

"Oh, you have workout clothes." He flicked on the light. There was an entire row of clothes for me.

"Where did all this come from?"

"I wanted to take you shopping while you were here, but I thought it would be too complicated. I had my assistant Keith shop for you."

"Keith has really good taste."

"Yeah, he does, much better than me."

I threw my arms around his neck. "Thank you so much. I love it. I love you." All it took was one kiss for us to heat up.

"Nia, you're killing me. I'm ready to take you right here."

"I'm all yours."

"You're trying to get out of going downstairs and eating something, aren't you?"

Busted. I shrugged with a big grin on my face. He shook his head and took me by the hand.

"Okay, I guess we're coming out of the closet."

He groaned.

"Come on, that was funny, I'm a hoot."

* * * *

When my eyes flipped open in the morning, everything was perfect, except I woke up alone. I rolled over and no Derek. It was already after ten. I slept a solid eight hours.

I padded to the bathroom and brushed my teeth. I didn't look nearly as haggard as yesterday. My eyes were bright and my skin retained its healthy glow. I was bouncing back.

However, Nick lingered in my mind. I had to tell Derek about him sending the yellow roses. I hated even bringing up his name.

Deep voices outside the door indicated Derek was not alone. I threw on a robe. I peeked out the door and Derek was there with breakfast. Like his house in Vegas, he had an upstairs balcony with a great view.

He came to me and pressed his lips to mine. "Good morning. Sorry I wasn't here when you woke up. I had some calls to make. I didn't want to wake you. How did you sleep?"

I snaked my arms around his waist. "I slept like a baby."

He played with my hair. "You looked like an angel."

I giggled. "An angel with horns."

"I wouldn't have you any other way. I hope you're hungry. Joe, my trainer, will be here at noon. You'll need to fuel up."

We sat down to a feast fit for a king. Omelets, waffles, fresh fruit. It was delicious. My appetite returned full force.

"Did you make all of this?"

"No, my housekeeper, David, is here. He made it."

"I thought I heard you talking to someone. So, your housekeeper and assistant are men, do any women work for you?"

"No, I find it's a lot less complicated that way."

"Why? Did you ever have a female employee?"

His body went rigid. "Let's say there was a situation a while back, and I needed to make some changes." He quickly changed the subject. "You didn't say much about the funeral. Do you want to talk about it?"

"Well, I'm glad I went. I was able to avoid my stepmother. I don't think anyone knew I was there. But something happened, and I'm sort of afraid to tell you."

He reached across the table and held my hand. "Sweetie, you can tell me anything."

"I went to the cemetery by myself. There was a huge spray of yellow roses at Dad's gravesite. They were from Nick. He signed the card, 'Mr. and Mrs. Ryan.' I think he was trying to send me a message. Yellow roses were my mom's favorite flower. They were in my wedding bouquet."

He leaped from the table. I went to him. "Are you mad at me?"

"Oh, God no, come here." He cradled me in his arms. "How did he find out about your dad?"

"The only way he could've known is if my stepmother called him. My dad would've flipped. He hated Nick."

"I'm with your dad on that one."

"I'm sorry. I don't want to start our day like this, but I thought you should know."

"I'm glad you told me. I'll do whatever it takes to keep you safe. I love you."

I beamed. "I love you too."

He endowed me with a tender kiss. I was so ready to rip off my robe and do it right there on the balcony. I untied the belt and it draped open.

"Young lady, finish your breakfast. You'll need your strength. Joe's workouts are rough."

"Fine by me, I like it rough."

"That's, my girl!"

* * * *

After breakfast, Derek had more calls to make, so I picked out something new to workout in. I chose the bootie shorts and bra top. They fit great, but were more revealing compared to my other outfits. It was almost noon, and I sent Derek a text. His house was so big I didn't even know where he was or how to find him.

He came back to the bedroom. "Wow! You look amazing." He sidled to me and his hands landed on my ass. "Maybe we should tell Joe we'll work out on our own."

David knocked on the door. "Mr. Pierce, Joe is here."

"Good things come to those who wait."

Joe Perez was super sweet and in great shape, probably an ex-athlete or something. They led the way to the gym. I followed behind, distracted by Derek's beautiful house. I was anxious for him to take me on a tour.

Derek's gym was impressive. The room was twice the size of the fitness room at the country club. It had a spin bike, *StairMaster,* and a treadmill. The floors must have cost a fortune. He also had machines, free weights, and mirrors on all four sides of the room. After our warm up, super-sweet Joe turned into a drill sergeant. It was like boot camp on steroids. I almost threw up.

There was a small part of me wanting to say, "Didn't you notice I'm a rather tiny person and Derek's like Hercules?" However, pride came to the rescue. I didn't give up. When it was over, I was exhausted, but wasn't about to show it.

Right before Derek walked him out, Joe said, "Nia, you did great. See you Saturday."

Holy crap...Saturday!

I grabbed a mat and set it down next to a weight bench. More stretches might combat the soreness I was in for tomorrow. I was lying on my back with one leg in the air, stretching out my hamstring when Derek returned.

"Are you okay?"

I groaned. "I think Joe killed me."

He knelt on the mat between my legs. "Let's see what we can do to bring you back to life."

"I'm all sweaty and gross."

"I don't care. I have to have you."

Derek ripped off his shirt. Just the sight of his sweaty rippled body made me wet. I sat up, lifted my arms and he snatched off my top. He eased me on the mat. He brought his mouth down on mine. Even his salty, sweaty kisses were delectable.

We rolled around on the mat. Now, I was on top. He slid hands underneath my shorts and cupped my bare ass.

"Well, what do we have here, a bad girl who isn't wearing any panties."

I owned my bad girl within, stood up, took off my shorts, and bent over the weight bench.

I offered myself up. "What are you going to do about that?"

He wasted no time peeling off his shorts and kneeling behind me.

"I'm going to fuck you."

Derek gripped my hips, securing me in place. His thick shaft poised at my slit. "Don't move."

I hung on to the bench, ready to accept my punishing thrusts. He delved inside and blasted my wicked cunt. It sent a surge of tremors firing through me.

I cried out, "Yes, fuck me, fuck me hard."

He plunged into me fiercer than ever before. It was good to be bad!

I craved more. "Ah, harder!"

He answered with demanding sharp jerks. My pussy seeped and clamped down on his cock. His barbaric rhythm trampled me. The noise of our primal groans reverberated in the room.

Derek grunted, "Is this fucking hard enough for you, because I can go harder."

"Yes, ah, I'm close."

His fingers drummed my clit. A thunderous rumble shuddered inside. With just a few more unyielding thrusts, I fractured into pieces. My walls pulsated and squeezed his cock so hard his release nearly obliterated me. Our breath was heavy and our bodies spent. The aroma of sweat and tangy sex filled the air.

He released my satisfied hole and cradled me in his arms.

A soft kiss adorned my temple. "You are full of surprises. I love it."

Still panting, I whispered, "I love you."

"I love you too, so much."

Chapter Fifteen

Before we hopped in the car to go to the set, Derek introduced me to his driver. Bernie was older than Derek was, maybe in his early forties. He was small in stature and very polite.

I was nervous and excited to meet the cast of *First Bite*. This was my first introduction to Derek's world. Could I prevent my mouth from embarrassing Derek and me? It was a tough order.

I wore one of the new outfits Derek bought me—a black, shoulder baring top with matching skinny jeans. Derek said I looked sexy. He was on the phone most of the ride. He was all business and in charge. Tonight he had two scenes to film.

I had a lingering question. "Can I ask you something?"

"Of course, anything," Derek said with a smile.

"In the scenes you're shooting tonight…uh… I sort of wondered if you would be naked or kissing anyone?"

"Why? Would you be jealous?"

"*No!* I thought I should know what to expect."

"No, I'm not kissing anyone, and for the record, I'm never completely naked."

"When I watched the show, in my head, you're naked in every episode."

"You're so adorable when you're jealous."

I folded my arms. "I'm not jealous."

"Good. Because I only have eyes for you."

When we arrived on set, I was overwhelmed. Everywhere I turned was a character from the show. I couldn't believe I was here. Derek held my hand and we walked right to his trailer.

Fifteen minutes went by and someone knocked on the door and told Derek to go to makeup. As soon as he left, there was another knock.

"Hi, you must be Nia, I'm Keith Johnson, Derek's assistant." Keith was African American, in his early thirties, about five feet eight, with a big smile and kind eyes.

"Hi, it's so nice to meet you, come on in. Thank you for the shopping spree, you have great taste. I love everything."

"Girl, I always have a blast shopping with Derek's credit cards."

Keith and I gabbed away like old friends. He told me he and Derek were buds since junior high. Keith said when he came out, Derek was the first person he told he was gay. He also said Derek introduced him to his partner, Tim Kane. Tim did wardrobe for the show. Keith and Tim had been together for three years.

They were ready for Derek on set. The first scene was in Derek/Drake's house. It was so weird. It didn't look like I imagined it. I sat off to the side with the producers. They were friendly enough and eased my nervous energy.

Derek was in the scene with four other vampires. Oliver Rock played vampire Seth. Seth was the youngest vampire, and one of the show's twenty something heartthrobs. Eliza Denton played vampire Natasha. Natasha was over a thousand years old and the matriarch of the group. Before things got rolling, Oliver and Eliza told Derek they wanted to meet me. I was thrilled to meet them. I was also proud of myself for not morphing into a total fan girl.

The other two vampires kept their distance from everyone. Apparently, they were already "in character" which I didn't understand.

I was fascinated while the cameras rolled. Derek was a brilliant actor. He mesmerized me. In between takes, he joked around and kept the mood light. When they said action, he transformed into vampire Drake Braden. His transition was effortless. *Talent is sexy!*

Eliza and Oliver were fun to watch as well. Those other two were a couple of crazies. They hovered alone in opposite corners. They would only answer if you addressed them by their vampire name. Funny, with all that focus and concentration they sure did forget their lines a lot.

They finished the scene and Derek escorted me back to the trailer

He asked, "What did you think?"

I flung my arms around his neck. "I think you're incredible."

He looked down at me with a sly grin. "Oh, you do?"

"And you're sexy and amazing and so fucking talented."

"Fucking talented? I like that."

I pressed my body up against his. "It's a real turn on. Have you ever done it in your trailer before?"

Derek's hands shot right to my ass. A knock on the door interrupted us. It was someone from the production staff. They changed Derek's dialogue in his last scene.

When we were alone again he said, "I'm sorry, I better look at this. I'll make it up to you later."

Derek studied his new pages while I curled up next to him. It was after eleven. I hit the wall and dozed off.

"Sweetie, do you want to stay here and sleep?"

"No, I'm up."

He stroked my hair. "Are you sure? It's kind of cold outside and you don't have a coat."

"I'll be fine."

I took my spot next to my new producer friends. It was chilly, but within minutes, Keith and his partner, Tim, brought me a coat. Tim was tall and slim, a little older than Keith, but super friendly and sweet.

Derek's last scene was with Madison Dale. She played Jennifer, the ingénue. She wasn't a vampire or anything supernatural, but she was the star of the show.

They nailed the scene in only a few takes. It was such a treat to watch them work together.

There was a break in the action and Derek brought Madison to meet me. She was even prettier in person, with dark hair and large green eyes.

I gushed. "It's so nice to meet you, I'm a huge fan."

Madison hugged me. "I'm glad to meet you too. It's nice to see Derek smile again. Last week he was an absolute bear to work with."

Derek asked, "Was I really that bad?"

"You were impossible."

She said she'd see us at the party and bopped over to the actor who played her dad. They were quite flirty with one another. Maybe they were an item.

I teased. "So, you were a bear to work with last week?"

"Hmm…Madison exaggerates."

The heat between us prickled. "Can I see your fangs?"

He obliged with a twinkle in his eyes. I touched them with the tip of my finger and begged, "Can you take these with you tonight?"

He dragged my hand to his mouth and bit it. Talk about enticing.

Derek whispered in a sexy tone, "I could, but then I won't be able to lick your pussy."

"Fuck the fangs! Derek we need to wrap this scene up!" I imitated someone from production, "Everybody, back to one."

I had no idea what I was saying, but Derek cracked up. I couldn't wait to get home.

* * * *

I woke up with my back to Derek's front and his arm flopped around me. I wasn't sure if he was still sleeping. Then his grip on me tightened. His giant penis said good morning to my butt.

I rolled over, reached down, and stroked his hard cock. "Who needs an alarm clock when you have that? Does it always wake up before you do?"

He gave me the sweetest smile. "Only when I'm sleeping with the girl of my dreams."

Once again, his words were enough to make me wet. He slid his hands down my body and dipped a finger inside.

I expelled a soft moan.

"It feels like you're awake too." He removed his finger and lay on his back with his head propped on the pillows.

He folded his arms on top of his head. "I'm all yours."

What was he doing? This was the only place I relinquished control. Derek was in charge and so good at it. Why mess with success? I hesitated.

He reached for my hand. "Come here. You're in charge. You're so beautiful. I want to watch you fuck me."

Holy shit! That was like a vitamin B12 shot to my pussy. I was ready to go for it. I straddled him and stuffed him inside my eager channel.

I started with a slow circular grind.

Derek grunted, "Good girl."

It was such a turn on to watch him enjoy every second. I kept up my slow grind and touched a bold finger to my clit. I was fearless.

A devilish grin crossed his face. "That's it, touch yourself."

My body flushed under my own hand. I exhaled. "Look what a bad girl you've turned me into."

"I think she was there all along. Maybe I flipped the switch. Come here."

I brought my lips to his and we sunk our tongues into each other's mouth. He slid a hand in between us and rubbed my clit. I dragged my wet hole up and down his cock. It slurped him deep inside. My pussy melted around him.

Derek broke our kiss and cupped my face with his hands. "You're ready. It's time for you to fuck me. Fuck me hard."

I sat up and accelerated our pace. Maybe I liked being in charge. This was incredible. Now that song "Save a Horse Ride a Cowboy" made much more sense. I rode my cowboy for all he was worth. I almost hollered, "Yee haw!"

Derek gripped my ass. "That's it. Fuck."

My cowgirl cunt sucked, bucked, and fucked him to the base of his rigid shaft. Derek was right. He flipped the switch. He awakened something inside me I never knew existed.

My hands flattened on the bed and I took him even harder. He yanked me to him in a frenzied state, lassoing our impending release. We busted with unbridled delirium.

My first time at the rodeo was *fuck-rific*!

I said in a muffled tone, "I don't think I can move."

Derek gently rolled me on my back and pulled out of me.

He stroked my cheek with the back of his hand. "Do you have any idea how fantastic you are?"

"It's because of you, I love you."

Derek pressed his lips to mine. "I love you too, so much."

He reached for his phone. "I'd love to stay in bed with you all day, but I can't." As he scrolled through his messages, tension filled his body.

"Is everything okay?"

He exhaled. "It's nothing for you to worry about. I have to finalize my itinerary for the summer. I need to get a copy of this to Brett, my pilot."

Translation—we would be apart.

I lightened the mood. "Speaking of Brett, I keep meaning to tell you how cool it was to fly on your plane."

"Did you like that?"

"I loved it. I just wished you were with me. I had to join the Mile High Club all by myself!"

Chapter Sixteen

"Can I get you anything else, Miss Kelly?" David said in a formal tone.

"No, I'm fine, thank you."

I was in the kitchen finishing breakfast on my own, while Derek tended to some business. Talking to David was like talking to a wall. He was a tough nut to crack. Maybe he didn't like it when Derek had houseguests, or perhaps I made more work for him.

I gave up on David and strolled about Derek's sprawling property. It was so lush and lovely. Derek had a pool at this house and the one in Vegas. I must admit I was never a big fan of the water. I never learned to swim. I spent most of my summer vacations at theatre camp. I didn't have time for swimming—until Ashley Dawson's family put in a pool and she was throwing a swimming party for her twelfth birthday. My mom signed me up for lessons, but I never made it to my first class.

For a moment tears welled up.

Then I spied Derek on the terrace. Just the sight of him faded my tears. He stood there with his hands on his hips, in shorts and a tank, looking so sexy. This magnificent man was in love with me. He knew the good, the bad, and the ugly. He accepted me warts and all.

I remembered how nervous he used to make me. Now I was so relaxed. We'd gotten to this fun, playful place, exploring each other's pleasures.

It was still hard to fathom I was here. Tonight was the wrap party, and tomorrow night Derek was hosting a dinner, so I could meet his parents. I couldn't wait to meet his mom. Valerie Bennett starred in an innocent romantic comedy called *The Royal Treatment*. It was a story about an American girl becoming a princess. It was my mom's favorite movie. We watched it every Valentine's Day. I mentioned it to Derek. Of course, he was so sweet. He said his mom would be flattered. Keith and Tim were coming for dinner tomorrow night too.

Although, we did butt heads about one thing. I offered to cook and Derek hired a professional chef. I suppose he was right. I would be nervous enough meeting his parents. I shouldn't add the stress of preparing the perfect meal.

I joined Derek on the terrace and we embarked on a tour of the house. Upstairs there were four other bedrooms, each with their own bathroom. In addition to the grand spiral staircase, I discovered there were stairs off the kitchen and an elevator. Derek had an upstairs and downstairs office. I preferred Derek's downstairs office since it had a library.

I was already familiar with some of the downstairs, like the gym, kitchen, dining, and family rooms. It was quite grand, but still had a homey feel. My favorite was his living room. There was something special about that room and its cozy fireplace. It would be a prime spot to sip red wine and make love.

Derek escorted me down a long hallway. I called it the "West Wing." To the right was a fantastic screening room. It looked like a fancy mini-movie theatre. It was awesome. To the left was his man cave. It was where he and his friends hung out and played darts or pool. I couldn't play either of those, but I saw something I could do really well.

I gasped. "You have a *Ping-Pong* table!"

"Yeah, why, do you play?"

"Yep and I'm really good."

"Is that a challenge, Miss Kelly?"

"Probably won't be much of a challenge for me." I strutted and picked up a paddle.

When I was in college, Julia and I went to this sports bar with *Ping-Pong* tables. I could beat any guy in the place. I couldn't put a spin on the ball, and I didn't have the greatest serve. However, I was quick and precise and wore my opponents out.

Derek got a kick out of this. "We'll see, let's play."

"You're going down, Derek Pierce."

"If only you would, Nia Kelly."

Oh snap! He went there. It was true. I hadn't gone down on him yet. Why was I so intimidated? My blowjobs received rave reviews. Although, Derek's dick was so big it could give me a tonsillectomy. Great, now I couldn't focus on the game. Instead, I focused on his giant penis. *Well played, Mr. Pierce!*

Derek gave me the first serve. Hmm...I hadn't played since I was twenty-one. I could be a little rusty.

I served the ball and Derek smashed it right across the net. Shit! Perhaps I overstated my ping-pong prowess. I served it again and the same thing happened. He didn't rub it in, but he was quite pleased with himself. He won the first game without breaking a sweat.

Then I figured something out. When he smashed it across the net and I was able to return it, I'd end up scoring the point. I'd also scored when I returned his brutal serve. I focused on those two tasks and won the second game. Of course, I took a victory lap around the table. He swatted my bottom with the paddle.

One thing was for sure, we both hated to lose. We battled it out for two hours. By the end, we were drenched in sweat. It was a blast even though I lost most of the games, but not by much.

Back in the kitchen, Derek asked, "Do you want something to drink?"

The only thing I wanted in my mouth was his dick.

"My throat is a little scratchy. I may need something to soothe it."

He furrowed his brow. "Like what? Do I have something you want?"

Derek stood by the refrigerator. I wiggled my ass over his junk in a playful manner. I opened up the freezer and retrieved a *Popsicle*. I licked and sucked it in a provocative manner. The look on his face was priceless.

He practically salivated. "Oh, to be a *Popsicle*. Is that good?"

"It's fucking great!"

He trapped me against the island. "What am I going to do with that dirty little mouth?"

I barred my teeth and chomped off the end of the *Popsicle*. Derek couldn't take it anymore; he pressed his sweaty body against mine and claimed my mouth. Before we succumbed to our passion in the kitchen, he grabbed my hand and we flew up the back staircase.

Screw the Popsicle!

We ripped off our clothes, jumped in the shower, and washed each other in our heightened state of feverish arousal. Derek gave me that carnal look of desire as I stroked his massive shaft. I had a plan for him, a devilish, delightful plan.

I took control and told him to lie on the bed. He happily obliged. I straddled him. My mouth and tongue worshiped every inch of him as I journeyed south to his hard cock.

In general, I rather liked to suck a dick. I found there was a certain art to it. The only thing I didn't like was paying attention to the dreaded nut sack. You never knew what you were going to get. There were the misshapen balls, hairy balls, scary balls, and the always unpleasant, sweaty balls.

I must say though, Derek's were delectable. His penis was spectacular so I went to work on him. I teased him, kissing and lightly licking his inner thighs. It totally made him squirm and want it more. I gently pumped his shaft while I tongued his balls. Then he gasped as I took his tip in my mouth. I ran my tongue around his ridge and he oozed a drop of pre-cum.

Derek hissed, "That's my good girl."

My lips and tongue ran up one side of his dick and down the other, like catching the melting drippings of an ice cream sandwich.

I slathered him in saliva and his pants grew to moans. My sex pulsed watching his arousal. My hands and mouth performed in tandem. Then I went in for the kill. I sunk all of him in my mouth and his cock fucked the back of my throat.

He growled, "Nia, ah Christ."

His bulging shaft glistened with my saliva. I strummed and stroked him into a stupor. It brought him to the brink, his veins swelling to break free. I pumped him again with my mouth and hand. He writhed beneath me, his cock straining and stretching.

My mouth descended on him once more. I inhaled and opened the back of my throat wider. His tip gagged me, and my eyes watered, but I didn't stop.

Derek fisted my hair. "Nia, I'm going to come."

With a firm grip on his cock, I heaved. "I want you to come in my mouth."

Sucking back inside my mouth, I suctioned him so tight his cock exploded. He convulsed and spurted, coming undone as I guzzled him down. His cum bathed the back of my throat. I drank in every drop as his body fluttered under my spell. I relished the site of my beautiful, satisfied boyfriend.

Derek breathed heavy. "Nia, you're superb, come here."

I wiped my mouth and lay down next to him with my head on his chest. I was super proud of myself. "So, you liked that?"

"Like it? I loved it. How did you…?"

"How did I go down so far?" He nodded, and I sat up. "When I was in college I took voice lessons and my teacher taught me how to open up the back of my throat. She was trying to get me to hit a high C."

Derek rolled to his side. "Well, did you? Hit a high C?"

"Hell no, but I can suck a mean dick."

He laughed. "Young lady, you've been holding out on me."

"I know and it's very bad. Maybe I need a spanking."

Every time Derek said the word spanking, I tingled. He popped up with his back leaning against the headboard and there was that look. Oh God, what have I done?

"That's exactly what you need. I'm taking you across my knee and giving you a good spanking. I insist." Derek held out his hand and guided me across his lap. He skimmed his hands over my bottom.

My body responded with an instant trickle of juices. *Sweet, fancy Moses, why was I so turned on?* My pulse raced as I waited for Derek to say something or do something. He was quiet while his fingers grazed my vulnerable cheeks.

"You've been a naughty girl. Exactly how many times should I spank you?"

Was he really asking? His hands disappeared. It was silent for a moment and then, smack. He spanked me, and I liked it! It wasn't that hard and it didn't hurt —it was like an endorphin rush. He rubbed the spanked cheek. Then he spanked my other cheek and rubbed it too. The next spank made my mouth yelp and my pussy gush. What was my body doing?

"Hmm…you have such a perfect little ass. I'm going to enjoy turning it a lovely shade of pink. Those first three were just a warm-up."

Eight sharp spanks followed in quick slapping succession. Each one drove me closer to the edge. Derek thrust two fingers inside my aching, needy cunt.

I cried out, "Yes, ah, ah."

"Look how bad you are. You're sopping wet."

His words worked me up even more. I rocked back and forth on his lap.

He pressed his other hand on my back. "Be still, sweetie." Was he joking? He removed his fingers and left me wanting, but not for long. "Spread your legs wider for me."

I opened up and his hand found my hungry clit. He massaged it. Fuck yes! I was close to imploding. His other hand spread the moisture to my anus. He was a man with a plan. I was totally down with it. I shamelessly pressed my pussy against his hand.

"Nia, don't move. Give yourself to me."

He ramped up his assault on my clit and stuck his thumb inside me. My pussy trembled and strained, firing toward my impending release. Then he took the tip of his finger and placed in on my tight pucker.

I wailed, "Yes, Derek! I want it!" He pushed his finger in my ass and I came like a raging inferno. I gave myself to him. I gave him everything.

I wriggled in aftershocks. My listless body was in a heap across his lap.

"Do you need some help?"

I could barely shake my head, yes. With one arm around my waist, he hoisted me up and swaddled me between his legs.

Derek brushed my hair off to one side and nuzzled my neck. "So, you liked that?" His fingers danced on my nipples causing them to pebble. His erection dug in to my back.

"Yes, and I think you liked it too." I turned to face him. His blue eyes penetrated me, and my body heated under his steaming glare.

In an instant, our flesh slammed together. Derek commanded, "I have to be inside you."

"Yes, make love to me."

He eased me on my back and entered me. My head was at the foot of the bed. I remembered when we were in my bed and I couldn't tell him I loved him. I wasn't sure if he loved me back, but he did. He loved me. He gave me everything.

* * * *

I was in the bathroom getting ready for the big party tonight. I wore my new black dress. It reminded me of the dress I wore to the benefit, only this one was short. It showed a lot of leg and my back was exposed. I also wore my new heels, which probably cost more than I made in a month.

Derek appeared in the doorway. Wow! He looked so damn fine. He was in a perfectly tailored grey suit and a black shirt with the collar open.

Just the sight of him sent a shiver up my spine. "You look so good. You should come with a warning!"

"A warning?"

"Yeah—may cause panties to drop!"

His lips brushed my cheek. "You are so sexy. I won't be able to keep my hands to myself."

He didn't. He ran his hands up my dress. They went right to my ass and he tugged on my thong.

I giggled. "What are you doing?"

"I'm making sure your panties didn't drop."

"I thought you were making sure I had them on."

"That too."

He took a step back and drank me in. "Tonight, when we come home, I want you naked except for the shoes."

He would get no argument from me.

Derek made sure I put the emerald earrings on, and now my outfit was complete. Before we climbed in the limo, Bernie told us it would take about an hour to get there, so as requested there was a bottle of champagne waiting for us. Everywhere you went in LA took at least an hour. It was nine o'clock and there was still so much traffic. The party was at a producer's house; one of the people I met last night.

I was glad Keith and Tim would be there. The rest of Derek's team was also coming. Season five of *First Bite* premiered on television in May. Derek would be traveling for that too. Until then, it sounded like we'd be spending a lot of time together.

We finished our second glass of champagne and drove up to this mansion. I'd never seen anything like it. Bernie dropped us off and we journeyed inside. Nervous jitters flashed through me. It was like walking into another world, a world where everyone was rich and famous except for me.

As we made our way through the house, my head swirled about. It was so much to take in. The house alone was so over-the-top. It looked like someone took Saint Patrick's Cathedral, and mixed it with some bling and a hint of brothel.

Everywhere I glanced, enormous fake tits threatened to poke my eyes out. I found it unsettling. The women also dripped diamonds and *Botox*.

Once we got outside, I breathed easier and released Derek from my death grip. "Sorry if I squeezed your hand too tight. That was like an assault on my senses."

He kissed my forehead. "I know, but I'm so glad you're with me." Derek snaked his arm around my waist.

I returned to my sassy self. "You're probably with the only woman who still has all her original parts. These boobs are small, but they're real."

"I love you and all your real parts."

We moseyed to the bar and chatted with Keith and Tim. It was a perfect place to people watch. Julia would love it. The music pumped and the partygoers let loose. Derek only left my side once to get us something to eat. Since I was such a finicky eater, he grabbed a little of everything. I settled on shrimp cocktail and of course, cheese.

As the evening wore on, I relaxed. It was nice to see Madison Dale again. She came right over to say hello. I was right. She was totally dating the guy who played her dad. Derek told me there was almost a twenty-year age difference.

The male executive types were a trip. The shorter and older they were, the younger their wives.

I'd looked forward to meeting Derek's publicist, manager, and agent, until I met them. They reminded me of an angry lollipop guild. During introductions, they looked past me, as if I was invisible. It was such a bad first impression. I didn't remember their names.

I was about to ask Derek to dance, when he said, "I can't believe she came."

"Oh, hell no," added Keith.

Gisela pushed her way through the crowd. She and her two girlfriends stumbled toward us with determination. It was like being in high school, and you knew the mean girls had their sights set on you. All three of them wore dresses two sizes too small. Their disheveled, wasted appearance was like watching an inevitable train wreck. Derek bristled and maintained a protective stance in front of me. Keith and Tim shot me a look that said they had my back. Was Gisela that bad?

Her friends hung back while she got in Derek's face and snapped, "I heard you had some girl with you on the set last night. Is that her? What is she, like twelve?"

It didn't happen often, but once in a while, I had a moment of brilliance. This was one of those moments. I put myself between Derek and Gisela and said, "Hi, you must be Gisela Monet. I'm Derek's cousin, Nia. It's so nice to meet you. You're my favorite on the show. You're even prettier in person."

Her mouth gaped open. "Oh, well, thank you. It's always nice to meet a fan. I'm sorry. I didn't know you were Derek's cousin. Anyway, I'm going to go."

She threw Derek a dirty look, tromped to her gal pals and took off.

Derek, Keith, and Tim instantly surrounded me. Derek said, "Nia, you are awesome."

"What else could I do? Gisela is literally bat shit crazy."

Keith put his arm around me. "Derek, this girl is a keeper. Come on, you're dancing with me."

He pulled me out to the dance floor and we tore it up. I sucked at many things, but dancing wasn't one of them. My Aunt Mary Jane used to tell me I was born with an "extra hitch in my get along." She would tease me and say I needed to spend extra time in confession for all of my "dirty commotions."

Keith and I had a blast. Some of the other cast members joined us. Derek stayed at the bar with Tim. His eyes fixed on me the entire time. After a few more booty-popping songs, a slow one played. Derek made a beeline for me. It reminded me of the benefit when we had our first dance. So much had happened in such a short amount of time.

He said to Keith, "You don't mind if I dance with my girl?"

I never tired of hearing that. Derek swept me into his arms and rested his hand on the small of my back. There were over a hundred people at the party, but as far I was concerned, we were the only two who existed.

"You are a woman of many hidden talents. I had no idea you could dance like that. I'm impressed with the way you handled Gisela. She was so drunk, it could've gotten ugly."

"Do you think she'll find out I'm not your cousin?"

"I doubt she'll remember coming to the party."

He drew me close and his cock swelled against my stomach.

I glanced up at him. "You're about to make my panties drop."

"I can't wait to get you out of that dress. Are you ready to go?"

I nodded. Fancy over-the-top parties were okay, but I would rather be alone with Derek than anything else.

We couldn't climb in the limo fast enough. Derek transfixed me with his eyes. He really couldn't wait to get me out of my dress. He wasn't even going to wait until we got back to his house.

He undid my dress at the neck. "I'm going to have you right now."

"What about Bernie?"

"He can't see us, and if we aren't too loud, he won't hear us."

The top part of my dress fell and my breasts were exposed. He treated them to light licks and flicks of his tongue.

I exhaled. "Derek, I'm not good at being quiet."

"Shhh... Sweetie, relax." He took off my dress and then my thong.

I was naked except for the shoes. The leather seats against my bare skin were chilly. Derek took his shirt off and laid it underneath me.

Then Derek discarded the rest of his clothing. "Lay back, I want to look at you." I stretched out, spellbound by him. His eyes lingered over my nakedness. "You're so gorgeous. I can't help myself."

He lifted my leg and glided his hand from the heel of my shoes to my expectant pussy. I was so lost in him I forgot I was in the backseat of a moving car, only we weren't moving. Derek caressed my clit with his exceptional tongue. I threw my head back yearning for more.

Then Bernie's voice boomed, "Mr. Pierce, there must be an accident ahead. I'm getting off at the next exit."

Derek's head popped up from between my legs. "Okay, thanks." It ruined the moment.

I giggled. "I was kind of hoping I'd be getting off at the next exit." We both chuckled.

I sat up. "So we've been sitting here next to the same cars? Can they see in the windows?"

"No we're safe. No one can see us."

"How long will we be stuck in traffic?"

"It could be a while."

I straddled him. "Whatever will we do to pass the time?"

Our lips pressed together. It only took a hot second to get back in the moment. Once again there was that look. The look that said Derek was going to fuck me. Would I be able to keep my big mouth shut?

He sheathed his hard cock inside me

I gasped. "Yes!"

"Shh... You have to be quiet for me. I'm going to take you slow."

His grip on me tightened. He was in control, rocking me with dutiful, seductive strokes. His hand slipped between us and circled my clit. I released muffled whimpers into his mouth. My walls zinged in tiny contractions, while divine, languid strokes rested on my naughty twat spot. My pussy flushed, leaking a small stream of my fluids. How was I supposed to be quiet?

"Derek, please."

"Please? Does my girl want to come?"

"Yes!"

"Not until I say so."

His strong hands steered me to his base. He held me still and pumped hard and fast.

Then he slowed. He was like the back of a shampoo bottle, lather, rinse, repeat. He took me to the brink and eased me back off, many times, too many times. I was in anguish, desperate to come.

He gave me wry smile. "I could do this all night."

I whispered, "Can I come now?"

"Only if you're good."

He grabbed my ass and ramped up our speed. My loud moans sounded in the limo.

"Oh, that's a naughty girl."

Grasping the nape of my neck, he anchored his mouth to mine. Maybe it was to shut me up, but it sent me to the cliff. He railed me up and down. When my pants grew to groans, he reprimanded me and spanked my ass. *Fuck yes!*

His hand caught my chin. His red-hot stare penetrated me. "Now, Nia, now you can come."

He gripped me to his root and blasted my pussy, double-time. I smothered my face in his chest to muffle my cries of pleasure. My orgasm flared and howled. Derek grunted and filled me with cum. *Limo sex... crushed it!*

He touched his lips to my forehead. "I love you."

"You love to torture me."

He patted my bottom. "Admit it, you loved that too."

"I love everything you do to me."

He was still inside me when Bernie's voice interrupted. "Mr. Pierce, the traffic started to move, we're at the exit and we just got off."

Before Derek could answer I said, "You can say that again."

"Thanks for letting us know." He shook his head. "You and that dirty little mouth."

"I'm sorry. Are you mad?"

"Of course not, I love you and your dirty little mouth."

Derek wrapped his jacket around me. I cuddled up next to him for the rest of the ride.

I'd fallen asleep. The next thing I remembered was Derek putting me to bed. I was under the covers. He sat on the edge of the bed with a washcloth taking off my makeup. It was so sweet.

"I'm sorry. I didn't mean to fall asleep."

"That's okay, close your eyes, go back to sleep. I'll be right back."

I waited for Derek to climb in bed so he could kiss me goodnight.

He held me close. "Goodnight, my sweet girl. I love you."

Chapter Seventeen

Morning arrived, and my eyes opened to a wonderful, familiar feeling—Derek's hard dick pressing into to me. From that day on, I referred to it as my alarm cock. Waking up in my boyfriend's arms and making love was the best way to start the day. I had the time of my life these past few days.

I was lying in his arms and simply said, "Thank you."

Derek was puzzled. "For what?"

"For everything. I didn't know I could be this happy. You're so good to me. Sometimes I don't feel worthy."

"You have no idea how phenomenal you are. I'm the one that's not worthy. I've never been this happy before, either. You know, this is only the beginning. I want us to experience everything together. I want to show you the world."

I let out a squeal, as if I was ten years old and hurled myself at him. "I love you!"

I kissed him all over, with absolute giddiness. Unfortunately, Joe was due in an hour to kick my ass. We hadn't even gotten out of bed yet. We dressed and headed downstairs. David fixed us breakfast, but didn't say two words.

Joe put us through our paces again. This time we mixed in cardio intervals with boxing.

After Joe left, I hit the shower. I asked Derek to join me, but he had some calls to make. I wrapped my hair in a towel, threw on a robe, and searched for him. He wasn't hard to find, he was yelling in his office. I haven't heard him that mad since I got drunk with Julia. I turned around and went back to the bedroom. I dried my hair. When I finished I found Derek slouched on the side of the bed.

"Honey, is everything okay?"

His eyes brightened. "Did you just call me honey?"

I shrugged. "A little something I'm trying out. What do you think?"

"I think it's adorable, like you."

"Good, I thought you'd like it as long as it was only honey and not Honey *Boo Boo*."

Only a slight smile touched his lips. Then he came to me and stripped off my robe. "Get in bed. I want you ready for me when I get out the shower."

Something wasn't right.

He joined me in the bed, we made love, but it was different. The way he immersed himself in me and said he loved me. There was desperation in his voice. Why wouldn't he tell me what was going on?

"Derek, I want you to know you can tell me anything. I'm not going anywhere."

"You realize you're using my own words against me."

"Would I do that?"

"I think you might. Something came up that I wasn't expecting, and I'm not happy about it. But it's not definite, so I don't want you to worry."

Now I was even more curious, but I didn't push.

I climbed on top of him. "Whatever you say, honey. I'm all yours."

Derek was back to his playful self. "In that case I'm going to have to have you again."

I slid down his sublime cock and got after it. It was so salacious! Then Derek slowed down and said my two new favorite words, "Turn over."

It was a quickie fuck fest of epic proportions.

He packed his cock in my tight hole and drummed it with force.

I screamed, "Yes, fuck me! Fuck me hard."

He poked, pounded, and plunged into my inflamed piqued pussy. Derek's fingers nursed my naughty nub to a hell's bells mother-fucking dandy of an orgasm. I wailed in delight. A loud grunt ripped from Derek's throat and he unleashed his load. We were lying in a heap when a knock on the door startled us.

David hollered, "Mr. Pierce, your chef Marcus and his staff are here."

"I'll be right down."

I laughed. "Do you think David heard us?"

"I think Julia heard us in Vegas. I'll be right back."

He got dressed, gave me a quick peck, and went downstairs.

After I got ready and donned another new black dress, Derek headed to his office, and I snuck downstairs to the kitchen. I couldn't resist. I had to see how they prepared the food. I introduced myself to Derek's chef Marcus, his sous chef Jarred, and Luke, the server for the night.

Marcus didn't appear thrilled as I hovered about, but everything smelled yummy. He whipped up filet mignon, scallops, roasted potatoes, and green beans. There was an appetizer and salad course, as well. I wasn't sure what was for dessert, because Derek walked in the kitchen and busted me.

"Marcus, is my girlfriend spying on you?"

Marcus shot Derek an unpleasant glance.

I said, "I'm sorry, Marcus. I'm kind of a picky eater."

Marcus replied with a sarcastic grin, "Mr. Pierce warned us about you."

Everyone chuckled a bit. It broke the ice. For once, my control freak nature came in handy.

Derek grabbed my hand and led me downstairs. He couldn't resist giving me a pat on the bottom.

I asked, "Did you really warn them about me?"

"Did you really spy on a professional chef?"

"Where are we going?"

"You'll see."

Derek opened the door to his glorious wine cellar. It was fantastic. Luke already set up a full bar, but Derek picked out a special bottle of red to serve with dinner. I couldn't even pronounce the name, so it must have been expensive.

"I've been saving this for a special occasion."

"I hope your parents like me."

"Sweetie, they'll love you."

The bell rang. It was Keith and Tim. I was so nervous, I went to the bar for a glass of wine. I took two sips and the bell rang again. My stomach flipped. Should I go with Derek to the door, take a shot of whiskey, or jump out the window? I opted for another sip of wine and the company of Keith and Tim.

Keith put his hand on my shoulder. "Girl, relax, I've known Derek's parents since I was a teenager. They'll love you."

Everyone was so sure his folks were going to love me, but me. My main goal was to survive the evening without saying son of a bitch.

I must say the sight of them together was majestic. They were all so tall. Even Derek's mom was at least five nine. Derek was a perfect blend of his parents. He had his mom's striking blue eyes and smile, with the masculine bone structure and build of his dad. They were in their sixties, but Valerie looked exactly like the princess from my mom's favorite movie.

Derek swallowed hard. "Mom, Dad, this is my girlfriend, Nia."

Derek's dad offered his hand and I shook it. "It's so nice to meet you, Mr. Pierce."

His mom smiled. "Please call us Charles and Valerie." She embraced me.

For a moment, a vision of Mom and I watching her favorite movie flew through my brain, and I choked up for a second.

Then Charles saved the day. "We're delighted to meet you, Nia. The last time Derek introduced us to a girlfriend she turned out to be a lesbian. So far, I'd say we are headed in the right direction." Everyone chuckled at Charles' offhanded remark.

In the dining room the oversized long table was gone, and replaced with an intimate table for six. Charles sat at the head of the table and Valerie was opposite him. Derek and I were next to each other on one side, Keith and Tim on the other. Keith and I were closer to Valerie. Derek and Tim sat closer to Charles.

The conversation during the meal flowed smoothly. Keith was a great storyteller and recounted some tales of Derek in high school. Tim chimed in with a few funny antics Derek did on the set of *First Bite*. His imitation of Derek, the first time he wore his fangs was hysterical. I laughed so hard I snorted, which made everyone else laugh even more.

On Derek's cue, Luke poured us a glass of the special wine. Derek stood to make a toast.

"I told Nia when we were down in the wine cellar I've been waiting for a special night to open this bottle of wine. And tonight is truly special to have you all here." He captured my eyes with his gaze. "Nia, from the moment we met, somehow I knew you and I belonged together. I've never been this happy. Thank you for loving me. You're my everything. Here's to my sweet girl. I love you."

He kissed me softly on the lips and we all clinked glasses. It was like something you'd see in a movie, only I wasn't watching it, I lived it. I had tears in my eyes, but I wasn't alone, so did Valerie. Keith folded like a cheap tent.

Luke returned with the main course and we resumed our meal and conversation. Everything tasted delicious. I ate every bite.

After dessert, Charles was chomping at the bit to hit the man cave and challenge someone to ping-pong. The men took off to the "West Wing" while Valerie and I visited in the living room with our wine.

She said, "Oh, I almost forgot, I have something for you. Do you know where Derek put my purse?"

I retrieved it. She pulled out a *Blu-Ray* of her movie, *The Royal Treatment.*

"I love this movie, thank you so much."

"Derek told me you and your mother used to watch it on Valentine's Day."

"You were my mom's favorite actress." A lump formed in my throat. "I'm sorry. I still get emotional when I think about her."

She took my hands in hers. "Of course."

The way she said "of course" reminded me of Derek. They had a similar comforting lilt to their voices. It must run in the family. She reached in her purse, took out some tissues, and gave them to me. It was such a nice mom thing to do.

"Derek told me that your dad just passed away too. I'm so sorry for your loss."

A few tears escaped from my eyes. "Derek's been so wonderful since I've been here. I don't know how I would've gotten through it without him."

"He really loves you. I've never seen him like this before."

"I love him too."

"It takes a strong woman to be with a man in this crazy business. You're stronger than you think you are, don't ever forget that."

We joined the boys in the "West Wing." They played ping-pong. Derek and Keith paired up against Charles and Tim. Tim wasn't having any fun at all. It was not his thing.

He pleaded, "Nia, you've got to rescue me. Derek and Keith are vicious."

I shot Derek a look, because I swore when I lost a point. He had quite a grin on his face and clearly couldn't wait to see what I'd do. I grabbed Tim's paddle. Charles and I clobbered Derek and Keith! I vindicated myself, and scored points with Charles.

After our victory, we all said goodnight. It was the perfect evening. I wasn't nervous. I didn't say anything embarrassing, and after meeting Derek's parents, I loved him even more.

We stood at the front door. The house was quiet. It was just the two of us. Derek pulled me into a knee-buckling kiss.

I looked up at him. "What was that for?"

"For being you. My parents adore you. I love you so much."

I jumped up and wrapped my legs around his waist. "I love you too."

Derek carried me upstairs. Whatever upset him earlier fell away.

We burned with desire. "Nia, I need to feel you."

In that moment, I didn't want to go back to Vegas. Couldn't we stay in our little bubble forever?

Derek was relentless. He couldn't get enough of me. It was like a dream. If only I didn't have to wake up.

Chapter Eighteen

I opened my eyes and I was alone. There was no Derek and no alarm cock.

We weren't flying to Vegas until this afternoon. He was spending the night and then heading to New York for a photo shoot.

It would be our first time apart since he said he loved me. I would miss him, but I was more secure than ever. I focused on that, slipped on my robe and searched for him.

He was in his office upstairs on the phone. He faced away from me. His beautiful broad shoulders rose in tension.

Derek turned and saw me. He softened somewhat and gestured for me to come in the room. He sat down on his office chair and invited me to sit on his lap. An invite I would never refuse. He wrapped up his call and curved his arm around me. I relaxed and nuzzled his neck, drinking in his clean Derek scent.

"Good morning, my sweet girl."

"I missed you this morning. I'm so spoiled, I hate waking up alone."

"I'm sorry. There's a lot going on I've been putting off. It's coming to a head."

"Can you please talk to me about it? I've been worried about you."

Derek set me on my feet. "I can tell you this. Brett called this morning and said they're expecting a windstorm in Vegas. We have to fly back right away."

Last minute changes were not my friend. My morning plan included sex on the desk.

I sat on the desk and undid my robe. "I'm sure we have a little time for a proper good morning."

Derek closed my robe. "No, we don't. I need you to go get ready."

"Just a quickie and then I promise I'll be good."

"Nia, please, I need you to do what you're told."

Rejected I slunk out of the office. Why wouldn't he tell me what was going on?

I showered and packed up my stuff. My stomach was in a knot, so I didn't go downstairs for breakfast. I stayed in the bedroom and waited for Derek.

From the instant I stepped off the plane, he was attentive and sweet. Now, he was bossy and sullen and refused to tell me why.

While I waited, I texted Brooke and Julia we were flying home early.

Derek returned to the bedroom. "Did you go down for breakfast?"

I shook my head.

He plopped next to me on the bed. "I really think you should go get something to eat."

"I really think you should quit ordering me around."

"Why are you being so difficult today?"

I jolted away from him. "I could ask you the same thing."

Derek rubbed his forehead. "You have no idea what I'm dealing with."

"That's right, I don't know because you won't tell me. I feel like you don't trust me or something."

He came to me and gripped my shoulders. "I'm trying to protect you. I need you to trust me."

"Please, tell me what's wrong."

"Okay, but remember nothing is definite. I don't want you to be upset. I'll tell you on the way to the airport. We need to go."

We gathered our things and headed for the airport. On the way, he told me there were issues with Eden. She was unhappy with the angry lollipop guild and sought new representation. I couldn't say I blamed her.

Before he could continue, his phone rang. Once again, Derek was furious with one of his team members. I dug into a protein bar I snatched from the kitchen.

By the time Derek was off the phone, we arrived at the airport. Brett was anxious to take off. He warned us it might be a bumpy landing and we should keep our seat belts fastened.

Brett performed his final safety checks while Derek told me more about Eden. After she acquired her representation, their public relationship would be finished.

"I don't understand why this is such a big deal for you. Can't you be single Derek Pierce?"

"I told them that. I also told them we aren't making our relationship public. I know I need to protect you from Nick."

"You didn't tell them about Nick, did you?"

"Of course not. I would never do that. But they had a lot questions about us that I couldn't answer."

It was time to buckle up for the flight. We faced each other, too far apart to hold hands, stupid seat belts.

I also had more questions. "I need you to be totally honest with me. Does your team have a problem with me?"

He exhaled. "It's not you. It's the situation. With Eden seeking new representation, they stand to lose a lot of money. They've been pressuring me not to take a break this summer. I've been adamant that I am. They think it's because of you. When I told them you didn't feel comfortable going public with our relationship, they called you a liability."

It hit me like ton of bricks. Maybe I was no good for him.

Derek took off his seat belt, leaned forward. "Nia, look at me. I love you. You're not a liability. You're the best thing that's ever happened to me."

"Do they want you to pretend to be in a relationship with another actress?"

"Yes. I told them I wouldn't do it. I need to tell you something else. If I'm being totally honest with you, I feel like I'm struggling with something."

My heart sank. "What? Please tell me."

"When I think about the awful things Nick did to you I get so angry. How could he have laid his hands on you?"

"I use to think that's what I deserved."

"No, sweetie, that's not true. I'm worried he might find you because of me. God, if anything ever happened to you…"

With urgency, he came to me, removed my seat belt, and sat me on his lap. Tears were in both of our eyes.

He lips touched mine. "I'm sorry I upset you this morning. It's not how I wanted to start the day."

"I'm sorry I'm causing you so much trouble."

"You're not, it's this business. You, my sweet girl, are perfect."

Gentle, loving Derek was back. I wasn't wasting a moment.

"Actually if you recall I wanted to start the day with sex. Perhaps if I had gotten a proper fucking, I wouldn't be so grouchy."

"Is that so? I'll have to remember that."

"You may also want to remember around this time every month I have PMS. You should put that seat belt back on. There could be a lot of turbulence."

"I will put it in my calendar and take cover."

That devilish grin crossed his face. "I don't know if this will be proper, but you are about to get fucked."

Plane sex, I was in, hundred percent. He stood me up and released the stowaway table

He slid to the edge of his seat. "Turn around. Bend over the table for me."

I heard him unzip his fly. He lifted my skirt and shoved my panties to the floor. His fingers opened me up and checked my readiness for his cock. He let out a guttural hum. "You look delicious. I have to have a taste."

He lavished his tongue on my silky wet folds. I writhed on the table. Long, luscious licks glided along my inner lips. Then his tongue flicked my clit, and my juices ran down my thighs.

"I think you're ready for me." His tip taunted my slit. I whimpered in my lust for him. He grasped my hips and embedded himself inside. Jesus, this position was so primal and raw.

"Is this what my girl needed?"

"Yes, oh my God, yes. It's so good."

"You're so good. I love watching my cock disappear inside you."

One of Derek's hands traveled to my aching clit. He gave me exactly what I needed. I used the support of the table and mastered this sultry reverse cowgirl. I cruised up and down him, sinking to his base.

I delighted in every stroke as we soared higher together. The pressure in my tight cabin contracted around his cock. I was ready for landing.

"Derek, I'm going to come. Oh God."

His firm grip on my hips tightened and his sharp thrusts peppered my hot spot, flying me over the threshold.

A heart stopping orgasm rippled through me like a rocket launching a space shuttle.

Derek didn't come yet. I lifted myself off him and spun around. "I want you to fuck my mouth."

I got on my knees and licked off my juices. I was delicious. Then I took him in my watering mouth and sucked him like the bad girl I'd become.

Maybe it was the plane. Derek had me *dick-matized*. Pleasing him set off a fiery sensation in my clit. It was some sort of *mouth-gasm*. I was aroused as he fucked my face. The sound of both of our moans filled the plane. My slick mouth encased him tight and my hand cupped his balls.

"Fuck, Nia, I'm going to come."

I drained him and gulped him down. I gasped and my sex twitched. I was on the verge.

I glanced up at him. "Derek?"

"Tell me what you want? Do you need to come again?"

"Yes I need to come, please."

"You are a greedy little thing. I may have to spank you again. Go ahead, bend over the table, I'll make you come."

I gave him my pussy on the table and he coated his fingers in my juices. Then he spread my lips and flicked his finger on my greedy clit. He rubbed and flicked and rubbed and flicked. His palm pressed and circled. I pressed back and it propelled me to the hilt. I pounded the table with my fists. Two fingers drilled me knuckle deep. I screamed and came apart on his hand.

"You are my saucy little vixen. Come here."

He tugged me up on his lap and wrapped his arms around me. "You never cease to surprise me. I love it."

I cuddled in. "I love it too."

Brett's voice sounded over the radio. "Mr. Pierce, we're about to make our descent into Las Vegas. If for any reason you unbuckled your seat belts, please fasten them now."

Derek patted my bum. "Let's get you in your seat belt."

I shimmied into my panties. He tucked the table away and locked me in place. "We have the entire day and night together. I promise to ravage you all afternoon." He sat on my armrest and brushed the hair off my face. "I'm turning my phone off so we aren't interrupted. I don't want you to worry about anything. I'm going to work it out."

"Thank you. By the way, am I an official member of the Mile High Club? Do I get my wings?"

"Yes, you're like an angel with wings."

"And a tarnished halo?"

Derek pressed his lips to mine. "One of the many reasons I love you so much.

* * * *

As we drove to the Mountain Heights Country Club, the windstorm gained force. The car rocked and rolled down the highway. We made a plan. I would run to the grocery store. Then head to his place, and spend the night there. Now he didn't want me to drive in the storm, so we changed the plan. I drove in one of these windstorms before. Some debris flew into my windshield, and almost caused an accident. I was happy to make the change. Derek arranged for a car and driver and asked him to stop at a hardware store.

When we pulled into the parking lot he said, "Can I have the key to your place?"

"Why do you want my key?"

"So I can have a copy, and I'll make you a copy of my key."

He already had the key to my heart. I was thrilled to hand over the key to Julia's guesthouse.

While Derek breezed into the store, I texted Julia and Brooke again and let them know we arrived safe and would be going to Derek's to cuddle up for the day. Julia texted she and Phillip had the same plan. Brooke texted the wind canceled her tennis lesson. It was a perfect opening to ask her about Tom Hyland, the tennis pro. I wrote back, "If you're not having a tennis lesson with Tom, will you be serving up anything else?"

Brooke replied, "You are so bad and correct."

Good for Brooke, she was such a great girl and had been through so much her with ex. Then she sent me another text, "Glad you're back. Sonya has backed off. I don't know why, but all is well at work."

What a huge relief. I had such a great time in LA, I forgot about Sonya. What I didn't forget was my dad. While the trip had been a wonderful distraction, I hadn't dealt with his death yet.

Tomorrow I would call the therapist who canceled on me. The downside to a new therapist was drudging up the past. It could trigger nightmares, like the one I had the night of the benefit after the Larry Wall incident.

When I first moved to Vegas, I had such terrifying dreams about Nick trying to kill me. I woke up screaming. It was awful.

I was able to brush that off, for now. Seeing Derek headed back to the car made me beam. The wind pounded him. Still, he had a big smile on his face. *God, how I loved that man!* Sometimes when I looked at my beautiful boyfriend, I still couldn't believe I was his girl. He made my knees weak, my heart melt, and my body smolder. He was magic.

He climbed in the car. "This is your key, and the key to my house." Then he held up my key, "And now I have a key to your place."

I leaned over and kissed him. "Please feel free to enter anytime."

"I usually do."

That was so true and delightful. Let the ravaging begin!

Once we settled back at Derek's place, I went to work on the grocery list. I suppose I should be grateful we could get delivery on a day this windy, but I hated not picking out every item myself.

He called the order in and I carried my things up to the bedroom. I was thrilled to see a brand new flat screen TV. This called for a little channel surfing.

Yes. I found a rerun of *The Doctor Is In*. It was the show Derek talked about the night he bandaged my knee. I hadn't seen it, but there was no mistaking his handsome face in a lab coat. I glued in to his scene with a dying female patient. The pretty patient may have been kicking the bucket, but her hair and makeup were flawless. Derek looked about my age and was so dreamy. Dr. Leif Stevens could breathe life back into a corpse.

A loud groan echoed in the room. "Oh God, what are you watching?"

"I believe that's you, Dr. Leif."

"I was awful on that show. Please turn it off."

He reached for the remote, and I put it behind my back. "No way, I'm going to watch you play doctor. I want to go to Dr. Leif. If I tell him where it hurts, he'll kiss it and make it better. I'll pull down my pants and he'll say ahh."

Derek laughed, retrieved the remote, and turned off the TV. "Come on, Shecky Green, you're coming with me."

"Who is Shecky Green…is he one of those stooges? You are so old."

Derek halted in the hallway, and pressed me against the wall. His eyes hooded with lust. "Someone needs a spanking."

Oh, hell yes! Whatever he had in mind I was all for it. He picked me up, and I snaked my legs around his waist. As Derek carried me to his office, his mouth took mine, ferociously, bruising my lips.

He plopped me down on his desk. It was the perfect place to start our afternoon delight.

I lifted my arms and he ripped off my top. I wasn't wearing a bra so his descent on my breasts was instant. I closed my eyes and leaned back. Derek was so talented he managed to keep my nipples hard while stripping naked. Forget playing doctor, I was ready for dictation.

I helped myself to his throbbing cock. "I feel like your naughty secretary."

"Sweetie, you're my naughty everything. Now turn around and pull your panties down." Excitement flickered as I obeyed his command.

"Now your skirt." My pussy dripped with moisture as I slid it to the floor. Derek smoothed my hair to the side. "Put your hands on the desk and spread your legs. Someone's been a bad girl."

A ragged breath escaped. What was he going to do to me? One thing was for sure, he was obsessed with my ass. His hands went right to it, making me squirm.

Derek said in a low sexy voice, "Hold still."

He plunged two fingers inside me, and I cried out in ecstasy. His other hand spanked my bottom. He stretched me open with a third thrusting digit. My ass burned in sinful pleasure. I loved it! Each sharp spank fizzed on my sex. I steadied myself, giving in to the intensity. My body absorbed its delicious punishment.

His fingers rubbed my billowy clit, working me into a crazy fury. I was on the cusp of an explosive orgasm that was almost too much.

As soon as Derek pushed his steely shaft inside, my release thrashed me. I screamed out his name and flattened flush on the desk. Derek continued his assault on my burning hole. His cock smacked my sweet spot head-on. My body convulsed and another orgasm lurked. I wanted it. I wanted everything he gave me.

"Does my girl want to come again?"

"Yes, oh fuck, yes!"

Teetering on the fringe of rapture, our bodies radiated molten heat. He grabbed my hips and slammed into me repeatedly. I let go like a wild savage! Derek emptied himself inside and came loudly. Still splayed out on the desk, the sensations of pleasure coursed through my body.

Derek's hands gently rubbed my ass. "Nia, you're amazing."

He was still inside me. His dick sputtered and sparked. He moved a little. *Holy hard-on!*

He was ready to go, again. "Sweetie, what are you doing to me, come here."

I turned around. He sat me on the edge of the desk and smoothed my hair. "Nia, do you have any idea how much I love you?"

"I love you too."

"I can't get enough of you. I'm going to take you again."

I whispered, "Yes."

He picked up my right leg and braced it against his chest. Lucky for me I was quite bendy.

"Lay back for me."

My left leg dangled off the edge of the desk. Derek leaned forward and squeezed into my ravenous pussy. What was it about my right leg being in the air? It was different in a new decadent way.

He moaned, "You feel even tighter, oh fuck."

He was in total control and knew exactly what to do. Our eyes fixed on one another as he slowly claimed me with every erotic stroke. The way my silky hole clutched his dick sent a roaring vibration streaming through me. His thumb rotated on my clit, driving me mad.

Utopia drew near. My milk and honey spilled out as his swift, rapid thrusts powered me onward.

Derek grunted. "Are you ready to come for me?"

I panted. "Yes, I'm ready for you."

He plunged hard and fast until our climax imploded and broke apart like shrapnel. I was limp like soggy spaghetti and positive Derek should buy a new desk. He took my right leg, kissed it, and put it back down. Any attempt to get up was pointless.

"Your naughty secretary can't move."

"Stay there, I'll be right back." He was back in two seconds with a warm washcloth. He cleansed me and helped me up. I was on my feet again with Derek's arms cloaked around me.

"Sorry about your desk."

He smiled, "Actually it was the Manning's desk." His hands traveled to my butt. "I'm sorry you had this paper clip stuck to your ass."

I giggled. "I thought there was something else poking me besides you."

I could have stood there, naked in his office forever, but the doorbell rang. The groceries had come and so had I—several times!

* * * *

Derek talked to his parents on the phone while I fixed lunch. I made what I called berry salad. It had blueberries and raspberries over greens with feta cheese, slivered almonds, and a champagne vinaigrette dressing. After the salad was complete, I went to work on Derek's grilled cheese. I used rye bread and a combo of provolone and Havarti.

He walked into the kitchen. "I'm turning off my phone for the rest of the day."

"I don't even know where mine is."

He scolded me. "We should probably talk about that. Since we can't always be together, it's going to be difficult to communicate if you don't answer your phone."

"I promise I'll be better about it, starting tomorrow."

He softened and came to me. "I need to know you're safe."

My situation with Nick terrified both of us. The least I could do was answer my phone.

I changed the subject. "How are your parents?"

He perked up. "They're great and they wanted me to tell you hello. They are quite smitten with you."

"Well, I am smitten with them too, and in love with their son." I flung my arms around his neck. "Are you hungry?"

"I'm always hungry for you, but we should probably eat first. We'll need the fuel for what I have planned."

That could've been the most arousing sentence ever; sex and a plan! Who needed a freaking berry salad? We sat down and ate anyway. Derek got us some wine and gobbled up his food.

"This is so good, what's for dinner?"

"It's a surprise."

Derek disappeared upstairs with the rest of our wine while I cleaned the kitchen.

When he returned to the kitchen, he had that look. My pulse quickened. He took my hand and led me upstairs. Candles illuminated his master suite and bathroom.

He ushered me to the bathtub filled with bubbles. I was fully clothed and so turned on. He rid me of my skirt and top, leaving me with just my panties. Derek got on his knees and slid them off in a slow titillating way. Then his hand worked its way up my inner thigh as he gently dipped a finger inside me.

"Nia, I love that you are always so wet for me."

Soft kisses traveled up my body and he captured a nipple in his mouth.

My whole body was flush with need. "Derek, I want you inside me."

His hands caressed my face. "Your appetite is insatiable. I love it."

He probably planned on a soak in the tub before making love again, but my craving for him took over. He stripped off his clothes. By the looks of his stiff cock, he craved me too. We had a quickie on the chaise longue before settling into the tub.

Derek poured us a glass of wine. We relaxed with my back resting on his chest. We sipped our wine and drank in the moment. I squirmed under long fingers grazing up and down my body.

He nuzzled my neck. "Can I ask you something? Have you always been this horny?"

"If I tell you something, you promise not to laugh?"

"Of course, you can tell me anything."

I faced him. "I don't think I ever came during sex, until I had it with you. Why do you think I had that vibrator?"

He chuckled. "You never had an orgasm with anyone?"

"If I did, I missed it." Gripped with emotion, I moved to my knees and confessed. "Everything is different because of you. The truth is, I've never been in love, until I fell in love with you."

He touched my face. "I've never been in love before either. You make me so happy." He swept me away with his kiss.

"Can we make love in the tub?"

"We could, but my girl is starting to prune. Come with me. Just like I promised, I'm going to ravish you all afternoon."

* * * *

"Do you want red or white wine with dinner?" Derek asked.

I stirred my sauce at the stove and he was behind me with his arms around my waist. It was hard to concentrate on the marinara, with Derek kissing my neck. Even though we made love all afternoon, we couldn't keep our hands off each other.

I didn't even bother to dress for dinner. I wore my soft, black robe. Derek was in a T-shirt and shorts looking delectable.

"I think red would be good. You should pick it out. You always know exactly what I like."

"I'll be right back."

We sat down to dinner. I made pasta primavera with yellow, orange and red peppers, and portabella mushrooms. I threw in spinach at the end, so it wilted up without getting mushy. I grated some Asiago cheese on top. The tomato salad looked pretty and was difficult to screw up, so if the pasta were a bust, at least the salad would be good.

Derek dove right in. He made many yummy noises, which pleased me. "This is so good. I think you're the one spoiling me."

"You know they say the way to a man's heart is through his stomach."

He reached across the table and grabbed my hand. "You've always had my heart."

We talked through dinner about a million different things. Derek told me about the magazine shoot. He had to be on set at six a.m., which meant getting up around four. He wasn't leaving Vegas until late morning.

Keith and Tim were going to fly into Vegas early, and catch a ride on Derek's plane. I must admit I was a little jealous. I would've loved to tag along if I'd known they were going. I mean, Derek and Keith would be working, but Tim and I could've gone to a Broadway show.

He would be back in Vegas on Friday afternoon. I was already counting down the minutes.

We cleaned up the dishes together and called it a night. We had to wake up at seven, because of my schedule. I organized my stuff for the morning while Derek was in the bathroom. Then I went to the bathroom and did my thing.

When I returned Derek was naked, sitting with his back against the headboard and grinning in that devious way.

I asked, "What's that look for?"

"I was thinking about what you said earlier in the tub."

I slipped off my robe, and mounted him. "Oh that. Yes, you and Buzz own all my orgasms."

His brow furrowed. "Who's Buzz?"

"My vibrator."

"You named your vibrator Buzz?"

"What was I supposed to name it…Irving?"

He chuckled. "What am I going to do with you?"

"Since you're leaving town, I'll have to do myself."

"I don't think so. I'm afraid Buzz has hummed his last tune."

"What do you mean?"

"I want you to save all your pleasure for me."

"Are you going to save all your pleasure for me?"

"Nia, I'm a guy, I have to do it."

"What? That's not fair. You've turned me into a human coming machine and now I have to be good when you're out of town?"

"That's right. I want you on the edge every time I return from a trip. If you are mine, your pussy is mine too."

His cock swelled beneath me. I guided it inside. "If that's the case, you better fuck your pussy, now."

"You are so naughty."

"Naughty and yours, all yours."

His hands cupped my ass as he controlled our pace. It shouldn't be possible to have this many orgasms in one day, but I was making up for lost time. Our bodies were so connected, so in tune with one another. We flowed in our perfect way. I was already close.

He slowed down and climbed on top of me. It was our last night together until Friday. We should make it last. His mouth was unyielding. Even though we slowed, I was still ready.

Then I had an idea. If one leg resting on his chest felt incredible, both legs would be twice as nice. I extended them to the ceiling.

"Good girl, I love the way you think."

He placed my legs on his chest and dove into me. Thank God, I was flexible, because this position and Derek rocked my world!

"Nia, come, come, my sweet girl."

I evaporated under his command and his thick stream of cum flooded me. We were still coming down to earth as I lowered my legs to the bed.

His gentle kiss touched my lips. "I'm going to miss you so much. I can't wait until Friday."

"I'm going to miss you too. Derek, can I...talk to you about something?"

He slowly pulled out of me and rolled to his side. "What is it, my angel?

"I need to go back to therapy. I'm going to call tomorrow and make an appointment."

The back of his hand stroked my cheek. "Do you want me to come with you sometime?"

"You would do that?"

"Of course, I love you. I would do anything for you."

"There's something else. A new therapist means drudging up the past. I'm afraid it might trigger the nightmares I used to have when I moved here."

"I hope I'm with you, so you're not scared."

"I hope so too. I haven't had one since the night of the benefit."

"I wish I wasn't leaving tomorrow."

"I'll be fine. You have to go do your thing. That's not why I told you. I'm trying to be more open and communicate."

Derek took my hands in his. "Okay, but promise me if I'm not with you and you have a nightmare, you'll call me no matter what time it is."

"I promise."

"Speaking of calling, I need to charge my phone. Do you want me to charge yours?"

Well, crap! Where was my phone? I draped the covers over my head.

He removed them. "You still don't know where your phone is?"

"Yes, I do."

"If that's true, I will lick your pussy in the morning before you leave."

"Um, it's in the car and I'm sure you don't want to go get it, so you'll have to take my word for it."

"Are you sure? That's your final answer?"

"Yes, that's my final answer."

He shook his head. "You left it in the kitchen."

"That's not fair. If you knew where it was then why did you ask me?"

"Because you need to know where it is. When's the last time you charged it?"

"I'm sure it's fine."

"Okay, but I know one young lady who isn't going to get her pussy licked in the morning."

I snuggled up to him. "Technically speaking I promised to be better about my phone after today, so you should totally lick it."

"You think so? I'll have to think about that. I'll call you and let you know."

I giggled. "I love you, Derek."

He kissed my forehead. "I love you too. Goodnight, my sweet girl."

* * * *

It was only six a.m. and Derek was still asleep. I woke up ten minutes ago with a naughty notion whirling in my brain. I slipped out of bed, went to the bathroom, and freshened up. I snuck downstairs, grabbed my phone, and crept back upstairs. I found my charger, plugged it in, and slid back into bed.

We faced each other. Derek's eyes fluttered open. I pretended to be asleep like an innocent cherub.

He reached for me and drew me close. "Good morning. How's my angel?"

I suppressed a giggle. "Hi, what time is it?"

His morning wood touched my tummy. "Hmm… The alarm cock says it is six-twenty."

He checked the actual clock. "You're right. How did you know that?"

My fingertips grazed his chest. "We angels have our ways. By the way, you mentioned you were going to call me and let me know if you were going to lick my pussy this morning. I thought you'd like to know, I'm charged and ready to receive."

I reached over and produced my phone. Derek smiled. He placed the phone back on the nightstand. "You're so adorable. How could I ever refuse you?"

Not only didn't he refuse me, Derek made my toes curl and my eyes roll to the back of my head. Then he made love to me for the last time until Friday. It was spectacular!

When we said our goodbyes, I wasn't tearful or even the least bit anxious. Of course, I would miss him, but our relationship was strong. A few days without Derek were no problem. I was fine.

Chapter Nineteen

"Nia, these are from all of us. We're sorry to hear about your dad." Sonya handed me flowers.

A smile replaced her usual scowl. Am I being punk'd?

"Thank you. That means a lot."

As my students filed in for Body Sculpt, the outpouring of sympathy overwhelmed me. Sue Peterson embraced me with tears in her eyes. It was too much. I excused myself and fled to the restroom.

Brooke wasn't far behind. One look at her and I broke down and cried. I should've been more emotionally prepared.

Brooke said, "Look, I can teach your class if you want. The first day back is tough, but it'll get better."

"I'm okay. I just need a minute. It's good for me to get back to my routine."

After a few minutes, I got it together and soldiered on. My classes pulled me out of my funk.

Back at the guesthouse, I checked my phone. I had a text from Derek. "Taking off, I will text when I get to New York. I love you, sweet girl."

We'd been apart a few hours and I missed him already.

Instead of texting him back, I stayed on task and called the therapist's office. Dr. Roma Laham didn't have any appointments for three weeks. I took the next available and asked if I could be put on the cancellation list.

Julia sent a text earlier saying she was home with nothing to do. It did bum me out she never came to my classes, but Julia wasn't a fitness class kind of girl. She preferred the great outdoors. She was an excellent swimmer and forever on my case for not being able to swim. One of these days, I would deal with that situation, but not today.

I went to the main house and we had a blast catching up. She loved hearing the stories about *First Bite* and the wrap party. Sammy stuck to me like glue.

The time flew by. I scurried to the guesthouse to change for my class on the other side of town. I was so mad at myself for not taking my phone with me.

I missed another text from Derek. "I made it to New York. I hope my girl is having a great day. Text back when you get a chance. I miss you."

A call from my therapist's office interrupted my text to Derek. It was good news. There was a cancellation and I jumped at it. My appointment was tomorrow afternoon at one o'clock.

I put my phone down, headed to the bathroom and there it was, my period. Thank God, it didn't come early this morning when I was with Derek. I would've been totally embarrassed. My period lasted only four or five days. It should be gone by Friday.

Running behind, I changed and hurried to the car. I was stuck in traffic. My phone beeped. It was probably another text from Derek.

By the time I got to the gym, I was stressing. I was usually there a lot earlier. I checked my phone. Sure enough, the text was from him. "Are you okay? I'm worried because I haven't heard from you."

I texted him back. "I'm sorry. I was with Julia and then I got a call from the therapist's office. I have an appointment tomorrow afternoon. I'm running late. I have a class. I love you."

After class, I checked my phone. Derek texted back. "I'm starting to wonder if I should have licked your pussy this morning. It's been fewer than twenty-four hours and you've already been naughty with your phone, LOL!"

Whew, he's being playful. I wrote back. "To lick or not to lick, if that is the question then *lick* is always the answer. You're so good at it…honey."

In two seconds my phone beeped. "Flattery will get you everywhere. I like it when you call me honey. It's adorable, like you."

I texted. "I love you. I'm getting in the car. Can you call me later? I promise I'll answer my phone."

He wrote. "Yes. You better or I will spank that beautiful bottom until it glows. I'll call you at seven your time. Drive safe."

It was Tuesday afternoon. I was anxious while I waited to meet my new therapist. The office was nice, very tranquil. I sent Derek a text to let him know I arrived and turned off my phone. We had a great chat last night, but he was tired and not looking forward to waking up at four a.m.

Before long, the receptionist took me down the hallway and introduced me to Dr. Roma Laham. She was quite striking with shiny, jet-black hair and beautiful, light-brown skin. She told me she read the paperwork I filled out a month ago when they canceled my appointment.

That was more than the other nut bags did after Dr. Kris Morgan left town. They were more interested in prescribing me medication. Working out was my anti-depressant.

Dr. Roma had a serene voice. "Nia, what would you like to talk about today?"

"Well, my dad just passed away."

"I'm so sorry for you loss."

"Thank you, we had a complicated relationship. I think I'm grieving the loss of what we could have had. Does that make sense?"

"Yes. Did you have a complicated relationship with your mother too? I read in your file she passed away when you were twelve."

"We had a great relationship. I feel like I'm grieving for her again too. I'm also in a new relationship that is amazing. Which is confusing, should I be this happy so soon after my dad's passing."

"Wouldn't he want you to be happy?"

"Yes, I just don't feel worthy."

"Then that's something we need to work on." She examined my file. "What about Nick? Are you still estranged?"

"Yes, he sent flowers to my dad's graveside. He's still looking for me."

"How does that make you feel?"

I sighed. "Scared, anxious, and frustrated. Seeing those flowers brought it all back. If it's okay, I don't want to talk about him."

"That's fine. It's our first day. We will talk about it when you're ready.

"I would like to tell you who I'm dating, but I need it to be confidential."

"Everything you say in our sessions is confidential."

"I'm dating Derek Pierce, he's an actor…" I didn't get the rest of the sentence out of my mouth.

Her eyes bugged out and she lost her cool, calm demeanor. "You're dating Derek Pierce?" She gathered herself. "I'm sorry, that was so unprofessional of me."

"No need to apologize. You should have seen me when he walked into my spin class the first time. I nearly fainted."

Dr. Roma's tone turned serious. "You mentioned Nick is still a threat to you. With Derek being in the public eye, doesn't it make it easier for him to find you?"

"It does. I'm being careful, but that's another reason I needed to see you. I can't tell Derek or my friends how scared I am. I don't want them to worry any more than they already are. I just want to close this chapter of my life for good."

Our time was up. I made an appointment for the same time next week.

As I drove home, I obsessed about Nick. I hated the hold he had on me. The entire time we were together, he controlled my every move and in some ways, he still was. I would love to shout from the rooftops I was in love with the most wonderful man in the world, and I couldn't. We had to hide our relationship, which also caused problems for Derek. It wasn't fair. Nick caused me enough pain to last a lifetime. When would I be free?

* * * *

I was in the fitness room setting up for class. Crap, I never turned my phone back on after my appointment.

I fired it back up and Sonya walked in. "Nia, it looks like you're going to have a full house. You'll need to set up all the bikes."

Distracted by two text messages from Derek I stared at my phone. "Oh, I'm sorry. My phone was off and I forgot to turn it back on."

Sonya smiled, again. "I do that all the time. Do you need any help setting up the bikes?"

"No, that's okay."

Sonya's new, cordial demeanor baffled me, although I couldn't dwell on it. After all, I wasn't fluent in crazy.

Wheeling out the bikes was time consuming and a bit of a workout on its own. Derek's messages would have to wait.

"Hey, Nia, it's been forever," Steve said as he plopped an arm around my shoulder.

Scott whispered, "Come over for dinner tonight so we can catch up."

I nodded with an enthusiastic yes.

After class, the boys walked me to my car to make a plan for dinner. They invited Julia and Brooke too. Julia would be there, but Brooke had a date with Tom. You go, Brooke.

"Thanks for invite. I'll be over right after I shower and make a couple of calls."

Steve couldn't resist. "Are you calling our favorite vampire? I know something is going on."

I shrugged. "Well, that depends."

Scott piped up. "Depends on what?"

"It depends if you two can keep a secret."

I smiled, climbed in the car, and totally left them hanging.

Before jumping in the shower, I checked my phone. Now I had three messages from Derek. I texted him a long rambling apology and he called me right away.

I didn't even say hello, I asked, "Are you mad?"

"No, sweetie, I was just worried. Do you like your new therapist?"

"Yeah, I like her a lot."

"Did you talk about Nick? Are you going to be okay?"

"I'll be fine, honey. Please don't worry about me."

"I'm only a phone call away if you need me. I love you, Nia."

"I love you too."

* * * *

"Inquiring minds are dying to know the real scoop!" Steve wasn't going to rest until he got the dish about Derek and me.

Steve and Scott were a riot. It was hard to imagine them in their serious chosen professions. Steve worked in insurance and Scott was a lawyer. Steve was tall with grey hair. Scott had a slight build and a perfect coif of red hair. I had no clue how old they were, it was a guarded secret.

Scott handed me a giant goblet of wine. They called it my truth serum. "No pressure, but if you would be so kind as to let us know, come on, Nia, spill."

"Yes, it's true. Derek and I are seeing each other."

They cheered.

I interrupted the celebration. "I do have to ask you guys to keep it a secret. It's really important."

"Got it, tick a lock. It's going in the vault," Steve said.

Julia chimed in. "Nia was on the set of *First Bite* and saw them film the finale."

The boys let out a gasp the size of Texas.

Scott exclaimed, "Tell Derek if he introduces me to Oliver Rock, I'll put him in my will."

It was after ten when we said goodnight. Julia walked to the guesthouse with me. She was there all of two minutes before Sammy scratched on the door. I let him in and he jumped on the bed.

Julia laughed. "Sammy, you're such a traitor!"

I crawled in bed with Sammy and flipped on the TV. Hypnotized by an infomercial my eyes grew weary. What was it about an infomercial late at night? I believed them. This thing could rotate your tires, bake perfect bread, and achieve world peace with a touch of a button. If my eyelids weren't so heavy I would've bought what they were selling for ten easy payments of only nineteen ninety-nine. I turned it off and went to sleep.

* * * *

I ran, but I wasn't moving. The hallway was long and dark. I had to get out of there. Oh no, my feet stuck to the floor. He was coming for me. I couldn't find my way. Please, God help me. He would kill me! *Somebody please help!*

I cried out, "Help me!" Sammy barked and it shook me out of my dream. "Come here, Sammy. Good boy."

The nightmares were back. It was five a.m. in New York. Derek would be up. I called him.

He answered on the first ring. "Nia, what's wrong? Did you have a bad dream?"

I answered in meek tone. "Yes."

"Oh, sweetie, I'm sorry. I wish I were there to hold you. Is Sammy there?"

"Yes, Sammy is right here."

"You want to talk about it?"

"No, but you said I should call you. I'm sorry. You're getting ready for your shoot."

"Don't worry about that. Hey, I just thought of something. This is the first time you've called me. You do know how to use the phone."

"You answered on the first ring."

"Of course. I'm always here for you. I love you."

"I love you too."

"Close your eyes and get some rest. I'll be in Vegas before you know it, goodnight, my sweet girl."

* * * *

Wednesday night I had another nightmare. It was three a.m. in New York. Derek would've been in bed, so I didn't call him. I didn't sleep a wink.

Thursday night, exhaustion set in. In my last text to Derek, I fibbed and said I slept great. I didn't see the point in worrying him. If anything, I worried I was too much for him. My insecurities and anxiety were getting the best of me.

Right before I hit the shower, Julia sent a text telling me Phillip was back. If Phillip was home, Sammy didn't come to sleep with me. I was on my own tonight.

I fell into bed and texted Derek to let him know I was home and in for the night. He usually texted back right away, but he didn't. I dozed off for a bit and checked my phone again, no word from Derek. Maybe he was out whooping it up in New York. Why haven't I heard from him?

I channel surfed for a while, but was so anxious I couldn't focus.

Frustrated, I called it a night. I plugged my phone in the charger, put it on the nightstand, and checked it one more time, nothing.

A cool breeze blew through the room. Was I still asleep? Was I dreaming? I saw myself in the bed. Oh no, the bed rocked like a boat. "I can't swim." No one heard me.

I drifted. My legs were heavy. My arms were immobile. I was still drifting. I couldn't see a thing.

Why was I so cold? Oh God, this wasn't good. I had to wake up. Was someone here? There was a presence in the room.

With a violent shake, I forced open my eyes. Someone was here! I let out a blood-curdling scream!

"Nia, it's me, it's Derek." He shook me and turned on the light.

I screamed, "Don't touch me!"

He backed off. "You're okay. It's me."

I held my arms out to him. "I'm sorry. I thought you were Nick."

He drew me close. "You're safe. I'm right here. I'm sorry I scared you. I sent you a text as soon as we landed to let you know I was on my way."

"I didn't get it."

Derek released me from the embrace and grabbed my shoulders. "If you didn't get the text, then why did you leave the door hanging open?"

"I didn't leave it open."

"Where's your phone?"

"It's right here." My nightstand was empty. I panicked. "Somebody was in here. I know I left my phone there. I know it."

Julia, Phillip, and Sammy flew into the room.

Julia asked, "We heard you scream, are you okay?"

Derek replied, "Something weird is going on. I came home early to surprise her, and when I got here the door was hanging open."

Phillip examined the door. "There are no signs of forced entry. Whoever opened the door had a key. Should we call the police?"

I protested. "What are we going to tell them? That someone who had a key unlocked the door and moved my phone. They'll think I'm nuts."

Phillip responded, "At the very least we need to have the locks changed down here and up at the house."

"Who would do this? It doesn't make any sense," Julia said as Sammy jumped on the bed by my side.

We talked in circles and got nowhere. Derek suggested beefing up security or hiring me a bodyguard. I was not interested in that. Finally, we all agreed the best thing to do was get some sleep. We said goodnight to Julia and Phillip. It took a bit of coaxing to get Sammy to leave my side.

After they left, I turned the place inside out and searched for my phone.

"Nia, I don't want to upset you, but are you sure you left the phone on the nightstand?"

I snapped. "Yes, I'm sure. Because I texted you tonight and I never heard back."

"Okay, I'm sorry. I didn't text you back because I was already on my way to Vegas."

"I thought you weren't leaving New York until tomorrow. Were Tim and Keith upset you cut their trip short?"

"No, at the last minute Tim couldn't go.

"Why didn't you tell me that?

"I wanted to surprise you."

"Well, here's a helpful little hint about control freaks. Sometimes surprises freak us the fuck out."

He draped his arms around me. "I will take that under advisement. I'm sorry I scared you. It's the last thing I wanted. I just couldn't take another night away from you."

"I need to tell you something. Last night I had another nightmare. I didn't call you because I would've woken you up."

"You should have called me."

"I know. I didn't want to worry you. Are you mad?"

"Why do you always ask me that?"

I choked back tears. "It's just... I made Nick mad all the time. I didn't mean to but I..."

He held me close. "Nia, I'm not Nick. I would never ever...you know that don't you?"

"I do. I'm sorry. I'm screwing everything up."

"No, sweetie, you're not. You need some sleep. We both do."

I went to the bathroom and found my phone on the sink...turned off.

Derek was in bed waiting for me.

I climbed in. "Look I found my phone in the bathroom."

He handed me my charger. "I found your charger by the dresser. Do you think Nick did this?"

"No I don't. If it was Nick, he would've…"

He opened arms to me. "Nia, come here. Put it out of your mind. I'm here now. You're safe."

I didn't move all night. Derek was still asleep. I slipped out from under his arm, trucked to the bathroom, and brushed my teeth.

"Nia, where are you?"

I came out of the bathroom. "I'm right here."

Derek slouched on the edge of the bed.

"Honey, what's wrong?"

"I thought, I don't know, God, I love you."

I went to him and pressed my lips to his. He caressed my face. Slowly we found our way. He stripped off his T-shirt and wrapped his arms around me. His kisses grew deeper. I slipped off my T-shirt. My puckered nipples craved his touch. Derek tended to them with gentle nibbles as he laid me on my back.

I exhaled. "Derek, I want you. I want you so much."

His fingers hooked the waistband of my boxers to glide them down. Then I remembered I still had my period. It was probably over, but I had in a tampon.

I froze up and Derek asked, "Hey, what's wrong?"

I put my hands over my face. "Um…I might…still have my period. I mean, it could be finished, I don't know."

He got off the bed. He came from the bathroom with a towel. "Sweetie, look at me. It's not a big deal. Lay on the towel."

I did, but I should've gone to the bathroom and taken out the tampon.

I sat up. "I'll be right back."

He stopped me. "It's fine, lay back, let me do it."

Off flew my boxers, he reached between my legs, pulled out my tampon and flung it in the trash. If it was possible to die from embarrassment, I was DOA.

"Oh God, what is happening?"

"Nia, I've been up close and personal with every inch of you. That was nothing. You could go to the bathroom in front of me and it wouldn't phase me."

"Well, I'm not going to…*ever!*"

He got naked and lay down next to me. I couldn't look at him.

He peeled my hands from my face. "You're so cute when you get shy on me."

We faced each other. He had that look in his eyes, the one that said he was dying to fuck my brains out. Instead, he was patient as he touched his lips to mine. They were tender and sweet. The way he tasted and his scent overwhelmed my senses.

I was totally lost in him. "Derek, I need you inside me."

He whispered, "I missed you so much."

He climbed on top of me and slid inside. I missed him too. I missed how nothing else mattered when we were together like this. I wasn't scared or insecure. I was his and he was mine. Together we were perfection.

Chapter Twenty

"What are you doing?" Derek asked.

I was in his kitchen early in the afternoon.

"I'm making a list so I can go to the grocery store."

Derek cocked his head to one side. "I thought you were okay with getting everything delivered."

"Well, that was different, because of the windstorm. I like to go. Besides, we don't even have anything for lunch."

He smiled in his sly way. "Yes we do. I already took care of it. I have a surprise for you." I shot him a disapproving glance. "It's a good surprise. I promise you'll like it."

He looked so adorable, how could I say no? Still, I teased. "Sorry, Mr. Pierce, I'm not available right now. I'm so grocery list busy."

Derek shook his head and hoisted me over his shoulder. "You're coming with me, young lady."

He carried me outside and I shrieked with delight. "Put me down, Derek Pierce."

He swatted my bottom and set me on my feet. It was a good surprise. He planned a picnic. A big thick blanket adorned with pillows lay before us. He had all my favorite foods and a bottle of wine.

I floated my arms around his neck. "This is so sweet. I love it. I love you."

I whispered in his ear, "My period's over."

"Good girl, you said that without blushing."

I stripped off my top. "How about that."

It was on. Our clothes came off in a flash. We stood naked in Derek's backyard. The sun bathed our flesh as a light breeze flowed over us. Derek laid me down on the blanket. It was so tantalizing and romantic. It was just like that old movie *From Here to Eternity* only better. There was no cold ocean and no sand in my butt crack.

Our passion revved up and boiled over. First Derek was on top of me.

Then he whispered, "Turn over." *Mother, may I?*

He plunged me from behind. I cried out, "Oh God, Derek, yes! Fuck me."

He reached around and fingered my wanting clit. It took me to the brink. "Derek, I'm so close."

He slowed down. "Don't come yet."

He pulled out of me and I turned to face him. We were on our knees. "Nia, I missed you so much. I need to see this beautiful face when you come."

"I missed you too."

"Come here, sweetie."

Derek lay on his back. I mounted him and glided him inside me. Our tongues entwined and we rocked at a leisurely, sultry pace.

He moaned. "Look how beautiful you are."

His words made me soar. It was liberating. With him, I was unfettered, brave, and super horny.

He bent his knees and spread me further. I braced myself on the ground and we surged in need. The air was filled with our groans and slapping flesh. He pulled me flush against him and drove his sweet tongue into my mouth. Together we unraveled from here to eternity and back again. Neither of us could move or even wanted to.

I lifted my head. "I like surprises now."

He smoothed my hair. "I'm glad." I slid off Derek and lay down next to him. He went from euphoric to serious. "I can't stop thinking about last night. I know the locks are being changed, but I don't know if it's safe for you to stay there."

"Where would I go?"

"You could live here. I want you to move in with me."

* * * *

Talk about surprises. I didn't expect Derek to ask me that. Actually, he wasn't asking, he was demanding. I couldn't do it. It was too soon. After a difficult negotiation, Derek and I reached a compromise. If he was in town and I was on dog duty, we would stay at my place. If I weren't, we would stay at his house. Then we hit an impasse. He didn't want to me to stay at the guesthouse alone. When I shared that with Julia and

Phillip, they got a security system for both houses. It satisfied him, for now.

We never found out who came into my room that night. At least, nothing else happened and the nightmares faded away. I was more secure.

* * * *

The next couple of weeks Derek stayed in Vegas, and I was in heaven. We settled into a routine. It was normal. Normal was exciting to me.

I loved watching him with my friends. It was as if he'd known them forever. I coordinated several TV binge-watching parties. We all took turns hosting, but I cooked most of the food and chose the entertainment. The night we hosted, I surprised Derek with a *Three Stooges Blu-ray* collection. I didn't get it, but the guys laughed their heads off.

It was also nice to see Brooke happy with Tom. It was funny how people commented Brooke and I looked like sisters, because Tom and Derek could have passed for brothers. Phillip was about five-ten. He teased he didn't want to stand next to those two.

Derek was a regular in my spin class. I got distracted if he was in class. It reminded me of how we met and of course, the man totally floated my boat. After class, he stayed and helped me put the bikes and mats away. One time, his eyes fixated on my ass during every song. It was such a turn on. After everyone left, we were in the equipment closet hoisting the mats to the top shelf. Derek was right behind me.

He coiled one arm around my waist, one hand on my butt and said in a sexy way, "The night we met, I wanted to take you right here. It was all I could do to keep my hands off you."

He slid my shorts off, bent me over a bike, and took me in the closet. It was awesome! I tried to be quiet, but when I came, I shouted, "Son of a bitch!"

* * * *

Derek was due back in LA. He asked me to come with him, but I flew to Wichita to visit Aunt Mary Jane and Uncle Bill instead. I only stayed a couple of days, but it was so good to see them. I brought along *First Bite – Season 3* so Aunt Mary Jane could see Derek. She was so cool and hip. The nudity didn't bother her at all.

There was a great shot of Derek's lovely butt and she said, "Oh my, that is one sweet ass. He would be worth shaving your legs for…above the knee. Good for you."

We cracked up. Uncle Bill would've flipped if he saw what we were watching. He didn't. He was taking a nap and snoring away.

Then, Aunt Mary Jane told me about her procedure. She confessed she had a breast cancer scare, but the biopsy came back negative. I was beyond relieved.

I made it back to Vegas on Tuesday in time for my therapy appointment. After my last class, I showered and went right to Derek's since he returned from LA. I was so excited to see him and tell him about my trip.

Turned out, he had some news of his own. The photo spread for a European clothing line was a go. The shoot was in Paris. He would leave on Friday morning and come back Thursday evening, two days before my twenty-fifth birthday.

"What's wrong? I thought you'd be thrilled to go to Paris."

"I'm happy to have the work. I just wish you were coming with me. Plus, I'll worry about you."

"Derek, I'll be fine. If it makes you feel better, I'll sleep at Julia's while you're gone. Phillip won't be in town anyway. It'll be like a slumber party."

"Is Julia going to be in town until Thursday?"

I curved my arms around his waist. "Yes. She doesn't leave until Friday. We're celebrating my birthday this weekend. Please, don't worry about me."

He played with my hair. "What are you girls doing?"

"Oh, you know, dance on table tops for dollar bills, like all our girl's nights."

He wasn't amused. "I seem to recall another girl's night. Someone got really drunk."

"If you must know, on Friday, Julia is having a spa day for us with massages and pedicures."

"Just who is going to be massaging you?"

"Nobody, I don't like anyone touching me unless they mean business."

"That's, my good girl."

"I was actually thinking about getting another Brazilian wax."

"Hmm…that's an excellent idea." His hand wandered up my dress and he brushed his fingers over my mound. "I'm touching you and I mean business. I'm taking you to bed for a happy ending."

* * * *

Over the next couple of days, we spent as much time together as possible. It was wonderful, but Thursday night he was preoccupied. He kept texting someone. It bugged me.

"Who are you texting?"

He glanced up from his phone. "It's someone from the shoot."

"Are you texting the photographer?"

"No, it's the other model."

"What other model? Is it a male model?"

He hesitated. "No. I'm shooting with Lena Rozwell."

Who the hell was Lena Rozwell? There were so many things to be mad about—I didn't know where to start. Should I be mad he didn't tell me about her or that he texted her all night? Would he have told me if I hadn't asked him? Are they staying at the same hotel?

Instead of flying off in a jealous rage, I marched to the bathroom and slammed the door.

Derek knocked on the door. "Sweetie, I don't want to fight. It's our last night together."

I yelled through the door, "Maybe you should have thought of that before you spent the night texting *her*. Why didn't you tell me you were working with a gorgeous model?"

"First of all, you're the most gorgeous woman in the world to me. Are you going to come out of the bathroom?"

"I don't know."

The door opened a smidge. "Do you mind if I come in?" He took a few tentative steps inside. "I messed up. I'm sorry. We're in such a good place and I—"

"You didn't answer my question. Why were you texting her?"

He came toward me. "She was texting me a lot of questions about the people on the shoot. I've worked with this fashion house before and she hasn't. It would've been rude not to text her back."

"Is she pretty?"

"Nia, I love you and only you." He wrapped his arms around me. "I wish you were coming with me. I want to make love to you in Paris."

Oh man, he was so impossible to resist. I wanted to make love to him right now. We did. It was fantastic! Derek loved me. I trusted him.

* * * *

Friday morning came too soon for me. It was time for Derek and I to say goodbye. His bags were packed, and a car waited to take him to the airport. We were at his front door.

He held me tight. "Hey, just think when I get back we can celebrate your birthday. Is there anything you want me to bring you from Paris?"

"Just you, I just want you."

"You have me. I'm all yours. Now remember Paris is nine hours ahead of Vegas. I'll try to call you when I can."

"I promise to answer my phone."

His tone turned serious. "I want you to call me if you have a nightmare or if anything happens. I don't care what time it is, understand?"

"I understand. I better let you go. I love you."

Derek caressed my face. "I love you too, so much."

Chapter Twenty-One

"And then he said she's only in town for two days. You don't mind if I take her to lunch." Brooke was pissed.

Things were going so well with Tom and now they hit a snag. A snag called Rachel, the ex. Both of my friends endured relationship issues.

Julia was at odds with Phillip. He wasn't too happy we were going clubbing tomorrow night. I would be fine if we just went to dinner, but Julia said dinner was out and dancing was in.

I'd only gone to a club in Vegas once, when I first moved here. Phillip wasn't happy that night either. Julia came home drunk and threw up. I didn't see what the big deal was—most of the time we acted mature for our age. It wasn't as if Julia threw up in the car or the hallway. She blew chunks in her flowerbed, like a lady.

While the girls got their massages and complained about the men in their life, I was on Julia's laptop. I logged onto her *Facebook* page since I didn't have one. I searched for Lena's fan page. Crap! Not only was she beautiful, she posted comments on her wall about Derek. I joined the "I hate men spa party" and read aloud what she wrote. "Leaving tomorrow for Paris with Derek Pierce, I'm so hot for him."

Julia popped her head up. "She's trying to be funny. It doesn't mean anything." I showed her Lena's picture. "Oh my God. Look at her body, she's freaking perfect. I hate her."

Then I showed the picture to Brooke. "Derek is madly in love with you. I can't believe you're worried about it. It's not like he's taking his ex out to lunch."

She was right. If you handed out a prize for who had the most right to complain, Brooke wins. Julia and Phillip will work it out, and I wasn't questioning Derek's feelings for me. Poor Brooke, her ex-husband jerked her around and now Tom. What was he thinking?

The mood lightened as the day turned into evening. We enjoyed our pedicures and lined up for the torture— the Brazilian wax. It didn't hurt nearly as bad as it did the first time. Turns out Julia had a secret remedy—a little ibuprofen and a lot of booze.

Before you knew it, we were in the TV room having our own little party. What would I do without these two girls? By one a.m., we were pooped and a little drunk, so we called it a night. Brooke spent the night at Julia's too. We vowed to get plenty of sleep, because tomorrow night we were dancing until we fell over.

* * * *

It was eleven o'clock, Saturday night. Tryst, the nightclub at the Wynn, was packed. Julia arranged for a table by paying a ridiculous amount of money for a bottle of vodka.

The weird thing was no one danced much. People stood eying scantily clad girls doing "dirty commotions" on elevated platforms.

Julia turned heads though when she danced. She said Phillip gave her the cold shoulder since we were going out tonight. I didn't even tell Derek our plan. He would worry, or scold me, either way, it was best if I told him later.

Brooke said Tom called her and she didn't answer.

While Julia and Brooke got after it on the dance floor, I took a break. I had on the same outfit I wore to Derek's wrap party. The super expensive heels were super killing my feet. My phone vibrated in my purse. It was Derek. Shit! I couldn't answer. The music was so loud I wouldn't be able to hear him.

Julia and Brooke ran to our table. Julia heaved. "Nia, you've got to come with us. You'll never guess who's here. Oliver Rock! You've got to introduce us."

"He's not going to remember me. I only met him once."

Brooke and Julia begged, so I went with them, although it was pointless. I didn't even see him at the *First Bite* wrap party. We left before he got there.

Oliver danced with a gaggle of girls and soaked in all of the attention. We danced close to his group. I waved at him. God, I felt like such a dork. He barely waved back. The next song cranked up, it sounded like the one before. I was about to give up. Then an arm wrapped around my waist. It was Oliver.

The music was so loud he pressed his lips to my ear. "You're Nia, right? You came to the set with Derek."

I introduced him to Julia and Brooke. He ditched his girls and danced with us. I moved so Brooke could be next to Oliver. She was full-on twerking it so hard, the scantily clad girls were jealous.

The amount of attention Oliver drew made me uncomfortable. Brooke was having such a great time. I stuck it out, until people took pictures. As soon as I saw the cell phones, I covered my face and took off. Julia wasn't far behind me. Brooke stayed and danced with Oliver.

Women went nuts for him. He was cute with his light-brown hair and hazel eyes. He had an all-American boyish charm, but he didn't do it for me. In person, he was so much shorter.

Julia and I plopped down and poured another drink.

She asked, "Are you okay? Do you want to go?"

"No, Brooke is having a blast. I don't want to make her leave. I'll steer clear of Oliver, so my picture doesn't end up on *Facebook* or worse."

Brooke returned to the table with Oliver. She was grinning from ear to ear.

They sat down and he asked me, "Hey, where's Derek? I thought he might be with you."

"He's in Paris doing a photo shoot."

"Who's he shooting with?"

"Lena Rozwell, do you know her?"

"Yeah, I know her. Everyone knows Lena."

A photographer approached the table and asked if he could snap a picture. That was my cue. I fled to the bathroom and listened to Derek's message. He said they were about to start shooting on location. He also wanted to know where I was and why I wasn't answering my phone. He didn't sound mad, just overwhelmed. I called him right back and it went to voicemail.

I texted. "Sorry I missed your call. I'm out with Brooke and Julia. I will text you when I get home. Everything is fine except I miss you. I love you, your girl."

It was best to tell Derek about Oliver when he was back in Vegas. Derek said some celebrities were media whores and loved to get as much attention as possible. Oliver could be one of those celebrities.

I came out of the bathroom and Oliver sidled up me. "Hey, Nia, where did you run off to?"

"I'm a little camera shy. I don't like to have my picture taken."

"You're not shy on the dance on floor. I was watching you."

"Well, my friend Brooke is a great dancer. She thinks you're pretty cute."

I walked past him and he grabbed my hand. "You don't think I'm cute?"

What was happening? He yanked me toward him and kissed me. He shoved his disgusting booze-soaked tongue in my mouth.

I pushed him off. "Oliver, what are you doing?"

"Nia, come on, it's no big deal."

"It's a very big deal. I'm with Derek, just Derek."

"You really believe that, don't you? If you think he's not going to fuck Lena in Paris, you're crazy. It's what everybody does. Hell, I've had Lena. I'm trying to help you even the score."

"Shut up! Derek is not like that. You don't know him like I do."

"You're so naïve. By now, she's been naked in his bed. You're the one who doesn't know Derek."

I slapped him across the face. "Fuck you!" I took off, with my heart racing and my hand stinging. I'd never slapped anyone before. I ran over to the table and said to the girls, "We need to leave...*now*!" I didn't wait for them. I hustled past the crowd. I didn't stop until I got outside. The girls told me to slow down, but I couldn't.

When we got in the car Julia asked, "What the hell is going on?"

"I ran into Oliver when I came out of the bathroom. He said Derek's going to sleep with Lena in Paris."

Brooke asked, "Why would he say that? That's so mean."

"And so not true. I'm sure you defended Derek," Julia added.

"I did, but he wouldn't let it go, so, I slapped him."

There was a moment of silence and then Julia said, "Good for you. Serves the dumbass right."

The ride home was quiet. After we dropped Brooke off, Julia and I flopped on her sofa. Before she went to bed, I confessed Oliver kissed me. "Do you think what he said about Derek is true? Is everyone in Hollywood like that?"

"Oliver is, but Derek is not Oliver. Don't let him mess with your head."

As usual, a Julia Dickson pep talk eased my mind. She headed upstairs and teased, "Goodnight, you little bruiser. I better stay on your good side."

I grabbed my phone and texted Derek. "Made it home safe, I'm going to sleep. I miss you."

I fell into bed. Perhaps I could put the Oliver mess and my insecurities behind me. Tomorrow would be a better day.

* * * *

It was about one-thirty Sunday afternoon. I'd just gotten home from spin class. Right before I stripped down to get in the shower my phone rang. It was Derek.

I answered, "Hi, honey."

His voice was stern. "Nia, I need to talk to you about last night. Were you out with Oliver?"

"We weren't really with him. We were at Tryst and he was there. Brooke and Julia wanted to meet him. Honestly, I didn't think he'd remember me."

Derek raised his voice. "Do you know there are pictures of the three of you with Oliver that went viral? Keith saw them. They're everywhere."

"Can you see my face? I covered it as soon I saw people taking pictures."

"No, you can't, but that's not the point. The point is; I can't keep you safe if you put yourself in potentially dangerous situations. Do you understand?"

"Yes, I understand."

"Do you want to tell me why I didn't know about your girl's night out?"

"I didn't think it would be a big deal. I didn't want you to worry. I'm sorry."

"Please don't do that to me again. When I saw the photos, I... Just don't do it."

"I won't, I promise."

"I can't believe you hung out with Oliver. He's such an ass. He's making a big story out of his Vegas trip to get publicity for himself."

"Do you two not get along?"

"I don't trust him. We've had some issues in the past."

Derek was so cold and distant. God, I hated the phone. "Derek, I don't think I feel very well. Maybe we should talk later."

His tone changed. "Sweetie, I'm sorry I was so rough on you. I'm not myself when we're apart."

"I'm not myself either. Is the shoot going okay?"

"It's been tedious and more complicated than I anticipated."

I didn't have the strength to figure out what that meant. When we said goodbye he told me he loved me and missed me. I said the same. I took a shower, climbed into bed and slept most of the day away. In the evening, I went up to the main house to have dinner with Julia. We were both out of sorts and turned in early.

* * * *

The next day was even worse. I was at Julia's watching one of those Hollywood gossip shows. It was like being on an old carnival ride with no safety harness. First, there was a story about Oliver's wild night in Vegas. There were pictures of him with assorted women including one with Julia and Brooke at our table. Thank God I went to the bathroom and wasn't in the shot.

The story prattled on for a bit and finished with a bang. "The *First Bite* star wouldn't confirm, but sources told us Rock was slapped in the face at the Tryst nightclub. Could it have been a jilted lover? We don't know for sure, but what happens in Vegas doesn't always stay in Vegas."

Oh, this sucked! Julia and I were stunned.

Her phone rang. "It's Brooke. I'll call her back later. I better call Phillip right away."

"Hang on a second. Now they're talking about Derek."

Eden issued a press release about their "break-up." I had forgotten about her moving on from Derek's team. She wasn't on camera. They showed an old picture of them and read her statement saying they would remain friends. That story segued into footage of Derek and Lena on set in Paris. There was behind the scenes video rolling.

The reporter said, "Derek Pierce doesn't appear to be taking the break-up too hard. Things appeared mighty steamy with model Lena Rozwell on their Paris shoot, a busy perhaps wild weekend for both stars of *First Bite*."

"Julia, I don't know if I can take this anymore. The night I met Derek's mom, she told me it took a strong woman to be with a man in Hollywood and I was stronger than I think. I don't know if I believe that."

"I do. You're the strongest woman I know. Look what you've been through and how you picked yourself back up. I couldn't have done that."

"I wouldn't have survived if it weren't for you."

"Listen, I'm going to give you some advice about Derek. Phillip and I are apart a lot and I hate it. What I've learned is when he's away; he's under a lot of stress. So I don't take anything he says to heart, because he isn't himself."

"That's weird, that's what Derek said yesterday on the phone."

Julia was proud of herself. "See, I'm always right. I'm also starting to think these Hollywood people are nothing but a stone-cold bunch of weirdos." Perhaps she was right about that too.

Julia went upstairs to call Phillip. I hung out with Sammy and Coco on the couch. I texted Derek to let him know I was going to bed soon.

He called me. His voice was softer. "Hey, are you doing okay?"

"I'm fine. Did you know you were all over the TV today?"

He sighed. "Yeah, I saw everything. Look, I'm sorry I didn't tell you about it. I got all the information after it happened because of the time change."

"They made it sound like you went from dating Eden to Lena."

"Trust me no one is happy about it, except for Lena."

"I looked her up on Julia's *Facebook* page. She's super sexy."

"Sweetie, she's a mess. She almost ruined the shoot."

"What happened?"

"We'll talk about it when I get back. Did you get your period?"

"Yeah, how did you know that?"

"You told me to put it in my calendar and believe me, I did."

"It should be over by the time you get back. I miss you so much."

"I miss you too. I'll be in Vegas soon. Everything is going to be okay. Goodnight, my sweet girl. I love you."

I went right to sleep that night and the two nights that followed. I couldn't wait to see Derek.

Chapter Twenty-Two

It was Thursday night. I was at Derek's, anxiously awaiting his arrival. I donned the same little black, easy access sundress that I had on at our first sleepover.

Derek sent a text about twenty minutes ago, saying he was on his way. I went upstairs, lit some candles, and did one more check in the mirror. I was nervous. Maybe because I still hadn't told him about Oliver, and we hit a rough patch while he was away.

From downstairs I heard, "Nia, I'm back."

It was music to my ears. I flew to the landing. He looked as handsome as ever. His dark-blond hair was wavy and loose, his ice-blue eyes sparkled when they met with mine. I bounded down the stairs like a kid on Christmas morning.

That same electricity sizzled in the air. Our connection was stronger than ever. I jumped into his arms and wrapped my legs around his waist. He crushed his lips to mine. His soft, minty tongue swirled in my mouth, invading my taste buds. It transported us to our bubble as he carried me upstairs.

He sat me down on the bed and undressed me. "I missed you more than you know. Lay on the bed. I want to look at you."

"Okay, but you've been gone almost a week. I saved all my pleasure for you. I didn't touch myself. There was no Buzz, or even a nip slip. I'm on the edge."

He delighted in my breathless state. I relished his naked body before me. Looking at his embodiment of perfection made my juices surge. He knelt on the bed next to me and grazed his fingertips over my flesh, causing little shivers in my stomach.

"Your skin is like silk. Being away and not being able to touch you has been driving me mad."

"Yeah, I'm going a little nuts here myself, mister."

His eyes glanced to my freshly waxed pussy. "Did it hurt?"

"Nope, hardly at all, so there's no need to be gentle."

He dipped a finger inside me and I gasped. "Oh, my sweet girl, you really are on the edge. You're drenched."

I panted. "I know. I need you inside me. Please."

My entire being filled with crazed desire. I whimpered in relief when he entered my primed pussy. He felt incredible. His thrusts were slow and steady. The way our bodies careened together was like a dance. He led and I followed. Our hips flowed and floated as one piece of well-oiled machinery.

I parted my lips and his mouth joined with mine. Our tongues probed and explored. I expelled quiet murmurs in his mouth, while his fully immersed strokes consumed me.

My heart beat so loud. I could hear it in my ears. God, I missed this. My body felt empty without him deep inside.

His lips made their way to my neck.

He took in a sharp inhale of breath. "Hmm…I even missed your scent. You smell amazing."

My fingers entwined in his hair as he took my neck voraciously. I coiled my legs around his waist, digging my heels into his back. Desperate to come, I arched my back and pressed into him with my insistent pussy until our pace grew more frantic.

The pressure built up and my walls trembled against his cock. "Ah, it's so good."

He lashed into me with hammering thrusts, rushing my orgasm forward.

Derek growled, "You're close, aren't you? I can feel it on my cock. You're ready to come for me."

I cried, "Ah, yes, ah fuck."

He swept me up and it tumbled me over the threshold. Derek rocked me feverishly as orgasms gushed, one right after another. I could have cried out, oh my God, The Father, Son, and Holy Ghost— Mathew, Mark, Luke and John—and all the animals on Noah's Ark!

When Derek climaxed, it set off another wave of jittery pulses. He held me tight as we milked every drop of our torrid pleasure.

Lush and gratified, I buried my face in his chest. His hands splayed on my back and calmed my quivering body.

After I rediscovered the ability to speak, I peeked up at him. "Now that's what I call a homecoming."

* * * *

"This is delicious. Thank you." Derek enjoyed the turkey burger, with sautéed mushrooms and sweet potato fries I made for dinner.

My stomach knotted.

I gave him half my burger and forged ahead about Oliver. "Derek, I need to tell you something."

"Of course, you can tell me anything."

"You know the story about Oliver in Vegas. How he got slapped across the face."

He chomped on my burger. "Yeah, what about it?"

"I'm the one who slapped him."

The expression on his face was hard to read. "Are you serious?"

"Like I said on the phone, I only hung out with him because the girls wanted to meet him. Brooke had a fight with Tom. I thought if he paid attention to her, it would cheer her up. The whole idea backfired. There was a photographer who asked to take a picture of the three of us with Oliver, and I left. I went to the bathroom. That's when I called you. When I came out of the bathroom he was there…and he kissed me."

He was pissed. "He kissed you? What a dick. Is that when you slapped him?"

"No, but I pushed him away and I said I was with you. He said I was naïve, and that you were going to sleep with Lena, because that's what everyone does. Then I slapped him. Oh, and I also screamed fuck you."

He flew from the table and paced.

"Are you mad?"

He kissed me on the forehead. "Not at you. I'll be right back."

Oh, shit! Derek grabbed his phone and headed upstairs. I was sure he'd track Oliver down and rip him a new one. I couldn't sit still, so I cleaned up the kitchen. Ten minutes later, he appeared in the kitchen sporting a sheepish grin.

"Is everything okay?"

"Yep, I just got off the phone with Oliver. He apologized to both of us. He said he only met you once and he didn't know we were in a relationship."

"I don't think Oliver knows what a relationship is."

Derek smiled as if he had a juicy secret.

"Did he say something else?"

"Yes, he did. He let me know you didn't just slap him. You slapped the crap out of him. He said it really hurt."

We chuckled a bit.

Derek pinned me against the kitchen island. "Such a hard slap from one tiny person, I'm proud of you." He leaned in for a kiss.

"Wait, I need to ask you something. I didn't make a big deal of it on the phone, because I didn't want to fight, but what happened with Lena?"

"She assumed since we were working together, we'd be sleeping together. When I told her no, she didn't take it well. She acted unprofessional. That's why she almost ruined the shoot."

"How did she assume? What exactly did she do?"

"Nia, it wasn't a big deal. I'm in love with you and only you."

"It kind of makes me crazy that she threw herself at you."

"It kind of makes me crazy that Oliver kissed you. I don't want to waste another minute thinking about either one of them. And by the way, you are adorable when you pout."

"I don't pout."

He threw his head back and laughed. "Okay. I'm sorry, you don't pout. That bottom lip is on the floor for an entirely different reason. I'm going to kiss that pouty lip of yours. Come here."

He hoisted me on top of the kitchen island. My hunger for him got the best of me. My pouty lip couldn't stop kissing him. The rest of my body succumbed too. I let him take me right on the island, even though he didn't answer any of my Lena questions.

* * * *

It was seven a.m. I slipped out of bed and got ready for work. Julia's morning flight left super early. I had to feed the dogs before my classes.

She sent me a text last night. She and Phillip smoothed things over. She was excited about meeting him in New York. I also got a text from Brooke. Tom saw the photo of her with Oliver and Julia on TV. It must have frosted his balls, because last night he showed up at her house with flowers.

I dressed without waking Derek. He was jet-lagged, but you wouldn't have known it last night.

I scribbled a note, put it on his nightstand, and crept to the door.

He called for me, "Nia?"

"Honey, go back to sleep. I have to go."

I kissed his cheek. He looked so cute with his sleepy face. He flung back the covers and revealed his alarm-cock. It was fuck-o'clock.

"Sweetie, come here."

How could I resist naked, hard Derek? "I have to go take care of the dogs and get across town. I'll be late."

He grabbed my hand and I found myself straddling him. "Let me take care of the dogs. I have to have you."

There was that look… I totally caved. However, if he took care of the dogs, I had a few extra minutes.

I ripped off my workout clothes. With a dirty gleam in his eyes, Derek took charge. He put me on my side.

We were spooning. I'd never done it in this position before. I was in!

I lifted my top leg and his alarm-cock slipped inside. He planted soft kisses on my neck and fondled my breasts. I savored every thrust. This was a new seductive sensation.

Then he rolled me slightly on my back. He was still inside me, our bodies tangled in an erotic knot.

It was like a naughty game of twister. My right leg was over his hip and his right leg was between my legs. Then it was a primal paradise. Derek went left hand tit, right hand clit! *Holy shit!*

He whispered, "Does, my girl, like it like this?"

I wailed in pleasure, "Yes! Ah, yes!" He ramped up his full court press as his swift strokes pushed me to the edge. His piston-like motion had me writhing. "Ah, I'm going to come!"

He cried out, "Yes, come for me!"

My orgasm blazed through me like wildfire as he emptied inside me. Our bodies were relaxed and sated. Derek pulled out of me, and I rested my head on his chest. I could stay here all day, soaking in this euphoric bliss.

Derek's fingers grazed my back. "I can't wait until your birthday tomorrow. Are you excited?"

Ever since my mom died, I hated my birthday. The birthdays with Nick were worse than the ones with my stepmother. Now everything was different. I was happier than I'd ever been.

I peeked up at him. "Yes, for the first time in over a decade, I'm excited about my birthday, and it's all because of you."

* * * *

Derek covered my eyes with a blindfold, and led the way. It was my twenty-fifth birthday. I had no idea where we were going. The only thing he told me was we were going out, but it would be private. I wore the new dress Derek bought me in Paris. It was short, flirty, and black, of course. The skirt had trails of twisted chiffon swirling down. I also wore the earrings and fancy shoes Derek gave me.

Before he blindfolded me, Derek looked delectable in a black suit with a black shirt open at the collar. He belonged on a billboard.

He enjoyed this part much more than me. "You realize, birthday girl, I'm in complete control. Are you freaking out?"

"You love this don't you?"

"Yes, I believe I do. We're almost there."

A door creaked open and shut behind me. Derek removed my blindfold and more than one voice yelled, "Surprise!"

We were in the private dining room at the country club. Brooke, Keith, Tim, and Marcus, Derek's chef, were there.

Brooke greeted me with a big hug. "Happy birthday. Were you surprised?"

"Yeah. I'm so happy to see everyone."

She escorted us to our table. "You sit right here as guest of honor. Derek flew Marcus into cook your birthday dinner, and Keith and Tim will be your servers."

"What's your job?"

"I'm the supervisor. That means no one comes into the room until I get a text that you're ready for the next course."

Keith poured our wine. "The wine is French. It's... um...it's very, *oui oui*."

Tim put the napkins in our lap. "I can't take him anywhere."

We giggled and Marcus said, "Miss Kelly, happy birthday, and no peeking in the kitchen."

"Derek, thank you so much, you made everything so special."

"The night is young. You never know what is going to happen."

I mounted him in the chair and took his mouth. "Remember when you kissed me in here at the benefit?"

"How could I forget?"

I put my hand on his already hard dick. "This is what I really wanted."

Derek grinned in that devilish way I loved. "You just can't behave, can you?"

He lifted my Paris dress around my waist. *Mon Dieu*! I brazenly pressed my arousal on his cock. His hands went right to my ass.

"Sweetie, you need to be fast. They're waiting for us."

"Oh, I can do fast. I got this."

His shoved my thong to the side. "Your panties are soaked through. I'm ripping them off."

Both of his hands went to the waistband at the back. He shredded the flimsy fabric and tossed the torn thong to the side.

It was so hot. More moisture pooled below. I reached for a cloth napkin and shoved it between us, to protect Derek's pants from my dripping pussy. "I honestly don't know why I bother to wear panties at all."

His hand clasped my chin. "Young lady, you'll wear them. And when I make them wet, I'll tear them off. Understand?"

I exhaled. "Yes, I understand. I'm going to have a lot of ripped up panties."

He smiled. "Good girl. Now, hang onto the back of the chair. I want you to come on my fingers."

His hands slipped down my cheeks and two fingers darted inside. They fucked me from behind. His other hand cupped my bottom, coaxing me up and down. I humped on his probing digits, delighting in our daring dalliance. How did he do this to me? How did he drive me to the point of no return so quickly? I bucked and bounced as my pussy spasms coated Derek's hand in juices.

"That's it, sweetie. I can feel it, you're close."

I gripped Derek's shoulders. He was right. A swelling pulse throbbed inside me. He brushed across my sweet spot. My cries of pleasure sounded in the room.

"You're almost there. Touch yourself. Let me see you work my beautiful pussy."

Derek sucked my fingers in his mouth. My hand pressed on my puffy clit. I rubbed and he thrust me, until my orgasm twittered and broke free. He nursed me to my final quake. It was extra bad since Brooke waited for a text message from us. I so didn't care.

He dried me with the napkin, tossing it on top of my ruined thong. "Maybe we should stuff those in your purse for a keepsake."

I giggled. "Or we could just kick them under the table and let people wonder."

He patted my bottom. "That's my bad girl. What will you think of next?"

I thought of it. I jumped up, unzipped Derek's pants, and got on my knees. His erection sprung forth. I teased him with my lips making him twitch and twinge. I let a heavy breath wash over his cock.

"Nia, what are doing to me?"

"You said I was bad."

My tongue toyed with his balls. Then I glided it lightly over his straining shaft.

He wriggled in his seat. "You're killing me. Be a good girl. Put it in your mouth."

I opened up and he grunted under my misbehaving, cock sucking mouth. I stroked him with my hand, and my tongue encountered his bulging main vein. He groaned when I treated him to a long lick, taking it to his tip. He was ready. It was time for my party dick trick. I took in a breath and the back of my throat entertained him. He fisted my hair and pumped my mouth. My saliva gushed and my hands joined the festivities.

He growled, "Fuck, that's it." He pulled my hair and then erupted in my mouth. I drank in every last drop. He was yummy.

Derek was still breathing heavy when I stood up, grabbed my phone and texted. "Salads please."

"The salads are on the way. You may want to zip your fly. I don't think you're allowed to sit around the country club with your dick hanging out."

He zipped up, pulled me down on his lap. "Well, there goes my big surprise."

"You mean very big...*huge!*"

He smoothed my freshly fisted hair. "Actually, you're the one that's full of surprises. If this is what you do on your birthday, I can't wait for mine."

"You mean when you're thirty-three. Will we have to start eating dinner at four-thirty so we can catch the early bird special?"

He shook his head. "If they weren't on their way with the salads, I'd take you over my knee and spank you."

"Damn it, I texted too soon."

Before Tim and Keith came into the room, Derek tossed my panties and napkin under the table. We exchanged knowing, naughty smiles when the boys brought in the salads and refreshed our wine.

After our salad, they returned with the main course. Marcus made the same meal we had the night I met Derek's parents.

While we sipped our wine Derek asked, "Do you want your birthday present?"

"You already gave me my present. I'm wearing it, and you flew everyone here. It's already too much."

He rose and strolled to the corner of the room. There was a velvet blanket draped over something. "Come here, my birthday girl."

I joined him, he lifted the blanket, and there were two road bikes. It totally blew me away.

I flung my arms around his neck. "Thank you! I love it!"

"Wait, there's more." He reached into his pocket and pulled out a card. I opened it and there was a picture of a beautiful house on a vineyard. "I made arrangements for us to stay in that house this summer. It's in Napa. We just need to pick the week."

Tears welled up in my eyes.

"Hey, what's all this? Are you crying? I didn't mean to make you cry."

"It's because I'm so happy. I've never been this happy before in my entire life. I love you so much."

He held me and stroked my hair with his chin resting on my head. "Do you want some cake?"

"There's cake too? This is officially the best birthday and you are the best boyfriend *ever*."

Brooke, Marcus, Keith, and Tim joined us for cake. Derek also invited Steve and Scott, but they had tickets to a show and couldn't make it. We had cake, wine, and many laughs. It was the perfect way to end the evening.

Keith, Tim, and Marcus were staying at Derek's for the night. After we said goodnight, they took the bikes and headed out. I gave Brooke a hug and thanked her for arranging everything with the club.

When we got back to the guesthouse, I ran in first to turn off the alarm. The dogs were at the main house. Sammy loved sleeping down here even if it was on the floor. Coco didn't like it so much. I took my shoes off and asked Derek if he could use his charm to woo her down here. I gave him the key and took off my earrings. He draped his arms around me.

Referring to my dress, he said seductively, "Leave it on. I want to undress you when I get back."

"Yes, I insist. Thank you so much for everything. This has been the best day of my life."

He pressed his lips to mine. "I love you, so much."

He took off to get Coco. I shut the door behind him. I placed the earrings in the jewelry box next to my mother's locket. There was a scratch at the door. Good old Sammy didn't need any coaxing. I opened the door for him.

It wasn't Sammy. The air left my lungs. He found me.

It was Nick.

Chapter Twenty-Three

I opened my mouth to scream, but nothing came out. Nick glared at me with a fiery hate.

He spat out in a sinister tone. "Happy Birthday, Mrs. Ryan. You don't look happy to see me."

Terrified, I shook. My legs nearly caved. Before I could react, he shoved me so hard I fell back on the bed. He was on top of me in an instant and backhanded me across the face. I screamed in agony and blocked my face.

He pinned my arms on the bed and yelled, "Did you really think I wouldn't find you?"

"Please, Nick, don't do this, let me go."

One hand covered my mouth and his other hand choked my throat. "Do you know what it was like for me to go back to the hospital and find out you were gone, like you vanished into thin air. No one would tell me anything. They treated me like a criminal." His face got close to mine. I smelled the alcohol on his breath. "Do you remember the last thing I said to you? Answer me!"

His grip tightened on my throat and he removed his hand from my mouth.

I choked out, "You said you weren't finished with me yet."

"That's right. Very good, Mrs. Ryan."

Nick smacked me across the face twice. Blood flooded the inside of my mouth.

His face split into a crazy smile. He gagged me with his hand. "I should give you your birthday present."

He unzipped his pants. I wriggled and fought. He tore at my dress.

I screamed, "Help me!"

He grabbed a pillow and smothered me. "Shut the fuck up!"

He shoved his knee between my legs to pry them open. I clamped them shut with all my might.

"You're my wife. Open your goddamn legs."

I squeezed harder and it pissed him off. He threw the pillow down and made a fist. I closed my eyes and braced myself for his punch. I heard a rumble. My eyes flipped open. It was Sammy. He barreled full speed and jumped on Nick. It stunned him and knocked him on the floor. I scrambled off the bed. Sammy towered over Nick and growled.

Nick yelled, "Get this fucking dog away from me or I'll shoot him." He reached behind his back. He had a gun.

I grabbed his collar. "Sammy, come here."

Nick pointed the gun at him.

"Nick, put the gun down. Someone probably heard me scream and called 911. The police could be on their way."

"Then we better hurry, Mrs. Ryan. My car is down the street. You're coming with me."

"Okay, I'll go with you. Just don't hurt Sammy."

I told Sammy to stay and shut the door behind me. Then I remembered something from a talk show. "Never let them take you to a second location."

I asked, "Which way is your car?"

"This way," he headed to the left.

I took off to the right and raced to the house. I screamed at the top of my lungs, "*Derek help*!"

The gun went off. I froze. He missed.

"Get back here, you little bitch."

Derek bounded down the hill. "Nia! Are you okay?"

When he got to me, Nick closed in. He pointed the gun at us. "Well, if it isn't, Mr. Hollywood. My new buddy Larry Wall said you were fucking my wife."

Larry Wall? It didn't make any sense. Derek took a protective stance in front of me.

"You're really willing to take a bullet for her? She's not worth it. She ruined my life. Larry's life. And she'll ruin yours too."

"You ruined your own life."

Nick cocked the gun. "Don't take another step, Hollywood, or I'll kill you too."

"I'm never going to let you hurt her again."

"Hurt her? She always plays the fucking victim. Did she tell you she killed our baby? How she can't ever keep her goddamn mouth shut?"

I was no victim. I stood in front of Derek and yelled, "Shut up, Nick! You shut the fuck up! You killed my baby! It was your fault. You're a monster!"

Nick advanced. He looked deranged. He leveled the gun at me. "I'm the monster? You disappear after you kill our baby and I'm the monster. I told you if you ever left me, I'd kill you. I'm a man of my word."

"Police! Freeze!"

Shots blazed through the air. Everything went black.

* * * *

My eyes fluttered. Where was I? It was fuzzy. Did Nick shoot me? Where was Derek? I pushed out a faint whisper. "Derek, where are you?"

"I'm right here, my angel. You're okay. You fainted."

My eyes focused. I was on the ground with a blanket and Derek's arms around me. I looked up at him. He had tears in his eyes.

"What happened? Are you okay? Sammy and Coco, where are they?"

"Shhh… We're all okay. Keith came and got the dogs."

"Sammy saved me. Nick tried to—"

A paramedic interrupted. "Mr. Pierce, we should take her to the hospital, just as a precaution."

"No, I don't want to go. Please, Derek, don't let them take me!"

"Sweetie, I'll be by your side the entire time."

"No, I can't. Please, don't make me go."

"Okay, let's get you inside, so they can check you out."

As Derek carried me back to the guesthouse, the flashing lights in front of Julia's house lit up the sky. Police were everywhere. Derek placed me on the side of the bed. My head throbbed, but I couldn't go to the hospital. That's where I ended up the last time.

Derek took a good look at my face and choked back tears. "Why did he do this to you?"

"I don't know. Did they arrest him?"

Derek sat on the edge of the bed. "Nia, Nick is dead."

"He's what?"

"He's dead."

I exhaled and my body slumped forward. I put my head in my hands. "It's over."

"Sweetie, what do you mean? Are you upset he's dead?"

I steadied myself and looked at Derek. "No, I'm... relieved. It's strange. Somewhere in the back of my mind, I knew someday it would be him or me. One of us would be dead. It's finally over. Did the police shoot him?"

"Yeah, Nick turned the gun on them and fired. He hit one of the officers in the shoulder, but he's going to be okay. They had to take him out. One bullet hit him in the leg, and he still wouldn't put the gun down."

The paramedics came in to the room with their gear and took my vitals.

The middle-aged paramedic with the soft voice said, "All your vitals look good. I'd like to check your ribs."

I removed the blanket. My Paris dress was in shreds. Nick's violent attack flooded my brain.

"He ripped my dress. He was trying to…" A fresh stream of tears threatened.

"Nia, did Nick…?"

"No, he tried to. Sammy stopped him."

The paramedic said, "I'm sorry I have to put you through this. It will only take a second. Let me know if you feel any pain."

Derek held my hand and he did a quick check. I was lucky. My ribs were fine.

I took the blanket and covered myself back up. The paramedics packed up their things and gave Derek a list of instructions for me.

As they left, the police came in and took our statements. While one officer talked to Derek, another police officer, a woman, was kind as she snapped some pictures. She told me her name was Ginny and made the process as painless as possible. I was calm as I recounted every detail of the night.

The police referred to Nick as "the deceased." They asked me if I knew how to notify his family in Pittsburgh. For the first and only time, there was a brief pang of sadness.

My mind wandered to a conversation with Nick's mother. When I had my first inkling he cheated on me, I went to her for support. It was a big mistake. She told me to keep my mouth shut and be a good wife. His entire family treated me with disdain after that.

However, no one should have to suffer a loss like this, even if he brought it on himself. I told them I didn't have any information and they left.

Derek and I were alone. We sat side by side in silence.

He said, "I don't want you to stay here anymore. Tomorrow, we're going to move all your things to my place."

"Okay. I want to take a shower. Will you come with me?"

Derek helped me to the bathroom. I saw my face in the mirror. My jaw quivered and a few tears escaped. I was swollen and bruised. It would look worse as I healed. I'd been down that road before.

Derek's gentle arms shrouded me. "I'm sorry, sweetie. I'm so sorry."

My voice trembled. "Please get me out of this dress."

He gingerly peeled me out of my ruined dress. Then I saw all the damage Nick had done. Even though my face took the brunt of the beating, the rest of my body bore some damage too. He turned me away from the mirror and led me into the shower. I lost my footing for a second and slipped. Derek kept me from falling.

He held me close while I wept. "Please don't let go. Don't ever let go."

"I won't, Nia. I won't ever let go. He can't hurt you anymore. No one will ever hurt you again. I'm right here. I'm never letting go."

He cloaked me in his love as the shower cleansed me body and soul. The warm water washed away the past and released me from the chains of fear. I was in Derek's arms. I was free.

Chapter Twenty-Four

"Nia, this is my fault, it's all my fault, I'm so sorry." Brooke's sobs were uncontrollable. It was Sunday afternoon. We were at Derek's, sitting on the couch. What she said didn't make any sense. How could anything be her fault?

She told me Larry Wall was out for revenge after his wife kicked him out. He was broke, desperate, and blamed me for destroying his life. He used Sonya to dig up some dirt. She didn't know what she was looking for, but she found it.

The Sunday I came to the club and discovered Brooke and Sonya arguing was the day Larry got what he wanted. Brooke gave her the big key ring so maintenance could get in the supply closet. She and I were outside talking. Sonya went into Brooke's office and unlocked the filing cabinet with all our applications.

My file said Nia Kelly on the folder but the application said Meagan Ryan. My address in Pittsburgh and Las Vegas was on there. Sonya gave the information to Larry.

After a little investigating, he found out about Nick. Larry contacted him, and for a price told him where I was. It was hard to wrap my mind around this.

"I can't believe it. Sonya really hated me that much?"

"That's just it, I don't think Sonya realized what she'd done until it was too late."

"How do you know all this?"

"She called me. Right after she turned herself into the police. Last night the news reported there was an officer involved shooting at the club, but they didn't release Nick's name. She thought you'd been killed."

"Would she have cared? It doesn't sound like it."

"She told me to tell you she's sorry. Larry played her for a fool. He promised to marry her after his divorce was final, and he told her Nick was a great guy who wanted his wayward wife back. In some way, she must've known she was in over her head. Maybe that's why she backed off and started acting nicer to you."

"Did she know something was going to happen last night?"

"All Larry told her was Nick wanted to be alone with you, so he could take you back to Pittsburgh. It was supposed to happen the night Derek came back to Vegas early and surprised you. Sonya unlocked the door and left it open. She took the key off my big key ring. I'm so sorry. I didn't even notice it was missing."

"Stop apologizing. You didn't do anything. Can you imagine if Derek hadn't come home early? I was a sitting duck. Did she say anything else about last night?"

"Larry instructed her to go back to the guesthouse and unlock the door, but the locks were changed. He called her a dumb bitch and said they were through. After all that, she still believed no real harm was going to come to you."

"I hope you told her she nearly got me killed."

"Don't worry, I did. She feels terrible."

"Did she ever say why? Why does she hate me so much?"

"I've always said she was jealous. Larry had a thing for you and who knows, maybe it ate her alive."

"I can't even process this now. I hope she goes to jail."

"I'm not sure what's going to happen to her. She's hoping there won't be any jail time if she cooperates with the police." Brooke paused and grabbed my hand. "Nia, I'm so sorry. I should've ripped up your application. If you need anything, just say the word. I'm here for you."

I embraced her. "Thank you."

The front door opened and slammed shut. It was Derek and Keith. They brought over the last load of my stuff from the guesthouse. Until Brooke arrived, Derek hadn't left my side. Keith carried my things upstairs and Derek came to check on me. Brooke and I filled him in on Sonya's involvement. He had the same reaction I did. It was too much to process.

Then he told us he called his publicist to let him know what happened. It was only a matter of time before the police held a press conference and released our names.

When Metro Police shot and killed someone, it was big news in Las Vegas. When the media found out Derek Pierce witnessed the entire thing, it would blow up all over the country. Brooke said she already saw local television stations parked outside the gates.

The bell rang and Keith went to the door. He was so sweet, going beyond his role as assistant. Tim and Marcus had to fly out this morning. Keith not only made breakfast and moved most of my things. He also volunteered to clean the guesthouse later that afternoon.

Steve and Scott joined us in the TV room.

Derek said, "Thank you for calling the police last night."

Their eyes took in the damage Nick did to me. I'd never seen their faces so sad.

Steve replied, "We'd just got home from the show when we heard the gun. I picked up my phone and we ran outside. Nia, I heard you scream. We both wanted to help you. The 911 dispatcher told us to let the police handle it and go back inside the house."

"You did the right thing. You could have been killed."

"We still feel awful," Scott responded.

"Please don't beat yourself up about this. Your phone call saved our lives. Derek and I will always be grateful."

Steve, Scott, and Brooke told me to get some rest and left.

Sammy stuck to me all day. Poor Coco was out of sorts. We called Julia last night, and she and Phillip were on their way home.

I phoned Aunt Mary Jane, and Derek called his parents. We didn't want them to hear about this on the news. Somehow, even in this nightmare, Aunt Mary Jane managed to ease my pain. She and Uncle Bill were a blessing.

I dozed off for a bit, but voices from the kitchen lured me awake. It was Julia and Phillip.

I sat up and called for her, "Julia, I'm in here."

She rushed to my side. "Thank God you're okay." She broke down in painful cries.

"Hey, I'm going to be fine. Please don't cry. You're Julia-tough-as-nails-Dickson, you don't cry."

"I'm sorry. I can't help it."

Phillip and Derek joined us. Their eyes were glassy with tears too.

Oddly enough, I did the consoling. "You would be so proud of Sammy. He was a hero last night."

Once we paid attention to the hero, Coco wiggled her butt for some attention too.

I looked to Julia and Phillip. "I want you both to know how grateful I am for you letting me live in your guesthouse, but I moved out. I can't ever go back there."

"Don't give it a second thought," Phillip replied.

"I'll burn it to the ground if that's what you want," Julia added.

"What I want is to apologize. You've both been amazing to me and I've repaid you by turning your house into a crime scene."

Derek jumped in. "If anything was damaged last night, I will gladly pay for it."

Julia grabbed my hands. "Nia, none of that matters. You matter. Nick didn't take you away from us. That's the only thing that matters to me."

After Julia and Phillip left, Derek and I sat on the couch in complete silence. Even though he was with me most of the day, he said very little. I worried about him. Maybe this was all too much for him. Maybe I was too much.

"Derek, I'm sorry."

"Sorry, what for?"

I stared at the floor. "For everything I put you through. I feel like I've caused you nothing but trouble since we met."

"I don't know how you can say that. You mean everything to me. If anything, I'm mad at myself for not protecting you. I'm the one who's sorry."

I turned to face him on the couch. "But you did. You've always protected me."

Derek rubbed his forehead. He looked lost. "After the gun shot, I ran down the hill and saw him ready to shoot you. I can't get that image out of my head."

I reached out and placed his hands in mine. "But I'm okay."

He took my hand and pressed it to his lips. His fingers touched the bruises on my wrists. "This is not okay. This shouldn't have happened. I should've been there." His hand caressed my cheek. His eyes scanned every wound on my face and a tear rolled down his cheek. "I'm sorry I wasn't there."

I brushed away his tear. "You were there. Nick wanted me to go with him. When we walked out of the guesthouse, I had to do something. I took off, and started running. I was running to you. You were there. You protected me. Because of you, I'm happy for the first time in my life. I wasn't going to let him take that away from me. I love you. I love you so much." I leaned in and kissed his cheek. For a moment, the sadness in his eyes lifted.

When we climbed into bed Derek clutched me a little tighter. "Goodnight, my sweet girl. I love you."

It was peaceful and normal—something I clung to in the difficult days ahead.

* * * *

"The deceased is thirty-one year old Nicholas Ryan of Pittsburgh, Pennsylvania." The police captain read a prepared statement to the press. Derek, Keith, and I gathered around the TV at ten o'clock Monday morning. As predicted, this was breaking news, garnering national coverage.

"When the police arrived, Ryan had the gun pointed at Nia Kelly and Derek Pierce. Officers Mendez and Grayson told him to freeze and drop his weapon. Ryan turned the gun on the officers and fired, hitting Mendez in the shoulder. Grayson fired, hitting Ryan in the leg. He would not stand down. Grayson fired again, hitting Ryan in the chest.

"We can tell you Mendez is in stable condition and will be released from the hospital later today. Derek Pierce's eyewitness account confirmed officers followed protocol. At this time I will take a few questions."

A reporter called out, "Do you have a motive?"

The captain responded, "According to the report, Nia Kelly was the estranged wife of the deceased. We have reason to believe she was the target. Kelly alleged she had been abused by the deceased and there was evidence of that on the night in question."

There must have been over fifty reporters crammed in the tiny room wanting answers. They asked if witness Derek Pierce was the Derek Pierce from *First Bite*. The captain confirmed that.

He did not comment when they asked about the nature of our relationship. He mentioned Derek was a member of The Mountain Heights Country Club, and I worked there.

The reporters hurled more questions at the captain. The captain wouldn't speculate. If it wasn't in the report, he didn't say it. The frenzied pace of questions grew.

The captain threw his hands up in the air in frustration. "When we get more information, we will let you know. According to the report, another suspect, Larry Wall, is under arrest in California. We will take no more questions at this time."

Thank God. Larry Wall was in jail where he belonged.

Derek's phone rang immediately. It was his publicist. Derek had to release a statement.

By evening, all the entertainment shows and national evening news programs showed clips of the captain's press conference.

They also read Derek's statement. "I would like to stress how grateful we are to Metro Police Officers Grayson and Mendez for their bravery on April twenty-eighth. They acted in self-defense and saved our lives. At this time we would like to respectfully ask for privacy as we deal with this tragic situation."

Everyone ignored his request. We were prisoners holed up in Derek's house. I couldn't go to work, to the grocery store or to my therapy appointment.

Reporters hounded our friends too. We were all on edge.

The cast of *First Bite* protected our privacy. The show's fifth season premiered in May. The publicity was in high gear. Every person associated with the show refused to comment about Derek's involvement that night. Even Gisela and Oliver told reporters to buzz off.

I went a little stir crazy. After I organized my things in Derek's bedroom, I rearranged the kitchen, twice. With everything in order, I expected applause. In reality, I made Derek nuts.

He was quiet and sullen. He told me he loved me every night before we went to sleep, but we hadn't made love since the incident.

He was slipping away from me. Nick was dead, but he still had this power over me, over us. I also obsessed about Nick's family. Would they seek revenge?

* * * *

Friday morning I stretched on a mat after my workout in Derek's gym.

He came in to check on me. "Hey, I hope you didn't push it too hard."

I sat up. "I feel fine. I'd really like to go back to work next week."

He offered a hand, and helped me up. "I don't know. I'll have to think about that."

Dejected, I plopped on the weight bench. "Derek, we need to get back to our routines. I don't know how much more of this I can take." I wasn't just talking about work. I was dying to see that look, the look that said he had to have me. Maybe he didn't desire me anymore.

When Derek didn't respond I went to him and touched my lips to his. "I'm going to take a shower. Please, come with me."

"You go ahead. I have some calls to make."

A lump formed in my throat. "Do you not want me anymore?"

"Of course I want you."

"Then why won't you make love to me?"

He rubbed the back of his neck. "I don't know, I'm stressed out. I can't talk about this right now."

"But we have to talk about it."

"Please, not now. I have a lot to deal with. Do you know how many appearances I've canceled this week to be here with you?"

"I never asked you to do that. You should go."

"I'm not saying I want to leave. That's not what I want."

"What do you want? Because I don't think it's me." I stood there for a moment willing him to say something, but he didn't. His rejection cut me to the bone. I ran upstairs, got in the shower, and bawled my eyes out.

I leaned against the wall. I couldn't stop crying. It was the longest shower of my life. I turned off the water, opened the door, and reached for my towel. It wasn't there.

Derek held it. "I'm sorry. Come here, sweetie." He wrapped the towel around me. His mouth came down on mine. He took it with burning passion. "Nia, I do want you. I've never stopped wanting you."

"I'm okay. I'm not going to break. I need you. I need you inside me."

He carried me to the bed, climbed on top of me and gave me the look. Oh how I missed that look! His skin was like heaven against mine. The weight of his body on top of me stirred our longing. We melded into one another. This is where I belonged.

His gaze captured mine. "I love you. I love you so much. Nia, I will always love you."

We were back. We were in that place, our place. We were one.

* * * *

Over the next few weeks, we found a new normal. I went back to work and therapy. Derek came to therapy with me when he could. It was humorous to see Dr. Roma blush like a preteen meeting a boy band when she shook Derek's hand.

Of course, it would take time to settle everything. The California authorities incarcerated Larry Wall. He pleaded guilty to charges of conspiracy to commit murder in hopes of getting less jail time. The longer he stayed in prison, the better. If he sought revenge before jail, what would he do to me when he was free?

Sonya received community service and probation for her involvement. I didn't give two shits where she was as long as she stayed away from me.

The requests for interviews never ceased. We said no to everyone. For the most part, everyone at the country club was respectful and didn't pry into our business. However, I discovered being in the public eye had consequences.

One day after class, the new girl, Shannon, who had Sonya's job, said a letter came for me. It was from my stepmother. My hands trembled as I read the note.

I saw the story about Nick on the news. I'm very sorry for what you went through. I'm sorry about many things. Enclosed is your inheritance, I hope you will accept it. Your father wanted you to have it. I would have sent it sooner, but I didn't have an address. They mentioned you worked at the Mountain Heights Country Club on the news. I want you to know how much I miss your dad. He was a good man. He loved you.

It was a check for forty thousand dollars! I was so sure she hated me. Why did she reach out to me now? I considered sending the money back, but I didn't. Maybe I could do some good.

The first thing on my list was repaying Julia and Phillip for everything they had done for me. Julia turned me down flat. I took some of the money and bought Julia and Phillip bikes, like the ones Derek got for my birthday, and invited them to Napa this summer.

Then I paid off my Honda. Derek gave me a hard time about it since he had five cars and said I could drive one of those. I was quite stubborn and told him my Honda would always be my "Swag Wagon" and he would just have to deal with it.

I still had twenty-five thousand dollars and itched to do something positive with it.

I received a call from Karen Reeder, the director at the woman's shelter. I met her earlier in the year when I volunteered for their annual fundraiser at the club. She asked me if I would do a public service announcement on behalf of the shelter. I happily agreed.

Afterward, she encouraged me to do one interview and share my story. If it made national news, it would go a long way to help all the women's shelters badly in need of funding. I did it. Phillip had an old friend, Jan Blake, who was a reporter at one of the local stations. It was someone he trusted. Derek came with me and so did his publicist Aaron.

Maybe Aaron wasn't so bad. It was his idea to bring Sammy, my hero. Sammy was a regular canine camera king. The piece ran nationally as expected. It was uncomfortable to put myself out there, but Jan did a great job.

After it ran, Sara from the Humane Society called. She asked me if Sammy and I would film a public service announcement for them. I was more than happy to champion the cause of adopting animals. Derek was too. Sara was thrilled to have all three of us in the spot.

Then, I got an idea. Karen told me some women stayed in their abusive relationship because they wouldn't leave their pets behind.

I hooked Sara and Karen up. We put our heads together, and formed a new charity called Sammy's Place, a safe haven for women, children, and their pets. It was my honor to give them twenty-five thousand dollars.

Good came out of evil. Giving back healed something deep inside. My past no longer defined me.

Chapter Twenty-Five

Who knew getting red-carpet ready was so much work! It truly took a village. Luckily, Derek hired the village people to keep me from looking like the village idiot.

It was Derek's *First Bite* season five red-carpet premiere. We were stepping out in public together as a couple for the first time.

I was excited, but exhausted. Once again, Derek hired all men and no women. They were brutal, and plucked, sucked, and tucked me within an inch of my life.

My favorite thing was the facial and hair. It was time for a change, so they chopped off a couple of inches of my long, out of control hair and added long layers and a few highlights. I loved it and Derek did too.

My least favorite part was the spray tan. Now I knew why those little pageant girls on *Toddlers and Tiaras* cried.

I didn't like picking out a dress either. The stylist suggested a loud print. When I wouldn't try it on, he offered an array of yellow and orange dresses. I would've looked like a creamsicle.

Derek came to my rescue and chose a gorgeous, deep-blue dress. It wasn't quite navy or royal blue, somewhere in between. It went with his suit. It was backless. That meant Derek's hand would be stroking my bare skin all night.

While the limo waited downstairs, I donned the expensive borrowed earrings that went with my borrowed dress, shoes, and bag. How did a girl from Pennsylvania end up here, in all this fabulousness?

Derek's footsteps sounded in the hall. "Nia, are you almost ready?" He stopped dead in his tracks when he saw me. "Sweetie, you're stunning."

"You are fucking hot!"

"You're going to get us bleeped off the carpet, aren't you?"

"I promise I'll be good. I'll be so nervous. I won't be able to speak."

He went to the nightstand and pulled out a small package. "I think there might be one more thing you need before we leave."

"Like a shot of whiskey or a muscle relaxer." He handed me a fancy package from a Beverly Hills jewelry store. I opened it. Inside was a diamond-crusted cuff. It was too exquisite for words. "Derek, it's beautiful. I love it."

He placed it on my wrist. "It's not borrowed, it's yours."

My eyes bulged right out of my spray-tanned head. "Derek, it's too much. I can't."

"I insist."

* * * *

In the limo, I studied a card the stylist gave me, so I could say who I was wearing. What if I ended up on some worst dressed "what the hell was she thinking" list?

We waited in a long line to get to the carpet. From where we sat, it wasn't glamorous. It was our turn. My heart was beating double-time. I let out a couple of deep breaths.

Derek kissed my hand. "Nia, you're going to do great."

He stepped out of the limo first. A wave of cheers filled the air. Derek offered his hand. I slid out and stood on quaking legs.

It was four-thirty in the afternoon. The sun's rays were intense.

Derek leaned down and I whispered in his ear, "It's hotter than balls out here."

He threw his head back and laughed. That little unguarded private moment between us calmed me down.

Aaron and his assistant Brad waited for us and told us the plan. There was a roped off area for fans, and the actual red carpet or step and repeat was for press. Derek would take pictures with his fans by himself. Then I joined him on the step and repeat. That was fine with me. If I had stood out in the hot sun for a glimpse of Derek, the last thing I would want to see was his girlfriend.

I stayed with Brad and Aaron, and Derek took off. The girls went nuts for him. Couldn't say I blamed them. The crowd held up signs with their favorite star's names on them. Derek did his thing signing autographs and taking pictures.

As he scaled down the line, a small group of signs shot up in the air. They said, "Way to go Nia. Nia Kelly is our hero." I looked at Brad with a confused expression.

Derek chatted with them and then he hightailed to me. He escorted me to the women with the signs. They saw the piece I did with the local reporter. They were survivors of domestic violence too. I was touched.

Derek said in my ear, "I'm so proud of you, sweetie."

Now it was the media's turn. They called it the "step and repeat" because every reporter asked the same questions. Derek repeated himself repeatedly.

They asked what fans could expect to see from his character, Drake Braden, in season five, and who we were wearing.

Aaron stood next to us like a bodyguard, making sure no one brought up the horrific night with Nick. Derek mesmerized me. He was so charismatic and smooth. His hand grazed my back or his arm was around my waist. I was his and he was mine. He never let go.

* * * *

"Thank you. I had the time of my life." I draped my arms around Derek's neck. My mouth hovered over his, craving him.

Back in the bedroom, our bodies were ripe with desire. Throughout the evening, we exchanged sensual touches and soft kisses. We stoked the fire and were ready to combust.

We resisted the urge to rip our clothes off since we borrowed my dress and Derek's suit.

Derek's lips danced on my shoulder blades while he unzipped me. My nipples grew taut and sensitive as he folded me out of my dress.

"Leave your panties and heels on for me. I insist."

"I insist on undressing you."

He grinned. "Whatever pleases my girl."

With his jacket already off, it pleased me to unbutton his shirt and reveal his brick like chiseled chest. It pleased me even more to run my fingers through the defined ridges and muscles on his incredible body. My mouth delivered feather light chest kisses. I drank in his scent. He smelled like Derek, clean like fresh air.

I peeked up at him with a randy smile, and undid his trousers. It pleased me to find a stiff present inside. I helped myself, and Derek hissed.

I got on my knees and slid them down, revealing his astonishing naked body. He stepped out of them and reached for me.

"My angel, it would please me to take you to bed."

He sat on the bed and I stood before him in my heels and panties.

"You were the most stunning woman there tonight." Derek's lips floated over my stomach making my pussy seep. I twirled my fingers in his hair, whimpering and squirming.

His fingers skimmed my thong. He dropped his hand between my legs. "What do we have here? Your panties are soaked."

He ripped my thong to shreds and tossed it. His hands clasped my ass. He pressed his face into my mound, and inhaled. "God, Nia, you are intoxicating."

He spread my pussy lips with his fingers and his tongue plummeted to my clit. It taunted and teased me. I could barely stand on my own two feet.

"Derek, I want to feel you inside me."

He stood up and sealed our bodies together. When he gave me that look, it inspired sheer wickedness. I put one foot up on the bed, and with my arms around his neck, vaulted myself. With both feet on the bed, I descended on him and mounted his cock. I was triumphant, like a gymnast sticking her landing! *Nailed it!*

Derek glided me up and down his massive shaft. His large hands spread my cheeks, driving me wild. He rocked me at a vigorous pace. My walls clamped down on his dick, we shuddered and shook. Yes, red-carpet sex ruled!

He slowed our pace and exhaled. "Hmm... My girl is so full of surprises."

I expelled a heavy breath. "Are you going to surprise me?"

He sat on the bed. "No, it's no surprise. I'm going to take you from behind."

"Abso-fucking-lutely!"

He grinned and patted my bottom. "Lay flat on your stomach. Spread yourself for me."

I scurried off him and flattened like a pancake. My legs opened wide. His tip touched my entrance and his hands palmed my cheeks.

"I'm going to fuck hard, Nia, harder than I ever fucked you before. What we've done so far, is only the beginning. I'm going to take you places, you've never been."

"Yes, take me."

His cock, still coated with my juices, swept inside my tight hole. He could take me wherever he pleased. Derek's slow steady thrusts were out of this world. My pussy pulsed and sucked him deeper inside.

His arm looped around my waist, drawing me to my knees.

"Are you ready for more?"

I heaved. "Yes."

He grunted, "Good girl."

He gripped my hips and took control. Derek pulled out and then plunged into me like a torpedo. A soft cry ripped from my throat.

He burrowed deep inside and pampered my hot spot with forceful short strokes. His fingers flicked my clit and I nearly splintered in two. My pussy flushed and contracted around him.

He settled into a firm, masterful pace. Our bodies were pure adrenaline, reeling in ecstasy. I pushed myself against him and he delved into me harder. His balls slapped my sex. My first orgasm built into a forceful crescendo of waves. I cried out his name as it rippled through me.

"That's it, my sweet girl."

He stalled his assault and his hand calmed my burning clit. Beads of sweat trickled down my back. My body shuddered in aftershocks.

"Nia, you're amazing."

His hands drifted to my shoulders and tenderly skated down my back in encouragement.

Once my body stilled, he gradually ramped up his speed. My body climbed with his. He pressed me flush to his chest. He grabbed my hair and anchored his mouth to mine. Our lips banged together in needy passion. Then he took my neck. My body transported into a haze of fiery pleasure.

"Do you want to come again?"

I whimpered, "Yes."

"Give me your hand."

Our fingers laced together and I sucked them into my mouth. Then they lowered and encircled my inflamed bundle of nerves.

He heaved. "Do you feel that? How swollen your clit is for me. It's ready to come on our hands. Let's make you come, together."

"Yes, ah, I feel it."

We rubbed and rocked my throbbing clit.

"See how good we are together."

"Yes. Ah, I'm close."

Our fingers threw me into a fury. Derek's thrusting cock increased its drive.

The combinations of sensations zinged and zapped me. I wailed and burst on our hands.

"That's, my good girl."

He clutched me to him. His lips pressed to my shoulder blade. He slowed his strokes.

My body trembled and quaked. I blew out a ragged breath. "That was so intense."

He wiped the sweat from my back. "Are you okay?"

I curved my face to his. "Yes, I want more."

His mouth came down on mine. "I love you. You're so beautiful. You're mine."

"I'm yours."

He put me back on my hands and knees. Fluent, easy strokes brushed against my sweet spot causing my walls to thud. My satiny hole siphoned him deeper inside.

Once I pushed back on him, he lavished me with reckless thrusts. My pussy squeezed his dick.

I panted. "Derek, oh God, I want to come again."

"That's my greedy little pussy. You're going to come again. You'll come when I tell you to."

I couldn't hold myself up anymore. I fell to my elbows and accepted his rough blows. Every cell in my body was insane with lust. I gripped the comforter and held on.

His thrusts pelted me, taking us to new heights. Our bodies strained against the reins. My cries were inaudible moans of scorching pleasure.

He was about to wreck my pussy.

I was delirious in my arousal. "Oh, my fucking God!"

"Now, Nia, come now."

One final blast of his cock hammered me and I ruptured into a million pieces, screaming and shrieking. Derek detonated inside me, causing an avalanche of climaxes as his powerful, creamy load overflowed.

Heavy breaths resonated in the air. There were no words, only love when he put me in the tub and tended to me.

He fucked me. He fucked me harder than ever before.

Chapter Twenty-Six

June brought many changes. Of course, I wasn't a fan of change, but these were all good, so I didn't mind.

Brooke received a promotion to Managing Director of the Mountain Heights Country Club. She, in turn, promoted me to Fitness Coordinator. The membership at the club boomed. I hired an assistant and more instructors to meet the demands. I quit my job at the gym across town, so I could focus on my duties at the club.

I was in heaven, organizing the schedules, ordering new equipment and working with the instructors. We put a plan in place to expand the fitness room, which also meant expanding the equipment closet. Even though I used to think of the equipment closet as a pain in the ass, it now had a special place in my heart.

I was excited about going back to school. I registered online for Statistics 2. I was determined to earn my degree. Oddly enough, my Business Management major was helpful in my new job. My dad knew best, after all. Although, I also vowed to take voice lessons again and hit that high C.

Not only did Brooke get a promotion, she and Tom were cohabitating and happier than ever.

Julia and Phillip were in a great place. They wanted to have a baby. I wasn't sure when they would start trying, but I was sure it would be the most loved child in the world.

Steve and Scott had additions of their own. They adopted two kittens from the Humane Society after we did the public service announcement. Ginger and Peachy were quite spoiled and very cute.

Derek returned on Wednesday from a press tour. I didn't mind the days apart anymore. I was secure in our relationship. Plus, absence made the heart grow fonder and his dick even harder.

It was Friday. Derek and I were hosting the gang for a barbeque. Much to Derek's chagrin, we planned to watch a new episode of *First Bite*. He didn't like watching himself. He was his worst critic.

It was four in the afternoon. Derek was out most of the day, while I organized the barbeque. Everything was done and ready to go. I was in the TV room watching one of those judge shows.

The front door opened and Derek called out, "Nia, where are you?"

"I'm watching TV."

"Close your eyes."

"Do I have to?"

"Just do it."

I relented. He told me to open my eyes. I did, and my heart melted. "Oh, where did you come from?"

It was the cutest, ball of black fur I'd ever seen—a little female puppy with a big pink bow. "I think I'm in love. Can I hold her?"

Derek handed me the puppy. "Her name is Molly. She's from the Humane Society, and she's yours."

Molly was about four months old and weighed around fifteen pounds. She was all black except for a white area on her chest.

"What is she, a lab?"

"Yeah, mostly lab, but Sara thought there might be a little cocker spaniel mixed in too."

"My dog, Sadie, was a cocker spaniel mix. You remembered."

Derek got on the floor with Molly and me. "I know we should've talked about if first, but I wanted to surprise you."

"This is the best surprise ever. She's perfect! You're perfect! Oh, Molly's going to need a million things. We better hurry since everyone's coming over."

"Relax, I took care of everything. Sara helped me. It's all in the car."

"You did?"

He smiled wide. "I did. That's right, Nia, I had a plan."

"I don't think I've ever been more attracted to you than I am in this moment."

"I don't know about that."

He picked up Molly and untied her big pink bow. There was something attached to it. *Oh my God! A ring! A big fat diamond ring!*

Derek got on bended knee. His voice trembled. "Nia Kelly, I love you so much. Will you be my wife? Will you marry me?"

"Yes! Oh my God, yes, of course I'll marry you!" Tears of joy flooded our eyes. His hands cupped my face and he pressed his lips to mine. It was the most fantastic kiss of my life!

He slipped the ring on my finger. "You are mine and I am yours."

"We belong together."

"I'm never letting go."

He drew me onto his lap and little Molly joined us in our cuddle.

"Do you like the ring?"

"Are you kidding, this ring is brilliant. It's beyond. I love it! I love you! *Son of a bitch!* We're getting married!"

We laughed and little Molly barked. I was so happy. I couldn't wait to be his wife.

* * * *

"Oh my God, it's bigger than mine," Julia said as she checked out my ring. For a moment, her bright-blue eyes turned green. She explained it was four carats, an emerald cut with a platinum band.

As everyone gathered for the barbeque, they gushed about little Molly and my ring. Fiancée was my new favorite word in the dictionary. We were all outside watching Molly, Sammy, and Coco play. Sammy and Coco were so sweet with Molly. They were fast, furry friends.

Many toasts and laughter filled the evening. As I glanced around the table, I smiled in sheer joy. This was what life was about, good food, good friends, and love, so much love.

* * * *

Later, Molly and I were in bed watching the news. Derek climbed in and gathered me close. "What kind of wedding do you want?"

"It doesn't matter to me. I just want you."

He kissed my forehead. "You've got me. Let me know what you want, and we'll do it. For our honeymoon, we can go to Europe or Australia, wherever you want. You should know you're about to become a very wealthy woman. Everything I have is for you."

A sly grin crossed my face. "You should know I'm not marrying you for your money. I'm marrying you for your giant penis."

We cracked up and he swaddled me in his arms. "I can't wait to be your husband."

He gave me that look and we made love. It was off the hook!

From this day forward, we would spend the rest of our lives exploring each other's pleasures. Derek was right this was only the beginning.

My head relaxed on his chest and he whispered, "Goodnight, my sweet girl. I love you."

There were moments in my life when I was alone. I had no one. My past was filled isolation and sadness. That part of my life was over. It was time to turn the page and write a new story.

When I gazed at Derek and Molly my heart soared. I would never be lonely again. We were our own little family. I was finally home.

THE END

Nia and Derek's journey continues in *Away With Him,* book two of the Swept Away trilogy...

Away With Him

Swept Away, Book 2

Inside their little bubble, newly engaged, Nia Kelly and Derek Pierce, are blissfully happy. Their passion reaches new heights as they explore each other in sensual, wicked ways.

Unfortunately, the rest of the world has not received the memo. They are hit with a barrage of attacks from Nia's past and Derek's pressure-filled Hollywood career. Their happiness and future are in peril at every turn.

Derek is steadfast in his commitment to Nia. No matter what, he will never let go. Nia is his and Derek is hers—they belong together.

Nia prays their love is enough. With everything she has, she holds on and vows not to run away. It's a promise she hopes she can keep.

Author Biography

Rosemary grew up in Pennsylvania, one of six children. Her parents, Charles and Dorothy, always supported all her creative endeavors, from acting to singing to Erotic Novelist. Yes, they are super cool.

She's been living in Las Vegas for over eighteen years with her husband Bill Johnson and their adopted pooch, Harley.

In addition to writing, she also teaches ten fitness classes a week. Her limited spare time is usually spent at home with her hubby enjoying a home cooked, healthy meal and all things HBO and Netflix. When she ventures out to a restaurant, she normally splurges on her favorite dish, mac and cheese. It's just as Nia says in *Running Away to Home*, "Sometimes it's good to be bad!"